Let It Be Me

Libbie Richman

Serenade Books

Nederland, Texas

ISBN 1-932300-02-3

First Printing 2003

9 8 7 6 5 4 3 2 1

Cover design by Talaran

Published by:

Serenade Books
PMB 210, 8691 9th Avenue
Port Arthur, Texas 77642

Find us on the World Wide Web at
http://www.regalcrest.biz

Printed in the United States of America

Acknowledgements:

I dared to dream and Renaissance Alliance Publishing, Inc. gave me the opportunity to fulfill my dream. To the entire staff of Renaissance Alliance Publishing, Inc., including Cathy, Barb, Casey, Donna, Lori, and especially my editor, Sylverre, I thank you for your assistance, persistence and confidence.

— Libbie Richman

This book is dedicated to Ross, who never stopped believing in me. I couldn't have done it without you. I love you.

Libbie

Chapter
1

The lights were dimming. Ronnie wasn't back in his seat yet. He'd said he wanted the aisle seat so he could stretch his legs. Lisa didn't care; she was thrilled just to be there. She moved to the second seat from the aisle.

The music was starting when a young couple approached her row. They didn't even say, "Excuse us,"; simply climbed over her legs to the two vacant seats beside her. The woman was carrying a large straw basket, and the young man held a neatly folded southwest blanket of teal and maroon across his arm. They looked very casual in faded jeans and worn sandals.

Lisa thought 0they were probably in their thirties. They had that 'yuppie' look about them. Both blended well with the majority of the audience. She smiled, trying to be polite, as they took their seats, murmuring, "You got here just in time. The show is just about to start." Neither responded.

The sky was not completely dark yet. A soft breeze made this warm June night comfortable for an outside concert. Lisa remembered a show she'd seen the month before. It had rained so hard, with thunder and lightning exploding, that most of the people on the lawn had left. Tonight, Lisa was glad to see Mother Nature cooperating. Conditions were perfect. The barometer was where it belonged, the air tranquil. She watched the sun descend behind the woodland which blocked the crossroads and parking facilities from view.

Nearly everyone was seated now. Lisa wondered why it was taking Ronnie so long to get back to his seat.

The music that had been playing stopped. A hush fell over the crowd as a deep voice ceremoniously announced, "Ladies and gentlemen. The Diamond Coliseum, in association with Parker Brothers, is proud to present the one, the only: Mr. Yale Frye."

Lights focused on center stage, an overture began. The

applause was deafening as Yale Frye appeared from behind a rising curtain. He was standing on a circular staircase designed to look like piano keys. With his arms extended, he began singing enthusiastically.

His voice had never been better, Lisa felt. A devoted fan, she had all his CD's and had attended many of his concerts. Lisa felt an excitement so intense, and was so caught up in the ardor of the moment, she didn't even notice Ronnie return to his seat beside her. Lisa recalled the time and money she'd spent to be here in these seats tonight. It was worth it, just for this very moment. She was clapping and cheering with everyone. Her face felt flushed as she watched her idol move to the music, and gyrate until the screams from the audience reached a fevered pitch.

Yale Frye waited for the moment—the second every great performer knows, when the audience is ripe, and ready. He reached out to grab and captivate his listeners, so he could give the audience their money's worth.

Ronnie smiled, watching Lisa's face glow with excitement. Her smiling face made him happy. He was glad he hadn't bellyached about being tired, or the junk she had bought before the show. He loved watching her have fun.

"Thank you. Thank you!" Yale shouted after he ended the opening number. He bantered about the trials of touring, mentioning the dilapidated trailer provided for him. He joked with the audience and the audience laughed with him. He smiled broadly, while walking toward a black grand piano to begin his next number.

Lisa looked over at Ronnie with gentle, smiling eyes. He leaned over to kiss her. She was in her glory. This was the night she'd waited for with such excitement and anticipation; she had marked her kitchen calendar with X's and a gold star on today's date. She reminded him of a child receiving an eagerly awaited present.

Yale Frye was more than good. He was a polished entertainer. Even Ronnie, who wouldn't have minded if he never went to another concert again, had to admit that he was one of the best performers around. His shows were always rated among the best in the business. He had established a strong following of both genders and all age groups, and aptly created fervor that few other performers could match. Yale Frye was famous for sparing no expense when it came to his productions. The extravagant staging proclaimed tonight's show was going to be no different.

Yale stood in front of the Steinway now, and his third number was a beautiful love song. The lights were illuminating the stage as the night sky darkened. Lisa looked up at Yale, dressed in a black and white pinstriped sport coat, black satin shirt opened generously at the neck, and black fitted trousers.

He wore no jewelry, and his hair barely touched the collar of the sport coat. His golden curls were styled away from his face, but perspiration caused strands to fall across his brow. He had long legs, broad shoulders and a compact ass.

Lisa smirked, wondering if he was less compact in front, while he swayed to the music, facing the twenty-piece orchestra, showing off his behind.

She opened her purse to take a cigarette from its case, and dropped her monogrammed butane lighter in the process. The Diamond coliseum was one of the few concert arenas that hadn't banned smoking under the dome yet. As she bent to retrieve her lighter, she noticed the young man next to her fumbling in the straw basket that was now in front of him. Minutes ago it had been between him and his date. He's probably searching for a beer, she thought, as she picked up her lighter and lit the cigarette. She considered asking the young man if he objected to her smoking, out of courtesy, but decided not to say anything.

Usually during concerts, Lisa at least chatted with people sitting near her. But the two to her left, obviously, had no interest in making conversation. Lisa noticed that the young man was fidgety and never applauded Yale's numbers. He probably didn't want to be there tonight, she surmised. At least Ronnie was polite enough to applaud, even if he, too, would rather have been home in front of the television, plugged into some sports show or half asleep by now.

Yale was introducing a new number that was going to be on his forthcoming album. As he was about to begin the song, he said, "Let me get a little bit more comfortable," and proceeded to remove his sports jacket, tossing it to someone in the wings. All the women, including Lisa, shrieked. Yale chuckled. They were eating it up.

The stage was black now, except for the spotlight directed on Yale Frye. He looked into the first few rows, flirtatiously bantering. "Wow! There are so many beautiful ladies here in Canton! I may never want to leave!"

Lisa's heart was beating rapidly. She was praying he would look at her, even for just one second. She was crazy about Yale Frye; had been for years.

Her friends thought her immature and obsessed when it came to Yale Frye. They often teased her about it. She always took the needling with good nature, often replying, "You're jealous that I

can still fantasize. Just remember, dreams do come true. One day
he'll sing to me. Just wait and see."

Yale bent now, accepting a long-stemmed red rose from a girl
in the front row. He gave her a kiss, and said, "Thank you, dar-
ling." Again, the women in the audience shrieked. He stood,
looked at the sold-out arena, and huskily said, "I like this next
song a lot. I want to dedicate it to all of you out there who are in
love, have been in love, or are searching for love." He added
humorously, "That should just about cover everyone."

One girl in the audience shrieked again. Yale stood with the
red rose in one hand, the microphone in the other, and began to
sway his hips as the music started. He lowered his head, smelled
the rose, and sang a beautiful new ballad. The song brought tears
to Lisa's eyes. She could see that Yale was putting his heart and
soul into presenting it to his captivated audience. When the song
ended, the audience stood, stomping and applauding in acknowl-
edgment. Yale stepped forward, smiling, as the audience roared
and gave him a standing ovation. He was taking a well-deserved
bow when the man sitting next to Lisa abruptly raised his right
arm, accidentally—but brutally—bumping into her. Jolted, she
turned toward him, and saw that he was holding a gun in his
hand. The pistol was aimed at Yale Frye.

Lisa screamed. "No! No!" She grabbed for the man's hand.
Only a few people close by heard her over all the applause and
cheering. She shrieked, "Yale! Yale! Get down!" but the audience
was still clapping, shouting, and screaming for more. Everyone in
the audience was standing, cheering, oblivious to the fact that a
shot had been fired. No one seemed to hear the gun go off again.

Lisa found herself on the ground after the second gunshot.
Applause was the last thing she heard before losing consciousness.

Ronnie was stupefied. He didn't know what had happened. It
had all happened so quickly. All he knew for sure was that he had
been knocked down; he didn't even know by whom. He struggled
to move, stunned to see Lisa lying next to him. He leaned over,
moving closer to her. He was just about to ask her if she was okay
when he saw that she was covered with blood. He started screaming her name, over and over again.

Suddenly, the police were there. Security people were all
around them. People were pushing, yelling, crying. There was
shuffling, and voices shouting to clear the area. A stretcher was
brought quickly. Lisa was placed on it. It was a nightmare. Ronnie
was being asked a lot of questions. He couldn't answer any of

them. All he could stammer was, "Is she alive? Is she alive?"

Someone took him by the arm. He tried to shake himself free. Strong arms were pulling him up from the ground. His legs felt weak. He wasn't sure he could stand. He felt sick. Everything was happening so quickly.

"Are you with this lady, sir?"

"Sir, do you know this person?"

He didn't know who was asking the questions, and was only able to mutter, "That's my wife."

Someone had a hand under his left elbow. Someone else was supporting his right arm. He was moving, but couldn't feel his feet. He was guided through the crowd toward a waiting ambulance. He was being pushed and pulled. His legs felt rubbery. People were all over him. He was assisted into the ambulance and was on the way to a hospital, with his wife lying on a stretcher. The sirens were blaring. Blaring. He wasn't sure what was happening. Someone was wiping his face with a cloth. Voices were mumbling all around him. Lisa was covered with blood. She wasn't moving. Ronnie's hands were shaking. His mouth was dry. He was both cold and sweaty at the same time.

The med techs in the ambulance were telling each other what they needed, and what to do. Ronnie sat very still. He was afraid to move. Lisa's normally twinkling eyes remained shut. Her lustrous auburn curls were now matted and void of sheen, her clothes saturated with blood. A voice said, "It doesn't look that bad. I think she's going to make it."

"Oh God. I don't believe this," was all Ronnie could manage. He wasn't sure what had happened. It had all taken place so quickly. But he knew he could handle anything, as long as Lisa was going to be all right.

Chapter
2

Yale was hustled off-stage by security personnel so swiftly that he was unaware of the danger that had just threatened his life. His personal assistant, David Ross, was shouting at a guard, and all Yale could gather from the string of vile profanities was that the coliseum had failed to provide adequate or substantial protection, and had unnecessarily put him in jeopardy.

"David," Yale called out while they hurried to the nearby trailer, "what is it?"

"I'm not sure, Yale, but I think some motherfucker got past the entrance gates with a pistol. Keep it together, Yale. I'll take care of it." They were ushered into the trailer. The door was shut with a slam.

"What else, David? Did you see anything?"

"I saw a standing ovation, Yale. I saw you grab and hold everyone out there. I saw you at your best. Don't get thrown, Yale. You've come too far to get rattled now." David steered Yale to a chair, handing him a glass of sparkling water. He turned to the three men who had entered the trailer with them and with honey-eyed sarcasm asked, "Don't you men think, maybe, you might prove more useful outside the trailer?" He opened the trailer door. "We would appreciate some privacy."

"We'll be right outside, sir," one of the men offered, "just trying to help."

"Fine. Thanks," David answered. He knew he had to remain calm and act unaffected so Yale would feel confident that everything was under control.

It had taken a great deal of persuasion to get Yale touring again. He was still fragile, and not completely over the fear of crowds that had kept him off the concert circuit for the last two years, though that fact had been miraculously kept from the tabloids. David worried that if some incident penetrated the smooth, pat format of this concert tour, Yale might never perform before a live audience again. He brought Yale a crossword puzzle book and pencil, knowing the familiar pastime would help Yale feel safe, especially after what had just happened.

David considered his employer thoughtfully for a moment. A sensitive man, Yale had first sought professional counseling after struggling against a severe depression he couldn't explain, understand, or dispel. In the last few years he had learned to understand himself much better, but he still didn't feel he had reached his potential artistically or professionally. David knew Yale was too hard on himself, but that was what made him so vulnerable, yet so likable.

Of course, there were other reasons why he was vulnerable. Yale had never known his father, the probable source of his blazing sapphire eyes and square jaw. He had been raised by his mother, still his harshest critic and his biggest fan. He adored her and she lived only for him, making sure she told him so often. And he was totally devoted to her. She was the number one woman in his life.

Screams sounded outside the trailer. Observing the tension in Yale's demeanor, David didn't open the door. Instead, he butted himself against the metal frame and yelled, "What the hell is going on?"

"It's okay, sir, just two women. Fans who wanted to see Mr. Frye. We're taking care of it. There's nothing to worry about."

David went back to the chair he'd been occupying without a word. Minutes later he calmly suggested, "Come on, Yale, lie down on the sofa, if that's what you can call this thing. I'll massage your neck. You look like you need to loosen up, and the puzzle book doesn't seem to be doing it."

As David rubbed Yale's neck and back, kneading the stiffness away, he hoped tonight's incident would prove to be of little consequence and they would be able to present the next concert tomorrow night, as planned on their itinerary.

"David, I have a feeling in my gut I don't like. Do you feel it too?"

"Relax, Yale. By tomorrow, this will be just another one of the many obstacles we're used to overcoming." David tried to sound convincing and transmit reassurance, suppressing his own worries.

David vowed to himself that he wouldn't allow Yale's fears to destroy their progress. They had come too far. Yale was more than just David's boss; they were friends, and David wanted Yale's comeback to succeed.

Chapter
3

It didn't take long for the ambulance to reach Beaumont Hospital, but to Ronnie, it felt as if an eternity had passed. He thought about how excited Lisa had been just hours ago, and couldn't believe what was happening. When he'd arrived home from the dusty construction site earlier, Lisa had already been in their bedroom laying out the clothes she had carefully selected for the concert. She had been smiling radiantly as she kissed him hello, and although he'd been exhausted from a trying day, her joyfulness had been infectious. He had laughed at the cuteness of this woman he adored as she sang along to a tune on the radio. He'd teased her for singing off-key and remarked that a weather report suggested it was going to rain that night. He remembered her reply vividly.

"I don't give a shit if it hails, Ronnie! Nothing is going to spoil tonight!" She, too, had worked all day at the accounting firm where she was a researcher, but was evidently too excited about Yale Frye's concert to be tired.

Ronnie looked at his wife's placid face as she lay still on a gurney now, feeling guilty that earlier he had wished he could have stretched out on the sofa instead of going out. "Damn," he said aloud. "If we had stayed home, she wouldn't be lying here now."

"Take it easy," one of the ambulance attendants said. Ronnie barely heard. He couldn't stand looking at Lisa like this. He couldn't help wishing she'd never heard of Yale Frye. Ronnie's eyes focused on the soft auburn curls of Lisa's hair, which normally cascaded to her shoulders, wishing she'd open those beautiful hazel eyes right now. Abruptly he shouted, "Can't you do something? Anything!"

"Calm down," an attendant softly responded, realizing how frightened Ronnie must be.

Lisa had spent an hour applying her makeup earlier. She'd

said she wanted to look good, in case Yale Frye looked her way. Lisa always looked good; she just never thought so. He always told her how beautiful he thought she was, but she had always been very critical of herself. In truth, no one believed she was thirty-eight, with two teenage sons. She not only looked younger than her years, but her jovial personality and exuberance added to her girlishness.

Ronnie stared down at his wife, and couldn't help smiling as he thought of the multitude of Yale Frye pictures Lisa had on the walls of their bedroom. There had to be at least a dozen. Lisa was enthralled with him, collecting everything he recorded on record, cassette, CD, and even the obsolete eight-track tapes. She belonged to his fan club, and more than a dozen times had waited in long lines to get his autograph, and have the chance to stand close to him.

Ronnie remembered, once, when they were playing 'True Confessions' in bed, after sex, Lisa had admitted that she often fantasized about Yale Frye. He had replied that he fantasized about several different women. She had said, "I only dream about Yale. Why do you think about a lot of different people?"

"I guess I like variety in my fantasies. It's more exciting."

Another time, he recalled coming home very late from work and finding Lisa curled up, upset, in their bedroom. He had thought she was disturbed or angry because he'd worked so late, and had neglected to call to tell her. She'd been mumbling, and it had taken twenty minutes before he could decipher what she was saying.

"I'm a Yale Frye reject," she'd pouted. "After all my efforts to find his home address, and all the letters and cards I've sent him, they are now sending my mail back stamped RETURN TO SENDER." Ronnie had thought she was overreacting, but had secretly been relieved that she wasn't upset with him. "Ronnie, I thought he liked hearing from me. I'm so stupid. Why should he care what a fan thinks anyway? He's probably the type of Hollywood star who thinks his shit doesn't stink." He had tried to lift her spirits by taking her to a movie, but on the way home her disappointment had still been evident as she said, "I'll get to him yet. If Yale Frye thinks he's heard the last from me, he's wrong; very wrong."

The ambulance halted. The doors opened quickly. Ronnie's heart was racing. He was still cold, although it was a hot summer night.

Lisa was rushed into the emergency room. People in white surrounded her immediately. Ronnie was asked to sit in a small room, by the side of the emergency room, and wait for someone to obtain the necessary medical information. Fear gripped his heart, while searing pain tore through him. Lisa was his whole life. He couldn't imagine a world without her in it.

He remembered just hours ago, when his sweet, gentle, big-hearted wife had been going from booth to booth purchasing all the latest Yale Frye souvenirs. She had been like a kid set loose in a toy store. She had even bought another stupid pin that she immediately attached to her expensive silk blouse, asking with sincerity if it was on straight. He felt guilty now that he had been impatient in the car because of the heavy traffic, and abrupt when he felt she'd already purchased enough junk. He should have been more tolerant, knowing her infatuation with this entertainer. He shouldn't have tried to rush her to their seats.

Ronnie knew he was lucky to have a wife who was so understanding of all his shortcomings. He had never even considered cheating on her, but was undeniably negligent about making her feel special or appreciated. She asked for so little and gave so generously. He could have at least pretended to be glad they were going to the concert. After all, it was Yale Frye's first concert performance in two years.

"Please, God," he said, praying Lisa would be all right. She had waited for three months for this night, and had so looked forward to seeing her idol. It just wasn't fair that she was hurt now. It just wasn't fair! "Please let her be okay," he silently begged God. "I'll never knock her for being a clean-a-holic, or pick on her for always being plugged into her music, and leaving radios on all over the house, or take for granted all she does. I'll be more supportive of her, and even help her with encouragement when she goes on another one of her stupid diets."

He was still praying when a uniformed woman with white hair and a bad complexion started asking him Lisa's medical history. He gave her perfunctory answers while growing frustrated by this woman's endless array of questions. She refused to find out for him where his wife was now, and what was happening.

Just as he was about to voice his irritation, a police officer approached him. He introduced himself as Sergeant Joe Daly, and he was holding Lisa's purse in his hands. Ronnie stood up as the sergeant asked, "Does this belong to your wife?"

"Yes, it does," Ronnie replied.

The sergeant asked him to sign a paper showing that the purse belonged to his wife, and giving the police permission to examine the contents.

Ronnie signed the paper placed in front of him, then was

directed to follow the officer to another room when he was finished. The uniformed woman, who looked like a walrus, flatly said, "We're done here for now, officer."

"Please follow me," Sergeant Daly directed. He led Ronnie down a corridor to a double door that had a sign on it reading UNAUTHORIZED PERSONS NOT PERMITTED BEYOND THIS POINT.

Ronnie's heart was pounding. "Is my wife okay? Do you know her condition? Please, can you tell me anything?"

"It'll be just a little while, Mr. Klein. Please, follow me."

They reached the end of another corridor and there was a second door that had a NO ADMITTANCE sign nailed to it. Sergeant Daly pushed the door open.

There was a sofa against a bleak wall, an end table, and an antique lamp on one side of the small room. A wooden table with four wooden chairs stood along the opposite wall. The walls were painted pale blue, and the floor was covered with the same dark gray tiles that had lined the floors of the corridors leading to this room. There was an ugly picture of a farmhouse on the wall behind the sofa. Otherwise, the walls were bare. Beside the lamp on the end table was a Newsweek magazine and several empty paper cups. Next to the magazine was a beige telephone with several extension buttons across the bottom. Ronnie sat on the sofa, and was about to question the sergeant when the phone rang.

Sergeant Daly picked up the receiver, said "okay" a few times, and hung up. He then took a statement from Ronnie. Afterwards, he stated flatly, "Please wait here, Mr. Klein. Doctor Feld has just finished examining your wife and will be in shortly." With that, Sergeant Daly left the room, leaving a badly shaken man sitting alone, in an unfamiliar setting, fearing the worst. Ronnie lit a cigarette.

"Fucking assholes! No one gives a shit about people anymore. Everything is a fucking bureaucracy." Fearfully, Ronnie switched his anger to prayer. "Please, God, let Lisa be okay." He knew smoking wasn't permitted in the hospital, but at the moment he really didn't give a damn. He'd been trying to kick the habit for years.

While Ronnie continued waiting for Dr. Feld with trepidation, he thought about how easily he and Lisa had fallen in love. She was a senior in high school when they first met, and he, being two years older, had already graduated and was working for an engraving company. He had lost his mother to cancer a month before his high school graduation. It still hurt, even now, that she hadn't lived to see him get his diploma. His father had remarried within a year and Ronnie had been lonely and unhappy at home. He had never been close to his father, and with a strange woman living in their home, he had felt like an outsider. One night, while he was having dinner with some friends at a local pizzeria, a cousin of his had walked into the restaurant with five other girls. He'd spotted Lisa among them.

Patty and her friends had been seated at a nearby table, and Ronnie hadn't been able to keep his eyes off Lisa. When she had risen to go to the restroom with one of the other girls, Ronnie had called Patty over and said he'd like to be fixed up with her, if she wasn't going with anyone. While saying good-bye, Patty had slipped Lisa's phone number on a piece of paper napkin into his hand. Ronnie had told his friends that night that he had just met the girl he was going to marry. He'd called Lisa the next day and asked her for a date for the following Saturday night. She had accepted.

Ronnie had devoted himself to Lisa from the time they started dating seriously. He'd had other girlfriends, and been popular in high school, but no girl had ever moved him the way Lisa did. He had learned quickly to distinguish between the girls who wanted to date you because of what you could give them, and the gals who really liked you for who you were. He'd known that Lisa was genuine from the beginning.

The door opened swiftly, bringing Ronnie back to reality. Overwhelmed by his fears, he wished he could have remained transfixed by past recollections, rather than facing the ugliness of tonight's events. He attempted to rise from the sofa but his trembling knees kept him glued to the seat. Dr. Jason Feld came over and placed a hand on his shoulder.

Dr. Feld was astute in evaluating situations. He did not waste time on introductions or social graces, simply stating, "It's okay. Your wife is fine. The injury is not life-threatening. I'm sure you must have been terrified, but I am certain she will be fine." Ronnie looked into Dr. Feld's eyes. The unabashed tears conveyed the thanks he felt, but couldn't put into words.

"Mr. Klein, your wife had a bullet enter her body below the shoulder. Fortunately, it pierced the flesh and exited behind the shoulder blade, causing loss of blood, but not damaging any bones or organs. The loss of blood will cause her to feel weak, but I don't feel a transfusion is necessary."

"Is she conscious, Doctor? Can I see her?"

"Yes, but not for a little while yet. I've ordered some x-rays.

As soon as that's completed, I'll have someone direct you to her room. I'd like your wife to remain in the hospital for a few days under observation."

"Doctor, are you telling me everything? Why are you taking x-rays?"

"Lisa is bruised in several areas and there are some lacerations. We'd like to be certain the bruises are superficial. Please, try to relax, Mr. Klein. Our procedure is to be thorough. Your wife is being well taken care of." Compassionately, Dr. Feld added, "the worst is over, Mr. Klein."

The expression on Sergeant Daly's face, who was standing in the doorway as Dr. Feld turned to leave, seemed to suggest otherwise.

Chapter
4

At the Diamond Coliseum, police and security personnel attempted to control pandemonium.

Squad cars were everywhere. There were conflicting reports from the many people questioned, and the puzzle seemed to be missing vital pieces. The area where Lisa and Ronnie had been seated was roped off. The surrounding areas, including the cement steps stained with Lisa's blood, were roped off as well. The police carefully scrutinized anything that might clarify the incident. Several people claimed to have witnessed the entire shooting. Officers diligently recorded their statements, documenting names, addresses, and phone numbers, in case they were needed for further questioning or corroboration.

Photographers were everywhere, with a multitude of equipment. Reporters were swarming, like bees to honey, for a story. Questions were coming from every direction. The person who knew the least, Yale Frye, was still inside the trailer where officers had whisked him after the shots were fired. Yale and David had been advised to remain inside until further notice. They were doing just that.

Yale was tense and annoyed. His patience was wearing thin. He attempted to recreate the moments prior to the sounds he had heard and the events that had followed. The only thing he really remembered clearly was a lot of yelling and what sounded like a firecracker. He told an officer what he had heard, and now waited for additional information. Meanwhile, David was placing phone calls, trying to find out whatever he could, with little success.

The two had been in the confining trailer for over two hours. Yale was not accustomed to being restricted and was becoming agitated. Earlier, he had been frightened. Now, he was angry. It reminded him of the time he had first performed in England. He hadn't had his own plane then and the chartered one was forced to make an emergency landing. He hadn't found out how close to death he had been until he heard a news telecast hours later. It seemed everyone had been trying to protect him. When he'd been told the complete story, he'd felt defenseless. His fear of crowds had intensified after that incident. That same feeling of helplessness was festering inside him now.

"Yale, I have someone from the office bringing over a television that works. Maybe we'll learn a little more than we know now. Are you okay?"

"Yeah, thanks, David. Next time we ask for a trailer, we'll have to be more specific about what we want it to contain, then have it checked before a show." Yale's voice rose. "This fucking trailer must be ten years old! Even the lighting is for shit!"

"I'll make a note of it, Yale. How about some fresh coffee?"

"No, David. What I want is a bottle to shove up the ass of the person responsible for this piece of crap."

David didn't say anything. He had been with Yale long enough to know Yale was not extremely particular about his dressing room accommodations while touring, and was just letting off steam. As long as the rooms were clean, and stocked with sparkling water, fresh fruit, and vegetables, Yale didn't make a fuss. Unlike many stars, Yale wasn't put out by something so inconsequential as the size of a dressing room. He was still amazed his success had reached a pinnacle beyond his wildest dreams.

David left the narrow sofa bed to answer a knock on the door. A young uniformed security officer stood outside. "Here's the TV you requested. Want me to hook it up, sir?"

"I can handle it," David replied, reaching to accept the small set from the guard. "Thanks," he acknowledged.

"No biggie," the young guard responded.

David closed the door of the trailer, found an outlet, and turned on the set. Both he and Yale laughed when every station David turned to had a commercial running on it. "Figures," David said.

"Where's CNN when you need it?" Yale quipped. Just then, David found a station with a local, unfamiliar newscaster reporting: "Our latest report verifies that the shooting, which occurred at the Diamond Coliseum, at approximately 9:40 p.m. tonight, has resulted in twelve persons being treated for minor injuries. One woman, believed to be directly involved with the incident, was injured by a bullet. She is still in surgery, at Beaumont Hospital, in Canton. Reports state mega star Yale Frye was targeted, but not injured. Police teams are currently at the Coliseum, where we understand a complete investigation is under way. It has not been substantiated, but word is that Yale Frye is still on the premises, under tight security. We go now to Larry Blue, at Beaumont hospital, for the latest update."

"Thanks, Jim. Right now, we are able to confirm that fourteen people, not twelve, as originally reported, have been treated at Beaumont Hospital for minor scrapes and bruises. All of them, I believe, have been, or are being, released. One woman stated that the security people made sure the area was cleared without incident, and she believed the majority of people were unaware of what had happened. She said an announcement was made, after Yale Frye was pulled off the stage, that the show would not continue, and everyone was asked to leave the arena. She also stated, Jim, that word spread quickly that there was a shooting near the stage, but most of the people apparently didn't know what was happening. She added that the police arrived quickly, and her bruises were the result of being knocked down on the concrete steps. People were evacuated quickly. Speculation spread that someone had been shot. But, apparently, no one knew who."

"Hold on, Jim. I understand Sergeant Joe Daly, of the Canton Police Department, is going to make an announcement regarding the shooting, with some new and pertinent disclosures."

The camera focused on the tall, uniformed police officer. "Ladies and gentlemen, I'm Sergeant Daly of the Canton Police Department. At 9:40 p.m., two shots were fired in the Diamond Coliseum, during a Yale Frye concert. Fourteen people—no, fifteen—were brought to the emergency room here at Beaumont Hospital, fourteen with minor injuries. Let me add, right now," Sergeant Daly continued, "it is remarkable so few people were hurt, considering there were over ten thousand people at the Coliseum during the incident. We can report there were no fatalities. However, I have been informed that there is one serious injury. A woman who appears to have been involved with the shooting is in serious condition. We have also received word that Yale Frye was not injured. We know of no other serious injuries. At this time, we have conflicting reports regarding what actually occurred. So, we'll have to wait until we know more before we make any additional statements."

Reporters began shouting questions. The barrage was relentless. Someone called, "Who is the lady who was shot?" Another yelled, "Was the woman shot in a struggle? We've heard she was shot while trying to shoot Yale Frye, then we heard she was shot instead of Mr. Frye. Can you comment on these rumors?"

Sergeant Daly yelled, "Hold on! Hold on." He took a deep breath. "We don't know the role of the injured woman in the shooting. All we know for certain is that she was the only person injured by a bullet, and is currently unable to speak with us."

"How soon before you can talk to her? Is she dead?"

Sergeant Daly was getting frustrated by the flood of questions. He held up a hand and yelled. "No! No. The woman is not dead. She was brought to the hospital unconscious, taken to surgery, and is in the recovery room at this time."

Previous experiences with the media had taught Daly that the 'vultures' wouldn't let up until they were forced to, and that being vague only made matters worse. He added firmly, "I am telling you the facts as we know them. As soon as we know anything more, so will you." Sergeant Daly was handed another slip of paper.

Someone yelled, "Sergeant Daly, does the woman have a name, or don't you know that, yet, either?"

The sarcasm didn't go unnoticed by Daly. He scratched his head, then calmly replied, "Yes. The injured woman has just been identified as Lisa Klein. As you know, we could not disclose the identity of the wounded party until her family was apprised of the situation." Daly waved his hand to indicate he was concluding his remarks, then turned and walked back into the hospital, while reporters continued shouting questions at him.

David looked at Yale's pale face and immediately turned the television set off.

Yale turned to David in the confinement of the trailer, feeling like his face had just been slapped. The reality that someone had aimed a gun at him had not penetrated the fog surrounding the events of the night until he watched the news broadcast. Now, he sat stunned with his jaw clenched. His face wore an expression of shock and horror.

"David, he did say Lisa Klein, didn't he?"

"Yes, he did."

"The Lisa Klein that has been sending mail to me is from Canton, Ohio, right?"

"Yes, Yale." David went to the door of the trailer and yanked it open. The guard in front of the door quickly turned around. Before he could say anything, David shouted to him, "You! Get the person in charge of the shooting investigation in here. And get me that person now!"

The stunned guard said, "I'm not supposed to leave my post, but I'll use my pager to get someone here right away, sir." David watched as the guard held up a hand radio and spoke, "This is Bill, the guard in front of Mr. Frye's trailer. You better get someone in charge of the investigation over here right away."

"Bill, what's up?" a voice questioned.

Bill saw the rage in David's face and said into the radio, "just get me a top dog, and do it fast. Okay?"

The voice responded, "I'm on it. Hold on."

David, feeling apologetic for shouting, said, "thanks" and shut the trailer door gently.

Within minutes, there were at least fifteen people in various uniforms outside the trailer door. When David opened the door, he couldn't help thinking that fame had some advantages. The 'ordinary Joe' certainly wouldn't get results this quickly. Then again, the 'ordinary Joe' wouldn't have been a target.

David looked at the face closest to the door and asked, "Are you in charge?"

"I'm Sergeant Bill Hill, one of the officers working on the investigation."

"Come in a minute, please," David directed.

Sergeant Hill went into the trailer and spoke with Yale and David for twenty minutes. After their conversation, Sergeant Hill picked up the telephone and had Sergeant Daly paged at Beaumont Hospital. Ten minutes later Yale and David, escorted by Sergeant Hill, were on their way to the hospital.

Sergeant Hill delivered Yale and David to Sergeant Daly at the hospital, then left immediately to return to the Diamond Coliseum. Yale and David spoke briefly with Sergeant Daly, reiterating what Hill had told him on the phone. Then the three entered the room, accompanied by Doctor Feld, to face a bewildered Ronnie Klein.

Sergeant Daly sometimes lacked tact, and often gave the impression of being more than a little pompous. He didn't mince words as he asked Ronnie, "Mind answering a few questions?"

Ronnie got up asking, "What's wrong?"

"Nothing. We just need a little information from you," Daly stated flatly.

"Well, I've been sitting here going crazy, waiting to see Lisa, and if you don't mind," he turned to Doctor Feld, "I really want to see my wife."

"She's fine, Mr. Klein," assured Dr. Feld. "I know you're anxious to see her. But since Lisa is sleeping right now, perhaps you'd like to answer Sergeant Daly's questions. Then I'll personally take you to see your wife."

"All right," Ronnie answered, feeling less apprehensive after

Dr. Feld's calming assurance.

Everyone but Ronnie sat around the wooden table that faced the couch. Ronnie sat back down on the sofa he had occupied for hours. He was not introduced to Yale Frye or the man with him. Both so far had been mute.

"Mr. Klein," the sergeant asked, "I take it you and your wife are fans of Yale Frye?"

Ronnie looked into Yale Frye's face and with a tinge of embarrassment said, "we both have always enjoyed Mr. Frye's concerts, but Lisa is the one who is nuts when it comes to him."

Yale Frye sat silently and expressionless. He did not acknowledge what Ronnie thought was a big compliment.

Sergeant Daly continued, "she's told you she's nuts about him?"

"Are you kidding? She's been writing him for years. She sends him cards, poems, presents, and has everything he's ever recorded on record, cassettes and CD. She's a member of his fan club, and there are more pictures of Mr. Frye than there are of me on our bedroom walls."

"Has she ever tried to meet him?"

"Sure. She has stood in lines for hours to get close to him, and get an autograph. At least three times I know of, maybe more."

"Really. That's quite a fan all right, Mr. Klein."

"Did it ever bother Lisa that Mr. Frye didn't write her back?"

"No, I don't think so. She said it made her feel good to write him. But I know she got upset a few months ago when her letters started coming back stamped RETURN TO SENDER."

"How did you know she was upset, Mr. Klein?"

"She said so. But you don't know Lisa. She said she'd have to think of another way to get to him. And if you knew my wife, you'd know that Lisa does not give up on anything easily." Ronnie was speaking with affection, and wondered why Yale Frye was just sitting there, not saying a word.

"Mr. Klein," the sergeant continued, "I know you gave me a short statement about what you saw take place when your wife was wounded. But I was so busy, and you were so upset, which is very understandable, I need to have the story right in my head before I type up a report. Could you tell me everything you remember again? Then we can all go see how Lisa is doing. Okay?"

"I told you. I really don't know very much. All I know is we were all standing and applauding for the number Mr. Frye sang. Someone shoved me, so I was knocked down in the aisle. I heard

Lisa yell "Get down!" and the next thing I see is Lisa on the ground, blood everywhere, and a lot of noise and pushing. I never saw a gun. All I know is that I thought she was dead. And all because of..."

"Because of what, Mr. Klein?"

"Nothing. Forget it. Can I see Lisa now?"

"What were you about to say, Mr. Klein?" Sergeant Daly persisted.

"All because of a fucking concert, and because of him!" Ronnie roared, looking at Yale Frye, who just sat there listening silently.

Ronnie got up, looking at Dr. Feld pleadingly. Dr. Feld rose, feeling sorry for Ronnie. He patted him on the back saying, "Come on, and let's go see if Lisa is awake."

Ronnie kept pace with Doctor Feld, walking closely beside him. Sergeant Daly, Yale Frye, and David Ross followed a few feet behind.

On the way to see Lisa, Ronnie remembered their first date, when they had gone to see a movie. He had been late picking her up, and when they had arrived at the theater the first show had been sold out. Ronnie had purchased tickets for the second showing. Lisa had admitted to him, years later, that she'd been worried they weren't going to have much to say to each other for two hours, until the second showing. She had been wrong. Her fears had faded quickly as she and Ronnie seemed to find endless topics in which they both were interested. They'd even missed the beginning of the second movie, still engrossed in conversation. Neither had minded. After the movie, they had gone to a restaurant and talked for another two hours. Ronnie had asked her out again when he walked her to her door that night. Soon they'd been inseparable. They had been married fourteen months after their first date.

Lisa was gentle, warm, and the first person, since his mother died, he felt good around. Her parents were Holocaust survivors. She resented how strict they were while she was growing up. Ronnie remembered back to when they got engaged. They were both nervous about telling their parents of their marriage plans. It wasn't because Lisa's parents didn't like him. Quite the contrary. They both liked him fine, and Ronnie's father liked Lisa. But both sets of parents said exactly what Lisa and Ronnie knew they would: "What's the hurry? You're both so young."

Initially like two kids playing house, they'd grown up

together and bonded, not just as husband and wife, but as best friends. They'd gone to Lisa's parent's house for Sabbath dinner every Friday night. They had purchased a little bungalow, turned it into a comfortable home, and started their family the following year. Their first baby had been stillborn,and Lisa had remained depressed until she found herself pregnant with Marc. It had been a difficult pregnancy, and they had both been nervous and frightened until the seven-pound bundle of joy was in their arms. Steven had been born the following year. They had both agreed then to count their blessings for the two healthy children they had been granted.

Lisa's health problems had begun after they'd celebrated their tenth wedding anniversary. First she'd needed gallbladder surgery. Then she'd had to have a tumor removed from her left ovary. The following year, Ronnie remembered, she'd had bouts of depression that left her feeling hopeless. Next came the tumor in her right breast, fortunately benign. And just last year, a hysterectomy.

Ronnie was thinking about how much Lisa had been through, especially for such a young woman, when the door to her room was opened. He was suddenly brought back to the ugly reality of the moment.

Chapter
5

"Do you have a suspect in custody?" Sergeant Daly heard as he walked back into the hospital. It infuriated him, having to admit they didn't.

He was going over the facts he had in his head. Too many things didn't add up. How did the gun get past security at the coliseum? That one was a no-brainer: smuggled in. Why was Yale Frye targeted? Easy, too: some nut wanted him immortalized or dead. It was not uncommon for a famous person to get death threats from crazed fans or lunatics. Look at the list of Presidents targeted since Kennedy was killed in 'sixty-three. And if someone could get close enough to shoot at a President, who the fuck was really safe? But something wasn't right; there wasn't enough evidence left at the scene. Nuts don't bother to clean up after themselves. One thing was certain in Daly's mind. This had been a carefully planned attempt, not a random shooting. This was a calculated, premeditated effort to eliminate Yale Frye.

The reports coming in all differed. The aisles were congested, since it was near the end of the first act, and Yale Frye was receiving a standing ovation, with a multitude of people applauding, cheering and screaming. No one saw a gun. Some reported struggling, but with so many people standing, no one could clearly identify the strugglers. Some said two men were fighting. Others said a man and woman were struggling, but no one knew for sure. Mr. Klein said he was knocked down. So what some had seen could have been Ronnie Klein being pushed to the ground. With the chaotic and tumultuous activity at concerts, how could anyone be expected to decipher excitement from anarchy?

No two stories matched. Some had heard one shot, some had heard two shots, and some had heard what they thought was the sound of a firecracker. Others interviewed stated that they hadn't been able to hear anything over the applause. They'd found a bloodied bullet, probably the one that had pierced the woman in the hospital, and they'd dug another bullet out from the underside of the stage. The second bullet looked like a match to the first. Still, there was no gun. Identifying anyone was going to be a bitch, because it had been so dark when the incident occurred. Daly was going to stay at the hospital until he could talk to Lisa Klein. It looked like she was the only one who might be able to give them some answers.

Sergeant Bill Hill had Daly paged an hour later from Yale Frye's trailer. He told Daly what Mr. Frye and his assistant, David Ross, had just told him, that a woman by the same name as announced on the television broadcast had been writing to Mr. Frye frequently. It was possible it was the same person; David had noticed her sitting near the front at the concert tonight, and thought he recognized her from prior encounters at autograph sessions. When David said he was sure he could make a positive identification in person, Daly advised Hill to bring them to the hospital immediately.

As the four men approached the room Lisa occupied in the hospital now, Sgt. Daly felt hopeful. He would get to the crux of this case and get some answers. There was a police officer sitting next to Room 235. Ronnie asked why he was there, not directing his question to anyone in particular.

"Just a precaution," Daly was quick to answer.

As Dr. Feld pushed the door open, the four men entered. Dr. Feld and Ronnie approached the bed. The doctor turned toward Daly, Yale, and David. "Give him a minute." The men stopped, standing against the wall, respecting the doctor's request.

"Lisa. It's Doctor Feld. I've brought Ronnie to see you."

"Lisa, it's me. Are you okay?" Ronnie asked, touching her hand and bending to kiss her cheek.

She slowly opened her eyes, inquiring, "Did they get him?"

"What?" Ronnie asked, not hearing her clearly.

"Lisa, it's Doctor Feld. I know you're tired, but are you able to answer a few questions?"

Slowly she became more alert. She looked at the doctor, then at Ronnie. "Did you call the boys?"

"Yes, honey. They're fine. Rose is going to run over to keep them company."

"She's such a good neighbor," Lisa said, a smile forming over her dry cracked lips.

"I told the boys I'd call them again after I saw you. I told them not to come to the hospital, since I wasn't sure when I'd get to see you."

"Good," she replied, trying to push herself up a little on the bed. "Ouch!" she screamed. Doctor Feld directed her not to move without assistance, since the area the bullet had pierced was going to be very tender, and recommended she lie on her right side for more comfort. As she slowly shifted, he propped an extra pillow behind her back. "That's better. Thanks," she said gratefully, more alert now.

She was about to say something when she noticed David Ross and Yale Frye standing near the foot of her bed with a policeman. She looked at Ronnie and back again to the three men. After the initial shock of seeing them subsided, she surmised quickly that they had come to thank her for stopping that man from shooting Yale. She suddenly felt uneasy, knowing she must look awful. She lowered her eyes to conceal the embarrassment.

The police officer spoke first and she turned her attention to him. "I'm Sergeant Daly," he began. "Can you answer a few questions, Mrs. Klein?"

"Okay," she replied.

"Do you know these two men?" he asked, looking toward Yale and David.

"Of course," she answered.

"Who are they, Mrs. Klein, and how do you know them?"

"Everyone knows who Yale Frye is, and I met his assistant, David Ross, a few times when I went to autograph signings. I've also seen his picture in Yale's concert souvenir books," she stated, wondering why he was asking.

"Mrs. Klein, it has been suggested that you have been writing to them for some time now, at a private post office box that is not known to the general public. You have also persisted in writing to that address, even after you were asked to stop. Is that correct?"

She looked at Ronnie, feeling betrayed, and simply answered, "yes."

The sergeant didn't give her time to think. He quickly asked, "Mrs. Klein, who went with you to tonight's concert?"

"My husband."

"Anyone else?"

"No."

"Mrs. Klein, do you hate Yale Frye for not writing you back?"

"Of course not. He's a very busy..." She stopped, suddenly realizing they weren't there to thank her. They thought she was somehow involved in the attempt on Yale's life. "Wait a minute," she said, anger in her voice, "what's going on? I got shot trying to stop some creep from shooting him, and you're talking to me like I'm on trial."

"If you have nothing to hide, Mrs. Klein, why would you feel like you were on trial?"

"Excuse me. I said that's the way you were speaking to me, not the way I felt. Now, if you don't mind, I'd like all of you to leave. I'm very tired."

"Mrs. Klein, do you own a gun?" Sergeant Daly persisted.

"Why don't you ask my attorney?" she retorted, insulted by his insinuation.

"Mrs. Klein, I understand you're under psychiatric treatment. Is that correct?"

She couldn't keep the tears from surfacing. She covered her eyes with a hand. "Get the hell out of here. Please! Get out. You too, Ronnie. Go! Please go."

"That's enough," Dr. Feld interjected. "Mrs. Klein is not strong enough to continue this conversation tonight. What she needs now is rest. Hold your questions for another time." He guided them, including Ronnie, to the door and into the hallway.

Ronnie was beside himself. They had used him. He'd helped them hurt Lisa. He'd stood there helplessly, and confided in people that were trying to blame her for something she was incapable of. He felt like a fool. He looked at Yale Frye, David Ross, and Sergeant Joe Daly, feeling humiliation. He hated them, and himself, for his gullibility.

Sergeant Daly asked, "You will be available if we have additional questions, won't you, Mr. Klein?"

Ronnie didn't answer. He turned away from the open elevator and walked to the stairway door. Before going down, he stood there and tried to regain his composure. Once outside the hospital, he realized he had come to the hospital in the ambulance. His car was still at the Diamond Coliseum. He started walking aimlessly.

A few minutes later, a cab stopped next to him. The driver honked the horn and Ronnie halted. Out of the cab stepped Yale Frye, speaking the first words he had uttered all night. "Mr. Klein," he said, "I'm really very lucky I had Lisa in the audience tonight or I might be dead now. Come on, we'll take you home."

Ronnie didn't know why, but he got into the cab. He let Yale Frye tell the driver his address and take him home. He could not remember a day when he had ever felt this dense. His stupidity had caused Lisa additional pain, and he had no one to blame but himself.

Chapter
6

Jeff Rose and his wife, Peggy, fought all the way home from the Yale Frye concert. Peggy had begged Jeff to sneak in a borrowed camcorder. She'd promised him the best sex he'd ever had if he'd get the concert on tape for her. He'd finally given in to her persuasions. It had actually been very easy to walk into the Coliseum with the camcorder buried beneath the family-size chicken order in a cardboard container. He'd also had a blanket over his arm. The jerks at the entrance just glanced at the tickets. None of them really give a shit anyway, he'd thought, walking casually through the gate.

Taking their seats at the concert, Jeff had sat in the aisle seat with Peggy beside him. When the show had been about to start, he'd taken the blanket and placed it over the armrest of the aisle seat. Peggy had surreptitiously handed the camcorder to him, and he'd wrapped the strap around the armrest until it felt tight and secure. He'd managed to turn the unit facing the stage, and turned it on. They'd been so close that he hadn't needed to use the light. As he was taping the show, he'd thought about how long he was going to have Peggy suck his dick when they got home.

At the end of the first act, Yale Frye had received a standing ovation with deafening applause. Jeff had remained in his seat so that he wouldn't destroy the positioning of the camcorder. Suddenly, a fellow behind him had lurched out and into the aisle. Jeff had turned in reaction. When the woman fell and he saw blood, he'd panicked. He'd yanked the camcorder free from the armrest and grabbed Peggy's hand, pulling her down the row to the opposite end of the aisle. They'd left before most of the audience even knew something had happened.

The announcement had been made to clear the arena as they were climbing the stairs toward the exit. Peggy had been so engrossed in the concert, standing and clapping for the ovation, that she hadn't known what was happening until they'd reached the car and Jeff had explained. He'd related what he'd witnessed, saying he had to go to the police. Peggy had pleaded for him not to get involved. He'd kept insisting that he had to.

They were still arguing about it when they reached their house. Once inside, Peggy changed her approach. She said that even though he'd only taped half the show, she'd still give him a blow job if anything came out on the tape.

He said, "Start sucking, baby," and started fondling her.

"Not so quick, buster. How do I know you got Yale Frye on the tape?"

"Well, I'll put the tape in the machine. But I'm only rewinding it a little, to prove I got the show recorded. Then, if you want the tape for keeps, baby, you're gonna have to earn it."

"So, show me how good you did, lover," she teased, pulling her blouse over her head, exposing firm ripe breasts and rigid nipples, "and I'll show you how good I am."

He was hard and horny. Quickly he took the tape and put it inside the VCR. He pushed rewind for a minute. She came over and started unzipping his pants. He moaned. She loosened her grip on his erection saying, "Play it again, Sam."

They laughed as he pushed the 'play' button. Both froze as they looked at the screen. Jeff had taped the entire struggle between the man and woman. They heard her yelling for Yale to get down, and they watched as she was shot during the struggle. He had taped the entire crime. He looked at Peggy, asking, "What now? You didn't want me to give a statement; do you want me to destroy the evidence, too?" Peggy started crying. Jeff continued, "We have to go to the cops with this."

She looked up at him tearfully, "We can't. I'll end up in jail."

"Why? Peggy, talk to me."

She looked at Jeff and sobbed out her story. "Jeff, I knew we couldn't afford to go to the concert. We never have any money for fun. We're always paying bills, working so hard all the time, to pay off all the loans. I just wanted a good time for us. You know I like Yale Frye, and you said you like his music too. So, I stole a jacket from work and traded it for the tickets, and if we tell the cops and they start checking us out, I'll be in trouble. Anyway, taping a show like we did isn't legal either."

"Okay," Jeff said. "This is kind of good...the tape, I mean."

"How do you figure that?" she asked, still crying.

"Look, we know we have to do what's right. I can drop the tape off in an envelope and they will have the evidence. But they won't know who it's from." Jeff couldn't chastise her about the jacket, realizing how little fun they had, and their seemingly endless financial strain. He realized that she was already feeling guilty and he couldn't stand to see her sobbing.

She started to regain some composure. She knew Jeff was right. "Now I know why I married you," Peggy said, drying her eyes, "'cause you are the smartest."

"Yeah. Well, does smart get rewarded?" he asked, pulling her closer.

She undressed him slowly, not caring at the moment how poor they were or what was on the tape. Forgetting everything, she moved over him, taking his hardness into her mouth. While her hands cupped his balls, she stroked his cock, and ran her tongue up one side, then down the other of his thick shaft. His groaning grew louder. She took him into her, as far as she could, moving her tongue expertly. His breathing intensified with his pleasure. He held her head as he exploded fiercely. "I love you so much, Peggy," he whispered, then moved his mouth down her body to please her.

The next morning, Jeff dropped the tape into the mailbox just outside the post office. On the envelope, he had written in bold letters:

Canton Police Department
Urgent
PRIORITY MAIL
Open At Once.

Once back in the car, Jeff drove to work feeling much better. He knew he and Peggy were doing the right thing.

Chapter
7

Early the next morning, Ronnie entered Lisa's hospital room. Ignoring the officer perched with a cup of coffee next to the door, Ronnie sheepishly approached Lisa and kissed her gently on the cheek. As he stood next to the bed, they appraised one another, realizing neither of them had slept much.

The untouched breakfast tray and numerous pieces of used Kleenex told Ronnie how his wife was reacting. He pulled a chair over to the side of the bed, feeling the strain between them, and asked if he could do anything for her.

"Yes. Shoot me and put me out of my misery," she answered tartly.

"I don't believe this whole thing. I don't even know what happened," he exclaimed.

"I know," she said, "it all happened so fast." She told him everything she remembered. He filled in what had transpired from the time she lost consciousness until he was allowed to see her.

"Should I get a lawyer?" he asked when they were both more relaxed, understanding more clearly the events of the previous night.

"Not yet," she replied. "They haven't charged me with anything. They just made awful insinuations." She felt prejudged, overwhelmed, and very tired.

The next half hour was spent discussing their boys, the calls Ronnie needed to handle, and what he could bring her from home. She asked if he would get her a newspaper from the gift shop. As he rose to comply with her request, Dr. Feld came into the room.

He examined Lisa, lowering the hospital gown from her left shoulder and carefully removing the bandages from the treated wounds. Ronnie stood on the opposite side, holding her hand, when Yale Frye entered the room without knocking. He was alone.

"I'm sorry," he said, taking a step backward, feeling awkward.

"For what?" she asked curtly. "For the present intrusion? For standing there last night, not saying one single word, while I'm being treated like a criminal? For your dumb assumptions? Or, perhaps, for thinking you're better than anyone else because you're famous?"

"I guess I deserve that. I'll leave if you want. I probably shouldn't have come."

"Gee, the PR will be much better now that you have. Hell, the big star visits wounded fan. That should make good copy, don't you think?" she spouted, feeling tears sting her eyes again.

"That's not why I came," he responded defensively.

"Well, you needn't have bothered. I don't know why I ever wrote to you in the first place. Elton John is much more talented. I should have written him instead," she said harshly, trying to hurt him.

"I agree. Elton John is much more talented." He turned and left the room. He walked to the elevator, took it to the main floor, and headed for the rental car. He got into the car, started the ignition. He couldn't help grinning when he heard the song playing on the car radio. Elton John was singing, "Sorry Seems To Be The Hardest Word." Yale turned off the ignition, went back into the hospital, and up to Lisa's room.

While Yale was going up one elevator to Lisa's room, Ronnie was coming down another, on his way to handle the various errands Lisa had requested.

Yale walked to Lisa's room. He acknowledged the officer stationed by the door, and decided, this time, to knock. She heard the knock, answering, "I already gave," thinking it was time for some other test, or for more blood to be drawn.

"I know you did, but can I come in anyway?"

She recognized Yale Frye's voice. Still testy, she replied with sarcasm, "Sure, if you like being abused."

"I'll take my chances," he responded, approaching her bed.

"So the man not only sings, but has balls as well," she countered, her voice still filled with bitterness. "Boy, talk about having illusions shattered!"

"I'm not really as awful as you think," he attempted.

"No, I know. That's not what I meant. It's just, for so long I've been playing these head games with myself, wondering, and making up scenarios of what it might be like if I ever got to meet you. We would have a conversation or something, and now..." she stopped, afraid her emotions would re-emerge.

He understood what she meant, seeing how hard she was trying to maintain control. "Well, I think we should start over," he said walking backwards to the door. He paused, cleared his throat, then slowly approached the bed, and bowed, "Hi, I'm Yale Frye. I'm here to express my sincerest gratitude to you for what you did on my behalf, last night. I know I should have said something sooner, but I sing better than I think, and that's not saying much if you compare me to someone like, say, Elton John."

She smiled for a second, sensing his sincerity, and couldn't control the tears any longer. He felt a tenderness he didn't quite understand. He sat on the chair beside the bed, leaned over to kiss her wet cheek, and softly said, "I'm sorry. I'm really, really sorry."

Needing to be comforted so badly, she instinctively put her arms around his neck and sobbed, "God. Oh God. I can't believe this whole thing!"

"I know," he whispered, allowing her to hold onto him and finding he was holding onto her too. For the first time since the shooting had occurred, he allowed himself to feel, really feel. Some tears of his own trickled down his cheeks. Together, at that moment, the impact of what had transpired, and how close to death they had both been, finally penetrated. They held each other for moments with mutual understanding.

"You know," she whispered when the tears subsided, "I normally handle things much better than this. Look better, too."

She let go as he sat up. He looked at her smiling, "Maybe I'll hang around for a while so you can show me." She reached for a tissue and handed one to Yale.

They talked about the shooting. She repeated what she remembered, then related what Ronnie had described. He offered what he knew, repeating several times that he thought she was really brave, but crazy, to risk her life. He spoke about having had death threats over the years, but never believing anything like this could really happen. Both felt better as they spoke. Yale was moved by her sensitivity, and Lisa became aware of how soft-hearted Yale really was.

Doctor Feld came back into the room around noon, followed by an orderly with a lunch tray. "You didn't eat breakfast. How about lunch?"

Lisa looked up at Doctor Feld, "I can't. Maybe later."

"You know, I meant what I said earlier. If you don't eat, I'm going to have to put the IV back."

She pushed herself up a little more, looked at the contents on the tray and made a face. She looked up at Doctor Feld and extended her arm. Yale and Doctor Feld laughed, glad to see her spirits improving.

"Lisa, I received the results of your lab work," Dr. Feld added. "Can we discuss it now?"

She understood that he was giving her the option of discussing her affairs in front of Yale or privately. Yale understood as well, interjecting, "I'll leave, if you'll be more comfortable."

She studied his face for a minute. "You don't want to leave, do you?"

"No, I don't. But I will if you want me to."

She understood what Yale was feeling. She looked at Yale, then up at Dr. Feld, "What the hell. Shoot, Doc." She giggled. "Oops, wrong choice of words, wouldn't you say?"

Doctor Feld was about to begin when Ronnie entered. His arms were filled with bags. He put them at the foot of the bed, asking if there was anything wrong. The doctor told Ronnie he had arrived in time to hear the medical and lab evaluation. Lisa, noticing concern on Ronnie's face, tried to lighten the atmosphere with wit.

"Well, doc, the good news is I know I'm not pregnant. So what's the bad news?"

"Your blood count has dropped dramatically since last night. You have a temperature, which suggests an infection in the body."

"Antibiotics for a few days, and I'll be good as new, right?"

Doctor Feld ignored Lisa's attempt to minimize her injuries, continuing in an even tone, "The wounds, where the bullet entered and exited the body, will remain tender, but should give you less pain in a few days, Lisa. The bruising on your body appeared to be superficial initially; however, the latest test results suggest otherwise, and there is some inflammation of the right kidney."

"Okay. I get the picture. Are we done?"

"There is also blood in the urine samples we tested last night and again this morning. Your medical history states that you had a hysterectomy a year ago, Lisa, and that they removed both ovaries. So you stopped menstruating at that time, correct?"

"Correct," she said flatly. "Are you done now?"

"Almost, Lisa. I need to know if you have had any vaginal bleeding since the hysterectomy?"

"None. I take Premarin Monday through Friday, stop for the weekends and feel fine. Are we done now?"

Doctor Feld saw the anguish Lisa was trying to mask. "We'll talk more later. Get some rest." As he walked toward the door, he motioned for the men to follow him. When they were in the hall, Doctor Feld said, "I don't want to alarm anyone, but she feels a lot worse than she is willing to admit. I wanted her aware that we know it. That's why I was deliberately probing. She has to be candid about how she's feeling. I'm going to order a few more tests for this afternoon. I think it would be a good idea to restrict her visitors for today."

"Thank you." Ronnie said. He understood that the doctor was trying to help by keeping intruders, including Sergeant Daly, out.

"See if you can get some liquids into her. I don't want to have to put her back on IV."

Ronnie and Yale walked back to Lisa. They found her fast asleep. She looked delicate and pale. The two sat in vigil, each with his own thoughts. Both feeling responsible for her condition, afraid to voice their fears. Neither able to express nor come to terms with their emotions.

Chapter
8

Sergeant Daly was annoyed. He hated being wrong, but had to admit the possibility that he had been completely off base, and that Lisa Klein was a victim, not a villain. He had told Hill as he left the precinct, "I was tough on the lady last night. I'm gonna see what she has to say today. Hopefully, she'll be feeling better and more like talking. You know, I got hold of her shrink and told him I knew everything he and Lisa discussed was confidential. But, off the record, in his gut, did he believe Lisa was capable of committing a crime like this one? You know what her psychiatrist said, Hill? He said, 'Lisa only hurts Lisa, and she'd sacrifice herself to help someone else if that's what it took.' While I'm gone, go over the statements and put a list of possible matches together. There's got to be more here than we're seeing."

Stepping out of the elevator on his way to Room 235, Sergeant Daly was halted by a security officer and asked where he was going. Familiar with procedures, he told the guy, "Room 235."

"I'm sorry, officer. The patient in Room 235 is on restricted visitors by doctors' orders. I'll have to ask you to remain outside that room."

"Look, you little shit," Daly sputtered, aware of the rules, but mad as hell for having to answer to some twerp. "Just get me her doctor. Fast! I don't have all day."

"Okay, officer. Please wait at the nurses' station while I have him paged."

Daly stayed where he was, leaned back against the wall with his arms folded, and retorted, "Go on, kid. I know the routine. Call for the doctor."

The security guard went to have Doctor Feld paged, completely intimidated. He was new to the job and didn't want any trouble.

"Don't worry, kid. I'll stay put," Daly said, slightly sorry for being rude. After all, he was only doing his job. Daly sorted through his notepad while the doctor was being paged.

"Shit," he said to himself, frustrated that so little was adding up. They knew the bullets came from the same gun, but they'd found no gun. The blood was the same type as Lisa Klein's, but A positive was a common blood type. She had been the only one shot that they were aware of. There had been a struggle, but between whom? So far, the descriptions ranged from a young guy in his twenties to an older man around fifty, with hair that was either blond, black, brown, or gray. Well, at least no one said the guy had red hair, he thought cynically. And what the fuck happened to the guy she was struggling with? If he was trying to stop Lisa, wouldn't he have come forward? On the other hand, if he was guilty of attempted murder or conspiracy, it made sense for him to vanish. With over ten thousand people at the Coliseum that night, how were they going to come up with a nondescript person smart enough to lose himself in the crowd and leave the Coliseum unnoticed?

A nurse passed him and went into Room 235. The guard had returned and was advising him that the doctor was on the way when Dr. Feld approached them. "Good work, kid," Daly mocked, then turned to the doctor.

"Hope your morning has been better than mine," he started politely, since he knew he was going to need the doctor's cooperation.

The doctor was about to speak when screaming filled the usually quiet corridors. The screams were coming from Room 235. Everyone in the area—Doctor Feld, several nurses, the security guard—rushed into the room. Sergeant Daly was right behind them.

Ronnie and Yale stood frozen in front of the chairs they had been occupying. The attending nurse was trying to calm Lisa. Lisa's screams persisted. The nurse turned toward Doctor Feld, "Her pulse is rapid. I haven't checked her pressure or temp yet, but she feels quite warm."

"Lisa, it's okay. It's Doctor Feld. Lisa, it's okay. Calm down, Lisa. It's okay. Everything's okay."

She opened her eyes, quieting some, but still breathing heavily. She looked up at Doctor Feld, who was holding her down. He had one hand on her chest and the other on her forehead. With terror on her face, she screamed, "He's coming after me! I know it. He's coming after me!"

Doctor Feld nodded to the nurse to go ahead and take her blood pressure. He continued to reassure Lisa with gentleness,

"You're safe, Lisa. It's okay. You just had a bad dream."

"One-sixty over one-twenty," the nurse stated clearly, putting a thermometer in Lisa's mouth.

Doctor Feld turned his head to another nurse, still keeping his hands reassuringly on Lisa, and didn't wait for the thermometer to tell him what he already knew. He ordered an IV, ten milligrams of Valium, and ice pads.

"A hundred four," Nurse Kelly confirmed.

Doctor Feld ordered the room cleared. Only the nurses went in and out. An hour later Doctor Feld emerged, put a hand on Ronnie's shoulder, and told him her fever was coming down. He felt Lisa was no longer in danger, but as a precaution against convulsing had administered Phenobarbital. "Ronnie," he reassured, "go in for a minute. Then I suggest you get some rest yourself. She'll sleep for some time. There's nothing else you can do right now. I'll have her closely monitored."

Ronnie went in and looked at Lisa, who was already asleep. He wept openly as he kissed her cheek, unaware that the doctor, Yale, and Sergeant Daly were behind him, and whispered, "I love you," to the fragile figure on the bed. Turning to leave, he looked at Doctor Feld, ignoring the others, and asked if someone would call him when she woke up. The doctor said he would take care of it. Ronnie walked away badly shaken, frightened, and needing to be alone.

Yale and Dr. Feld looked at the sergeant. Daly knew positively then what the other two had realized before him: the woman in the bed was a victim, not a perpetrator. Daly said, "I'll call to see how she's doing in the morning," and left.

On his way out of the hospital, Sergeant Daly stopped in the gift shop, picked out a plant with some pretty flowers mixed in the pot, and asked for it to be delivered to Room 235. The cashier handed him a card on which he simply wrote, "Hope You Feel Better Soon". He left the card unsigned, put it in the envelope, and left the building. He had never done anything like that before.

Yale had gone into the men's room before leaving the hospital. On his way out he also went into the gift shop. He picked out a stuffed animal. A koala bear. He was going to have it sent to Lisa's room, but decided to take it up to her room himself. He needed another look at her before he went back to the hotel.

He walked past the nurse's station and the guard carrying the bear. When he went up to Lisa's bed and placed the bear beside her, she opened her eyes briefly. He bent and whispered, "I'm so sorry."

She smiled weakly and whispered, "You owe me another concert," and went immediately back to sleep.

He looked at her, whispering now to the sleeping figure, "I owe you a lot more than that."

With an ache in his heart and a lump in his throat, Yale left Beaumont hospital and drove back to the hotel.

Chapter
9

George and Mary were silent until they were outside the Coliseum grounds. It had been a relatively simple task to join the many pushy patrons as hysteria broke out after the gun was fired. Of course, it didn't hurt any to make certain several people were quickly knocked down to enhance the confusion. The two of them, joining in the panic, pretended to be confused spectators. As the crowd grew larger, they were able to retreat as part of the mob vacating the premises. Mary had grabbed the basket and blanket when she became aware of the struggle between George and the woman who was seated beside him. George had been able to drop the gun into the basket unobtrusively once the woman was off of him. They had used the basket to push people aside, providing extra space for them as they calmly walked to the car. They'd stayed partnered with the crowd, keeping pace with the majority of people, while security personnel directed them to the nearest exits.

It wasn't until they were on the highway that George lost his temper. Slamming his fist against the dashboard, he shouted, "Fucking, stupid bitch!"

Mary didn't say a word.

"I would have had him. I had a clear shot until that cunt jumped up. Shit!"

Mary still didn't speak.

"You know, it would have worked. I thought Peter was crazy when he picked the Coliseum. But did you see how the people swarmed in the area, causing chaos? You know, being that close was smart, too. All the farts up front directed their attention solely to the performance on stage," he rambled on. "The fools around us had no idea what was happening."

Mary spoke for the first time since they left the Coliseum. "Where was the silencer, George? If you had used the silencer, the way you were supposed to, you could have gotten him."

"I couldn't have gotten him." He spat the words at her. "You saw that bitch lurch at me out of nowhere."

"Peter is not going to be happy, George. Not only is Yale Frye still alive, but now there is a witness who can identify you."

"I had no way of knowing the silencer wasn't still on. I secured it, you know that," he said, doubt evident in his voice. "And maybe the bitch is dead," he stammered, now feeling anxious.

"You know, George, if she's not dead now, she's going to have to be almost immediately," Mary said, looking in the side view mirror to see if they were being followed by anyone as they veered off the dark highway. "Any way you look at it, George, you fucked up. Peter is not going to like it."

"We can fix it. It won't be so bad." He tried to sound more confident than he felt, wishing he could tell Mary to fuck herself. She sat smugly beside him. He was aware that he had to treat her well. After all, she was Peter's woman, and had more influence with him than anyone else.

It was astounding how dramatically his life had changed in the last two years. So much had happened. He was a different person. His existence had taken on a new purpose. He felt visionary.

"The world will be alerted. Evil will be addressed. We will remove the ugly and corrupt. We will eliminate the inferior. We will expand the horizons of beauty. We will stomp on power. We will destroy the notion of equality. White supremacy will rule." George repeated some of the mottoes Peter had presented as a guide to the seven who had joined forces over two years ago.

They had met at a party. It had been late into the night and there had been only eight of them left. Suddenly, one had risen, drawing attention to himself. Peter. "My whole life is a facade. I do all the things I'm supposed to do and I hate it. Like a puppet, I follow rules I didn't have any part in establishing, and I try to earn the respect of others, as if it were important. Bullshit!"

He had stood up from his seat, holding a fist up, "I'm not going to live the rest of my life like that. I am going to make myself count. I will validate my existence."

Those listening that night had felt exactly as Peter did. One by one, they had voiced their opinions, their sentiments. The host of the party, an artist, had risen from his seat, the pain of illness etched on his face. In a voice filled with anguish he had said, "I wish I could live to see change. It is within your reach. Apply the principles you carry within to alert the world before the eve of destruction. The way to begin is with the destruction of the power structure in this country. Knock out a few bricks on one side of the structure and it loses strength. The government may well be the roof of the structure, but a roof needs a solid foundation. It is not always necessary, or wise, to aim for the jugular when amputating a foot can obtain the same results."

Turning to leave the room, he had continued, "Peter, your life can be substantially more, with some effort. The problem is, everyone has opinions. But as you have all heard before, opinions are like assholes. Everyone's got an asshole! What is required is action. Speak less, Peter, and do more while you are able, my friend."

About six weeks after they'd formed P.A.P., People Against Puppetry, Peter had announced that he had received word of the artist's death and cremation. Peter had further related that he had received a certified letter from an attorney stating the artist had left this world as he had entered it, alone. All his earthly possessions had been left to Peter, with the stipulation that the world must be bettered by the inheritance. Peter had understood.

Peter had become the organizer and leader of the group. He was the oldest, at thirty-three, and the most self-assured. He had financial control over the farmland and the fifty thousand dollars bequeathed to him by the artist. Peter had also claimed the only woman in the group, Mary, as his from the outset.

They'd devised a scheme whereby each picked an eminent black or Jewish person who would be missed. They'd each selected a target for elimination, then dropped their choice into an urn from which Peter had randomly selected a name.

The first person selected by PEOPLE AGAINST PUPPETRY had been a black female soul singer who had been actively promoting racial equality. Her demise had gone easily and smoothly. Late one night, after she left a party, her car had simply lost control on a winding road. They'd stilled her voice permanently.

The second target had been more difficult. He had been a popular, renowned, black comedian. He was outspoken, had a top rated television show, and was far less accessible than the singer had been. He was always surrounded by people, because of his influence and power. This choice had certainly been a challenge! They'd decided that Otto, the biggest of them, would have to devise a way to get beside the entertainer and inject him with a lethal dose of cocaine.

It had been a rewarding experience when the comedian was found dead. At first, it had been assumed to be a heart attack. But when an autopsy was ordered, it was discovered that he had a large amount of cocaine in his system. There were several needle marks under his nails and between his toes.

The entire Hollywood community was shocked. The comedian had publicly said on several occasions that he denounced the use of any illegal substances, and that those who used drugs were sick. He'd been presumed to be living by respectable standards. The papers had had a field day, exposing his 'long-time addiction'. His family could not understand it. His fans were calling him a hypocrite.

So much for promoting better education for inferior races that dared to call themselves 'minorities'!

The members of P.A.P. were thriving on their victory. They were anxious for plans to be completed for the elimination of number three. Decidedly, the next public figure would have to be eliminated with a great deal of publicity and exposure surrounding the circumstances. After all, the impact would be so much greater. It was also true that the risks provided stimulation and produced a euphoria they believed they deserved. George had felt that euphoria tonight, before the shooting. He had felt a rapture and elation that was beyond anything he had ever felt before.

The wheels of the car screeched as George turned into the parking lot of the car rental agency. As he glanced toward the adjacent airport, he felt apprehensive about returning to Los Angeles, trying to figure out how to approach Peter with this failed attempt. He felt Mary might betray him if she could, just to humiliate him.

Mary slept for the next four hours, while he sat awake on the flight, planning what he might say to Peter.

Chapter
10

In his hotel room, Yale was updated on specifics. David had had Yale's business manager cancel concerts until further notice. The only person Yale had to call again was his mother. David reported that she had called four times in the last two hours.

Meanwhile, at the Klein home, the phone was becoming part of Ronnie's anatomy. He was tired of repeating the same story. He filled the boys in, but remained vague when he spoke to Lisa's parents. He didn't want to alarm them, knowing how protective Lisa was, and their tendency to overreact.

Later that day, when Ronnie and the boys entered Lisa's room, they found that a reporter had just awakened her. He had managed to get past the guard stationed at the door by claiming to be Lisa's brother. Once inside the room, he'd started snapping pictures of Lisa and asking questions. Lisa's screams had alerted the guard, who had removed the impostor. Her husband and sons did not find her in good spirits. Lisa ended their short visit on a sour note, telling them to leave. To Ronnie she added, "Just go to work tomorrow. I need a paycheck more than I need to have you hanging around here." Her good-bye to her sons consisted of, "I can hardly wait to see the pig sty at home. Well, if nothing else, I don't have to hear the two of you fighting for a few days."

They went home disappointed by the visit. Ronnie had only been in the house five minutes when the phone started again. He decided to ignore it and let the answering machine take the message.

Lisa was calling to apologize. But when she heard the recorder, she hung up. As she turned on her side crying, Yale Frye entered her hospital room. She didn't hear him.

"Anything I can do, Lisa?" the voice she used to dream about inquired.

"Yeah, go away. I'm not good company right now."

"I'll take my chances."

"Look, Yale," she turned her tear streaked face to him, the pain of moving evident, "you've got better things to do with your time. I'm getting tired of looking like a 'damsel in distress' every time you see me. If you want Sarah Bernhardt, go rent a fucking movie, okay?"

"Actually, if I were to rent a movie, I would like something with some humor. Probably a Woody Allen movie. Do you like Woody Allen movies, Lisa?"

"Some. I can relate ethnically and understand his pain."

"Me, too," he said, taking a Kleenex from her tray table and handing it to her. "I think he's an extraordinary satirist. He can take painful personal feelings, analyze them, and transfer them onto film. He exposes himself, shamelessly, through his work. But he is capable of distancing himself from the public, maintaining a high degree of respect from his peers professionally while doing whatever he wants privately."

"Well, I think he's as screwed up as the rest of us, Yale. He's just willing to admit it, instead of denying it."

"Then he's already a step ahead of most of us, isn't he?"

"Yale, what do you want? Why did you come back here tonight? What's with all the crap about Woody Allen? I forgive you for not being hurt while I was. Okay? Is that what you need? You are not responsible, and if you need someone to help you get rid of some guilt, call a shrink, okay?"

"I don't know why I came back. Obviously, I shouldn't have. Feel better, Lisa. I'll call, if that's okay, to see how you're doing." He was confused himself as to why he felt compelled to be with her. Maybe it was guilt. Maybe he really should call his shrink. Maybe his ego was so big that he believed she'd be glad to see him. "Goodnight, Lisa", he said, turning to go. "You know, I came here concerned, thinking you might need a friend. But the truth of it is, I needed your friendship more than you needed mine."

He was leaving the room when a nurse collided with him, dropping a tray. She was so flustered about bumping into a famous star that she became very clumsy. The scene was so comical, Lisa couldn't keep herself from laughing. "Does this sort of thing happen to you often, Mr. Frye?" Lisa teased, still giggling while the nurse disappeared.

"Yes. One of the hazards of being a familiar face. People are easily intimidated, I guess."

"I'm sure the advantages outweigh the disadvantages," Lisa countered.

"Well, maybe if you hadn't gotten involved, my death would

have proven how wrong such assumptions can be."

Lisa was quiet, feeling at a loss for words. Finally, she asked, "Can we start over, Yale?"

Smiling, he walked toward the bed with a hand outstretched. "Hi, I'm Yale Frye." Taking her hand in his, "May I sit and talk to you a while? I heard there was a special lady in this room, one worth knowing."

"I'd like that. Thank you." For some reason, she was becoming emotional again. He understood as she lowered her eyes.

He sat on the edge of the bed and lifted her face with a gentle hand. He waited until her eyes, filled with unshed tears, were facing his. "Can I hold you for a minute?" he whispered, his face close to hers.

"Only if you won't let go until I'm ready," she answered, as the tears fell.

"I've got you," he repeated, over and over again. He held her close to him, not knowing who was getting the most comfort from the moment. Silently, he was hoping they could just stay that way a while longer.

The nurse came back with another tray, breaking the magic of the moment. "Mrs. Klein, I have your medication for tonight. Dr. Feld said to let you know he is coming to see you in a few minutes. So if you want to wait before taking the sleeping pill, that's fine."

The nurse was taking Lisa's vital signs when Doctor Feld entered. She marked the chart and handed Lisa the paper container of medication.

"I'll take them later," Lisa said. "Thank you."

The nurse looked at Dr. Feld. "It's okay. Leave the chart with me, Lorraine. I'll bring it to the station in a minute. Are you on the night shift, Lorraine?"

"Yes, doctor. All this week."

"Good. After I talk with Lisa, I'll talk to you. If she gives you a hard time and doesn't follow instructions, we'll order several other unpleasant tests to torture her with," he said with good humor. The nurse left. Yale sat down, indicating that he had no intention of leaving, and waited for Dr. Feld to continue.

"Lisa, Ronnie called me very worried and upset. He said you were hard on him and your boys, and that you asked him to go back to work tomorrow."

"Look, doctor, he can't do anything by sitting here. The bills don't stop just because we stop working. So that's what I want."

"I told Ronnie you were not to be left alone for the next two weeks, or until I say it's okay. Your fever went over one hundred four earlier. You lost a great deal of blood. You're weak, in pain, and you have limited use of your left arm. I left instructions for you to be monitored closely until morning, and you are not to leave the bed without a nurse present for any reason." He stopped briefly, waiting for an outburst. He was surprised when she said nothing. "Any questions, Lisa?" Doctor Feld risked asking.

"No," she replied. "But if I feel I am here longer than I need to be, I'll order an AMA and leave."

Yale interjected with, "What's an AMA?"

"Against Medical Advice form. I hope Lisa won't request one, and that she'll be smart enough to work with me, instead of fighting me. After all, we are on the same side."

Yale looked from the doctor to Lisa, "Do you always give everyone such a hard time?"

"Stick around and find out, Yale. Or am I scaring you away?"

"Doctor, I can't walk away when challenged. Is it okay if I stay a while?"

"Only at your own risk, Mr. Frye," the doctor answered, winking at Lisa. He left the room to answer a page.

He returned a minute later. "I've ordered the IV and catheter removed, and liquids for tonight, Lisa. Your fever is down. I'll see you in the morning. You can take the medication after Mr. Frye leaves. Try to relax, your pressure is still too high."

"Okay, doctor. Thank you."

"Doctor, can I talk to you for a minute?" Yale asked.

"Sure. Come on, I'll buy you a cup of lousy hospital coffee while the nurse tends to Lisa."

They walked down the hall to an empty lounge and Doctor Feld got them each a cup of coffee from the machine. "What's on your mind?" he asked Yale.

"I'd like any bills for Lisa's care sent to me, if you could arrange that confidentially."

"She's got insurance, Yale. It should cover everything. Personally, I think there's more to what's bothering Lisa than Ronnie's paycheck."

"Doctor, do you know something you can tell me? I'd really like to help her," Yale rushed on.

"She's very bright, Yale. I think she feels Ronnie said more than he should have to Sergeant Daly and to you. I also think she's scared. More, much more, than she's willing to admit to anyone."

"Scared of what, doctor? I'm sure she was responsible for saving my life, not for trying to take it. And I got the feeling earlier that Sergeant Daly knew he was wrong in his first assumption, and realized Lisa wasn't the kind of person to hurt anyone. He was just doing his job."

"Yale, I think Lisa is afraid because she doesn't know who to trust right now. She's acting tough to conceal her vulnerability."

"Can I do anything to help?"

"Yes, Yale. Be honest with her. Perhaps she'll start to trust you."

Yale and the doctor walked back down the hall toward Lisa's room. Nurse Lorraine was walking toward them, on her way to the nurse's station.

"Everything all set?" Doctor Feld asked her.

"Yes, Doctor Feld, but she's very depressed. She wants her phone to remain disconnected. I asked if she'd like to look at the cards from the plants and flowers sent to her. I thought she'd want to know who they were from. She responded with, "Who cares?" and started crying. I thought it best to leave her alone for a while. But before I left the room I asked her if I could do anything or get her something. I really didn't understand her response. She asked me if I had any Woody Allen movies?"

"Mr. Frye is going to stay with her for a while. I'm leaving the hospital, but I'll check with you later. She's still on restricted visitors until I advise otherwise."

Yale returned to Lisa's room to find the bed vacant. He turned around as she was coming out of the bathroom. "Do you ever follow instructions?" he asked.

She got back into the bed, hoping he'd notice an improvement in her appearance. She had hurriedly brushed her hair, put on a fresh nightshirt, and sprayed herself generously with cologne.

Yale sat down in the chair next to the bed. Nothing had gone unnoticed. He decided not to comment on her appearance, or on the scent of Obsession that engulfed the entire room. Instead he casually asked if the television worked. She shrugged. He suggested, "Let's check it out, okay?" He handed her a glass of water and the container of pills. She shrugged again. He picked up the remote and turned on the set. "Look, Equal Justice. Great show, it's just starting. Mind if we watch it?" She shrugged once more, and slid down in the bed, while he pretended to be engrossed in the program. She fell asleep within minutes. He sat beside her and watched her sleep, not at all interested in the show.

Nearly an hour had passed when another nurse came to check Lisa's vital signs. She checked her pulse, then began wrapping her arm to check her blood pressure. Lisa woke startled and began screaming. It took several minutes to calm her. The nurse completed her duties while Yale sat on the bed, stroking Lisa's hair. The nurse returned with hot decaffeinated tea for them, and left when she was sure everything was under control.

"Why the hell are you still here?" Lisa snapped, "Equal Justice must be over by now!"

"I thought I'd catch the news," Yale said calmly. He continued stroking her hair. His smile mocked her outburst.

She let his gentle touch soothe and quiet her. She didn't take her eyes from his. She looked at him long and hard. When she felt more controlled, she said, "I'm okay now. Sorry." He didn't move and his eyes didn't leave hers. "Yale, it's not over. He's going to try again. I know it. I'm scared."

"I've got you," he whispered, bending and holding her close to him again. "You're okay. You're safe."

Her body trembled. "I'm cold, and I don't feel safe," she said in a voice that was almost inaudible.

He tucked the thin sterile blanket around her, and remained beside her. He felt her shiver as his body touched hers. "I'd better call for the nurse," he whispered.

"No, please. Just hold me. Please. I'm scared. God, I'm so scared." She put her good arm around him. After holding her, he looked at her face and kissed her gently on the cheek. He looked at her again, her eyes meeting his, "Please, Yale. Stay close for a few minutes."

He moved so that he was almost lying beside her, trying to comfort and warm her with his body. She snuggled closer. Slowly, she relaxed and the trembling diminished under the calming arm that held her. She was breathing more easily and shut her eyes. He kept repeating, "It's okay. It's okay now."

She fell asleep with Yale holding her, his body against hers. He didn't want to move. He was afraid he might wake her. He tried to stay alert, dozing off for only a few minutes. He wondered if she felt the uncontrollable stirring of arousal in his loins. Was it his imagination or did she move her body closer, against his hardness? He held her and together they found solace and slept.

When the nurse came back later to check her vital signs, Lisa did not scream in fear again. She felt safe being close to Yale.

In the morning, she wondered what time he'd left. She had slept so soundly that she hadn't felt him move from her side. She touched the koala bear, now on the spot Yale had occupied, and was glad that Yale had turned out to be so kind.

She felt better this morning, and knew she was improving when she ate everything brought to her on the breakfast tray.

Chapter
11

Yale climbed out of Lisa's hospital bed to use the bathroom around three-thirty in the morning. He stood looking at her peaceful face, feeling surprisingly protective for someone he'd just met. She made him aware of all the lonely nights when he'd needed the closeness he'd just felt, and had opted instead for a one-night stand. He decided to go back to the hotel, placing the stuffed bear beside her before leaving.

He turned the key and entered the posh hotel suite, heading toward his bedroom. He flicked on the light next to the telephone to see if David had left him any messages. A slip of paper indicated that his mother called, and asked him to call her in the morning. Another message said the press was pushing for a statement from him. He crumpled the paper and aimed for a basket with it when he heard sounds of rowdiness from David's room. Noticing a light coming from under the door, he knocked twice, then turned the knob when no one answered.

David was on his knees on the bed, a buxom redhead beneath him, lying on her back with David's dick in her mouth. She had her feet on the wall and was rubbing herself with her right hand. She pushed back and forth, squeezing her thighs together, giving herself the friction she obviously wanted. At the other end was a young man. He stood at the foot of the bed, with his organ in David's mouth. His buttocks were tightening and relaxing as he pushed himself in and out between David's lips. David turned when the door opened. Taking the hard, wet penis from his mouth, he laughed. "Come on, Yale. I found some friends at the bar. Cindy here will help you feel good. Won't you, honey?"

She slid a finger inside of herself, "I'm wet and ready, baby. Come fill me with something hard." She continued to move her hips, spreading her legs wide.

"Some other time," Yale answered. "Have a good time. I'm just too tired." He closed the door, went to his room, and got undressed. Once under the covers, he felt the exhaustion of the day taking its toll. He turned on his side, cradling the pillow, but found sleep elusive. Normally, he might have dropped his drawers to be sucked off but, tonight, his erection had started in the hospital when he was beside Lisa. It had lasted all the way back to the hotel as he thought about her. There was a gentleness about her that was different from the women he was used to. She understood his need to be close to her and wasn't afraid to admit that she needed him near. She evoked emotions that were foreign to him. And even now, when he wanted to sleep, the throbbing persisted.

When they were touring, David usually found fun people who liked to play. Neither he nor David cared who wanted to suck them, as long as it felt good. They both thought sexual preferences were only relevant to people hung up on labels. Sometimes a guy understands what another guy needs better than a woman would, just as sometimes a woman better accommodates another woman's needs. In the last two decades he'd seen and done it all. What he needed tonight, however, was not his for the taking.

Before drifting off, his last thought was of Lisa snuggled against him, needing his comfort and protection. His body against hers. Her vulnerability. When he woke a few hours later, he realized he'd just experienced a nocturnal emission. It was the first time that had happened in years.

At the police station, in the late hours, Sergeants Daly and Hill were going over the similarities from the statements taken after the shooting. Daly needed to talk to Lisa, not as a suspect, but as the only person who could clearly identify the assailant. He was plagued by the fact that with so many people sitting close together, there was less to go on than in some instances when no one was near the crime scene.

"Calm down, Daly," Hill tried, "you know how people are. They don't want to get involved in anything ugly. Something will pop."

Officer Randall walked in. "This just came from a carrier," he said, handing a package marked URGENT to Daly.

Daly opened the package, removing a videocassette with a note attached:

PLEASE VIEW. VITAL. YALE FRYE CONCERT.

Daly ordered a VCR brought in and put the tape in the machine. "Son of a bitch! Some motherfucker wasn't afraid to get involved. Hill, get the photo lab on this fast. I'm going to need blowups, stills, copies. The works. Randall, get on the phone and get a description out, and have the mug books checked for a match. I'll be back in an hour. I'm going to see Frye and ask him to look at the tape. Hell, maybe he knows the motherfucker that tried to kill him."

At Peter's house in California, the atmosphere was less jubilant. By the time George and Mary arrived, Peter and the other P.A.P. members were assembled. They discussed the television broadcast that had described the failed attempt on Yale Frye's life.

George argued for continued action, for the demise of Yale Frye and the woman. He claimed that getting rid of both Yale Frye and Lisa Klein would attract even greater attention and create widespread panic. He pushed on, arguing that this failure could be turned into a bigger victory than the original plan. "Listen to me," George persisted, "fame and power do not equal safety. We can eliminate them both."

Peter suggested that they meet in two days and devise their next plan of attack.

With Mary beside him in bed, however, he spoke differently. "This failure could delay the group's actions. George will be identified. We have no choice but to eradicate him so we can continue our efforts."

Mary, fearing for her own safety, moved closer to Peter. Placing his hand on her stomach, she said, "I hope our child has your wisdom." He turned his face to hers with surprise. She took advantage of the moment, saying, "George was inept. He is stupid. He jeopardized my safety and that of our child. We can do without him." She moved a hand slowly up and down his penis until his hunger grew. He was moving her down. "Suck, suck." She ran her tongue around his dick, gliding her tongue up and down the shaft. She slowly moved up, kissing his body, while her hands methodically intensified his desire. She pushed a finger up inside his rectum, the way he liked. She licked his body. She forced her tongue in his mouth. "I've missed you. I've missed the feeling of you deep inside me. Enter me, so I feel your hardness close to the child you created within me. Peter, I want you. Fuck me. Fuck me, hard."

He entered her and she wrapped her legs around him, thrusting vigorously until he came inside her. Silently, she prayed that tonight she would conceive the baby she had just told him she was carrying.

George knew that Peter would retaliate in some way for his failure to eliminate Frye; he had to act quickly if he was to remain unharmed. He had to protect himself, and if he was going to be punished, he'd make sure Peter would feel pain, too. They all would.

The first thing George did when he got home was to dictate a tape detailing the organization's inception, plans, motives, objectives, and accomplishments to date. Also included were the names of the seven members and their addresses. Copying the tape, he placed one in an envelope to be mailed to his attorney, with instructions for it to be opened only after his death. He put the other tape in an envelope with a note attached, which read: "If I'm a friend, I'll be one you defend, but if you pretend, we will all meet our end." He sealed the envelope and decided to have it delivered by certified mail to ensure that she signed for it. He addressed it in care of the art studio Mary operated.

Next, George wanted to 'thank' Lisa Klein for her intervention. He purchased several newspapers and magazines until he found an article identifying her husband as Ronald Klein. Then he called every Ronald Klein in Canton until he located the right house. The neighbor, Rose something, was eager to help the florist, which he professed to be, with the correct address. She also said Lisa would probably be in the hospital another day or two.

"Well, Lisa, a nice note should arrive at your house about the time you come home from the hospital," George said to himself as he proceeded to cut out all the letters he needed from the magazines. He glued them on a piece of paper to read, "YOU TRIED TO SAVE FRYE, NOW BOTH OF YOU WILL DIE." He placed the note in the envelope, then removed it, and added in ink at the bottom of the paper, "Your neighbor Rose is nice. Don't tie up the phone, I'll be in touch." Just an extra touch to scare the lady a little more, in case she thought it was only a prank. He sealed the note inside a brown envelope and wrote CONFIDENTIAL in bold letters. He put the envelopes on his dresser and went to sleep.

In Room 235, at Beaumont Hospital, Doctor Feld was examining Lisa. Ronnie came in carrying lilacs in a glass vase.

"I guess you didn't need more flowers," he laughed sheepishly, looking around the room. It was filled with plants and floral arrangements. There wasn't much space for his offering.

"You know lilacs are my favorite. Put them on the tray-table, next to me, so I can enjoy their fragrance. Thank you, Ronnie."

Ronnie felt better, realizing that she really did appreciate his effort. He kissed her and was happy to see her so cheerful this morning, after her anger the previous night.

"Lisa, I've got good news for you and Ronnie," Doctor Feld began, "your vital signs are good and your fever is down. I expect that with continued administration of antibiotics, your temperature will be normal by tomorrow. I understand you're requiring less medication for pain, which is also a good sign. If things continue on course, you should be able to go home tomorrow morning. That does not mean resuming normal activity, though. You lost a lot of blood. But I don't think you'll have to remain hospitalized. I suggest you walk a little today, assisted, and if everything is okay when I see you in the morning, Ronnie can take you home. Any questions?"

"What about the stitches?"

"You can come back in a week or so to have the sutures removed. There shouldn't be any problems. The areas are healing nicely. Anything else?"

"No, that's it. I'll be glad to get home."

"Okay. I'll see you tomorrow then."

"Thank you, Doctor Feld," Ronnie and Lisa said simultaneously. Lisa leaned over to smell the fragrance of the lilacs, feeling good. Ronnie asked who had sent all the flowers and plants and she answered that until now, she hadn't even felt like reading the cards.

One by one, Ronnie handed Lisa the cards attached to each arrangement and she responded how nice it was for everyone to think of her. Ronnie handed her the next card and Lisa commented, "That's funny, this one's not signed. All it says is "HOPE YOU FEEL BETTER." I wonder who sent it. Ronnie, is there anything else on the plant?"

"No, Lisa. Does it have the florist's name on the card anywhere?"

"On the bottom it says Beaumont Hospital. It must have come from the gift shop."

"Maybe Yale had it sent up."

"Maybe."

They talked while walking the hallways. Then Lisa asked Ronnie to get things in order at home and to do some marketing. Before leaving, he bent and kissed her, "I'm glad you're better, honey. I'll see you later."

She looked at Ronnie's face, admiring the all-American good looks that had first caught her attention years ago. "No, Ronnie, just call. Get some rest. You've been running around enough. I'm fine, honest."

"Okay, I'll call you later then."

After Ronnie left, she called the gift shop, thinking maybe they would have a record of who had sent the plant. The woman she spoke with said she remembered who paid for the plant. It was the same policeman who made the televised statement the night she was brought in by ambulance. Sergeant Daly.

"Are you sure?" Lisa questioned.

"Oh, yes. I'm positive," the voice answered.

"That's funny," Lisa said, wondering why Sergeant Daly would have sent her a plant.

Pondering, she fell asleep.

About an hour later, voices woke her. Outside the room, two guards were talking.

"She know anything?" one asked. Lisa froze.

"Nothing. I had her TV cut off when she walked the halls with her husband earlier, and they are holding all calls at the switchboard. Daly has the entrances covered and security tight. No visitors. Everyone's being checked. It's been quiet so far. Even the nurses were told to stay calm and say nothing. She's been sleeping for over an hour."

"Good. Maybe they can catch the fucker. I heard Frye is in bad shape."

Lisa felt like the air was being sucked out of her. Her heart was pounding. She peed all over herself and the bed. She was afraid to move and afraid not to. She had to find out what was going on. What did the guard mean when he said Frye was in bad shape? What didn't she know?

She waited. Nothing else was said. She took a few deep breaths, calming herself. She got out of bed very quietly and put on her robe. She tiptoed to the bathroom, placed a towel across her arm, a bar of soap in her hand, and casually walked out. She strolled past the door saying, "Be back in a few, I'm going to shower down the hall. Mine is broken."

The guard caught her by surprise, "Hold on, miss. I'll get someone."

"It's okay. I know where it is." She kept walking, not having the vaguest idea where other showers were, but looking for the nearest exit. Spotting the exit sign at the end of the hall, she increased her speed in order to reach it. She was trying arduously to turn the knob when two arms grabbed her around the waist. She started yelling and wrestling to free herself. People were all around her. She felt like she was falling and couldn't decipher what anyone was saying. Everything was getting fuzzy. She lost consciousness.

When she opened her eyes, Yale was looking down at her, "Where were you going, Lisa? Is the service here that bad?" He tried to make light of the situation.

"You're okay? I heard the guards talking. Someone said that you were in bad shape. I heard someone ask if I knew anything."

"You made it to the exit, but the door was locked. I had just come up and heard you screaming when you couldn't open the door. I ran to you. The guard caught you before you fell. You passed out from the exertion. The guard helped put you in bed."

"I heard voices. I felt hands. I couldn't understand."

"It's okay, Lisa. It was the nurses. You were wet. They changed you and put fresh sheets under you. That's all. You're okay. Lie still. I'll sit with you."

"Oh, God. I thought someone went after you again. They said you were in bad shape." She was drifting off from the sedative they'd injected to relax her. Her eyes closed. Yale put his face in his hands, venting his own anguish, his feeling of responsibility for Lisa's condition. He thought she was asleep when she gently whispered, "It's okay, Yale. Only those without heart don't cry."

Chapter
12

Lisa woke to find herself surrounded by Yale, his assistant David, Sergeant Joe Daly, Ronnie, and their two sons. She looked around at the somber faces and quizzically probed, "This looks serious. Give it to me straight. How much time do I have left?" Her words hung in the air like dense fog. She pulled herself up to a sitting position and waited.

Sergeant Daly was the first to speak. "Lisa, we received a package at the precinct today containing a video of the struggle between you and an unidentified man at the Diamond Coliseum. We are taking the necessary steps to identify the male suspect, and hope to have him in custody soon. Meanwhile, however, you were involved in the struggle and prevented what might have resulted in a serious injury or death. We therefore fear that the information released to the press, and the photos shown on TV today, could jeopardize your safety. We want to keep you under protective custody until we locate the suspect and ensure that you are in no way endangered."

"Gee, Joe," she said sarcastically, "two nights ago I was a suspect, or at least under suspicion. And I was referred to as Mrs. Klein, who had her personal belongings removed for inspection, her feelings scrutinized, her motives in attempting to contact Mr. Frye questioned, and her psychiatric history divulged. Now, it's 'Lisa, we want to protect you for your own good.' Get out of here! All of you! You all make me sick!"

When they stayed, waiting for her to calm down, she resumed her original horizontal position, pulled the covers up around her, and asked them again to please leave. She felt violated and impotent.

"Lisa," Sergeant Daly continued, "you're right. I understand your anger. Please accept my apology. I'd like to move you to another room, ask you a few questions, and have someone stay with you."

"Go to hell, Sergeant! I don't want your fucking apology. It's a little late for that, don't you think? I've had my picture in the papers, my privacy invaded, my character questioned, and the sad thing is, you don't get it! I have family, friends, children, co-workers, parents, all who have been affected by this. And you want me to accept your fucking apology. No way, buster, not until my reputation is restored. You make a public statement so everyone realizes I was a victim, not some loony. Then come talk to me."

"I already have, Lisa. I tried to clarify everything. We also sent copies of the video to the local television studios so the public could see what happened. We hope others will come forward to help us find the suspect."

"Why am I the last to know anything? Why was my phone turned off? Why was my television disconnected? And why should I believe you?"

"Lisa," Daly went on, "I gave those instructions in case you were not physically or emotionally strong enough to relive the incident. Believe it or not, I am human. You gave everyone a good scare the other day. If I was wrong, again, I'm sorry." He picked up the phone in Lisa's room, pushed three numbers to an inside extension, and told someone at the other end of the line to bring a wheelchair to transport Lisa to a private suite usually reserved for VIPs. They were also told to make sure the TV, phone, and radio were operable. Daly further requested an empty elevator, and advised the person on the line that he'd get back to them as to who would be staying with Lisa tonight. He hung up and turned to Lisa. "No more secrets, okay?" He continued, "You have to be moved for security purposes, but if you don't want to talk to me after that, I'll go."

While contemplating the sergeant's words, Lisa changed the subject and directed her conversation to her sons. "Well, guys, what have you been up to?" They both began updating Lisa on their current activities, filling the room with animation and laughter. She apologized to them for being so nasty the other day. After all, they were her reason for living, and she didn't want to alarm them.

"Mom," Marc said, excitedly, a few minutes later. "Yale knows everybody! He knows Billy Joel, and you'll never guess what! He said, he could get me and Steve tickets to see Ted Nugent the day after tomorrow. We can each bring a friend and get passes to go backstage. Right, Yale?"

"I said, if it was okay with your parents," Yale said, defending himself.

"Dad said he'd see how you felt about it. And, you know, you are going to be real surprised when you come home tomorrow and see how clean our rooms are. Right, Steve?"

"We even washed all the stuff in the hamper today," Steve added.

"Well, there's one more condition you have to agree to before I say yes," Lisa said. She tried to remain serious, but was glad to see her boys happy and exuberant after the last few trying days.

"Oh-oh," the boys said, looking at each other.

"You have to bring me home a souvenir t-shirt."

Marc looked at Yale, "I told you it would be okay. Our mom is the best."

The wheelchair was brought in. All of Lisa's belongings were gathered, and the entourage accompanied her to the large private room she would be occupying for the night. It looked more like a hotel room than a hospital room with its sofa, chairs, and small refrigerator. The walls were a pale yellow and the floor fully carpeted. Lisa was helped into bed. The sergeant turned on the TV to make sure it was working. The news had just started. Sergeant Daly was preparing to turn it off when Lisa asked if he would leave it on. He did. They all focused on the broadcast.

Lisa answered Sergeant Daly's questions for the next sixty minutes. When she showed signs of fatigue, Sergeant Daly ceased the questions, asking if she needed anything. She replied, "Yes, Sergeant Daly. I need it to be over."

"Soon, Lisa. It will be over soon." His words were not convincing. Lisa insisted they all leave. She claimed that she wanted to sleep and needed some space. With a guard posted at her door, they all left.

When David and Yale reached the hotel, Yale dropped David off and said, "Don't wait up." David knew where Yale was going.

Yale walked into Lisa's room when she didn't respond to his knocking. He walked to the bed, sat on the chair closest to her, stroked her hair as he had done before, and asked if he could stay. "I'll go if you want, Lisa. I guess I've become a pain, but I need to be here." She didn't say anything. "It's just, after I watched the video earlier, I couldn't believe what I was seeing. How do I ever repay you? How do I thank you?"

She looked up at his sad eyes. Her heart fluttered. She wanted him to kiss her, hard, right then, and felt embarrassed by her thoughts. She tried to mask her feelings with humor, "Well, you could start by getting me front row tickets to an Elton John concert."

"Go ahead, stab me in the heart. If it makes you feel better, I can handle it," he replied, smiling at her.

"Forget it, Yale. Guilt doesn't work on me anymore."

"Gee, wish I could say that. Guilt follows me around wherever I go. Okay, two Elton John concert tickets. What else?"

"Well, a pizza would be great. I'm starved."

He laughed and kissed her nose. She named her favorite pizza, and forty minutes later a nurse brought it to the room with the bill. He reached for his money clip, then remembered that he had left the hotel without it. With embarrassment he asked, "Will they accept a credit card?"

Lisa couldn't control her laughter. She asked him to hand her the purse, took out two twenties, and passed them to him still laughing. Yale handed Lisa's money to the nurse and told her to tell the delivery person to keep the change. "Sure," she teased, "go ahead, be a shooter with my money." They devoured the pizza, both of them hungrier than they had realized. They felt comfortable in each other's company.

They talked about their childhoods, reminisced about teenage experiences, reflected on moments, people, and ideals that held special meaning. Yale turned on the television when the nurse came to check Lisa, afraid he was revealing too much about himself. Being a celebrity had forced him to become guarded long ago, and the barriers he had placed around himself were beginning to crumble. After the nurse left, he told her to get some sleep and that he'd go now, hoping to see her in the morning.

"It's hard, isn't it?" she said as if she was reading his mind, "You never know who you can trust anymore. People only see the glitz and glitter. But everything has a price, doesn't it? One way or another, we all pay."

"When I saw the way your boys related to you earlier, I felt sad about all the things I'd never know. I made my choices a long time ago. But sometimes, as you get older, you question those decisions. I'm grateful for what I have, don't get me wrong. But there are days when it's not enough. Who knows, maybe I'm one of those people that feels nothing is ever enough."

"Do you believe in destiny, Yale? That fate is responsible for much of what occurs in our lives?"

"Depends what day of the week you ask me. My opinions change like my moods," he answered honestly.

"You just said something important about yourself. I think flexibility allows a person to grow, develop, question, pursue, challenge, and create. I really believe people who box themselves in stagnate."

"The same boxes can provide safety, shelter, protection, and security, Lisa."

"True, but they can be stifling. It seems to me life should be a constant quest, Yale. An adventure, not a rut."

"Maybe the answer is to remain open, searching, and exploring. But to know the box is there, if and when you need it."

"Idealistic, Yale, but not realistic, unfortunately. We're oftentimes marionettes, and someone else controls our strings. We allow ourselves to be manipulated."

They were aware they had just exposed a great deal about themselves and that trust was developing. Yale went out on a limb, took a chance. "I don't want to leave yet, Lisa. I'd like to stay and I'd like to hold you."

"Come on." She made room for him on the bed. "I need to be held, right now." She liked his candor and sensitivity, she realized. He made her feel special, unique, and feminine, something she hadn't felt with Ronnie for a long time.

She was beneath the sheet, he on top. But it was going to take more than a sheet to separate the desires building between them. She was cradled in his arms, feeling his heart next to hers. His breathing warmed her. He touched her face, looked into her eyes, and traced the outline of her lips with his finger as she turned her face to his. The room was quiet, the scent of flowers sweetly filling the air. They both felt the fire building as their bodies touched. The sheet did not hide the hardness of him against her.

She pushed against his loins, feeling herself breathing harder, wanting him. They were afraid to move. Their eyes remained fixed on each other. Neither had to speak. Yale kissed her gently on the lips, kissed her cheek, and again kissed her on the mouth, harder this time. She opened her mouth to his hungry tongue, kissing him back with volcanic passion.

They continued kissing, pressing their bodies together, feeling the urgency mounting. Yale put a hand on her breast, circling her nipple gently. He pushed against her several times, needing desperately to be held firmly. She returned kiss for kiss and heard him whisper, "I want you. I want you." He put his hand beneath the sheet, searching between her legs until he felt her wetness. "Touch me," he said as he covered her mouth again with his.

"Stop! Stop!" she urged suddenly, afraid of her own feelings and knowing that soon she wouldn't be able to stop. "I can't, Yale. I can't. Please." He removed his hand and sat up abruptly. A few minutes later she whispered into the silence of the room, "I'm sorry."

"No, Lisa. I'm the one who should be sorry. I'd better go." He got up, tucked his shirt back into his pants, ran a hand over his hair then left without another word. He felt ashamed for taking advantage of her susceptibility, feeling disgusted with himself. He had no right to push himself on her. He hoped she'd be able to forgive him.

Lisa was confused, feeling stupid for her outburst. She wanted him. She needed what he was offering. After twenty years of marriage, passion was no longer a part of her life with Ronnie. Sex was infrequent and had stopped being good a long time ago. They no longer discussed it, just accepted it. After all, they were best friends, and had a lot more than many couples.

She didn't sleep much that night. Her thoughts wandered. She felt like a silly schoolgirl. This was a new millennium. People had affairs. Monogamy was an unrealistic concept anyway. No wonder Yale had left. No wonder he'd said he was sorry. He didn't need some ditz afraid of her own feelings. He didn't need to be stopped or denied. He could have anyone he wanted. After all, he was Yale Frye.

Chapter
13

The following morning, Lisa was discharged into Ronnie's care. She was testy all day. Ronnie, trying to remain patient, attributed her foul disposition to stress resulting from the ordeal. She found fault with everything. She didn't eat, wouldn't accept phone calls, and refused to have visitors. She stayed in bed with the lights off, but didn't sleep. By evening, Ronnie and the boys were apprehensive about asking her anything. She knew she was being a bitch, but didn't care. She was angry at herself for not seizing that special moment with Yale the night before. She wanted to be left alone, but was upset at the end of the day that Yale hadn't called.

At the hotel, Yale fidgeted. Now that Lisa had been discharged, he feared public confrontations disrupting everyone's privacy. If he went to her home this could easily occur. Maybe, he decided, it would be best not to visit her today. He thought about sending flowers, then changed his mind after telling David to send her roses. He felt the gesture might be misconstrued. He felt indecisive, bored, and confined. Every meal ordered up to the suite was left untouched. He couldn't concentrate long enough to read even one chapter of the book he had been engrossed in only days ago. He wanted to call Lisa, but decided against that idea, too.

At the precinct, Sergeant Daly had lost his temper with everyone by late afternoon when no new evidence shed any light on the Yale Frye case. Eventually, he just sent everyone home. He wanted to talk further with Lisa Klein, but her husband told him she was not strong enough for visitors. He went home after seven, without having dinner, and went straight to bed.

At the Rose residence, there was a celebration in progress. Jeff and Peggy were glad they had mailed the tape of the incident at the Diamond Coliseum. They had heard a news report indicating that an anonymous video had been received by the Canton Police Department. As a result of the video, the police were confident that the suspect would be apprehended and questioned soon.

However, that was not the primary reason for Jeff and Peggy's celebration. Their festivity had begun with the letter Jeff had received in the morning mail, announcing that he had passed the California bar exam. They could go home to California now, and Jeff could begin his career as an attorney. All the years of hard work, studying, and scrimping had paid off. Jeff called the law firm in Canton, thanking them for his apprenticeship. They wished him well. Peggy had already given notice at work. By next week, they would be home in Los Angeles starting a new life.

George had started his day favorably. He had mailed one tape to Mary via certified mail, and the other tape to his attorney's office. He'd also mailed Lisa Klein his specially designed note. She'd pay for fucking with his plans, he thought to himself on the drive to Peter's house.

Peter answered the door in torn jeans. He wore neither shoes nor shirt. George followed him into the library, considering the incongruity of the man. Peter's house was always meticulously clean with everything in its proper place. Yet Peter himself always looked unkempt. He was rarely clean-shaven, and he either wore the same torn jeans repeatedly, or owned several in identical condition.

Peter sat in a high-backed leather chair and told George to take a seat. He pointed to a sofa that was surrounded by shelves of books. George felt encased every time he sat there, but even more so now. He felt that a distance had developed between himself and Peter because of his failure to complete the last mission successfully. He waited for Peter to speak first, so that he could assess his mood.

Without a word, Peter handed George the morning paper, scrutinizing his reaction. George's picture was smeared across the front page, showing his struggles with Lisa Klein. Peter remained quiet until George finished reading the article, which established that he was being sought for questioning.

"George, it appears you are going to require plastic surgery, immediately. I assume you agree?" Peter regarded George with contempt and disdain, having no respect for the fool he seemed.

"Okay, Peter. I slept last night and had no idea..." He couldn't believe he had been observed and photographed that night; he had no idea how this could have happened. He sat back, visibly shaken.

"We have no time to waste. You will be ready to leave the

country by dusk. You will be taken home now to pack. I will take care of the necessary arrangements. You will not talk to anyone. You will not see anyone. Wally will drive you to a plane, which I have already chartered. We will not see one another, or have further communication, until I ask for you. Nothing else need be said." Peter stood, indicating that the visit was over. He walked to the front door, and held it open for George.

Wally stood next to the limo waiting for George. George's car was not in sight. Wally opened the back door to the limo and waited for George to enter. He got in beside him and they drove off. It wasn't until they were some distance from Peter's house that George looked at the driver and saw that it was Otto. Hesitatingly, George spoke, "Unfortunately, my mission was not completed as planned. I suppose some other scheme will be developed regarding Mr. Frye." Wally and Otto exchanged glances through the rear view mirror. Neither spoke. George became uncomfortable when they arrived at his house. Wally directed Otto to drive around the block once slowly. "What's going on? Wally? Otto? Come on, we are all one team." Suddenly George knew that he had become the next target for elimination. He tried to jump out of the limo.

Wally grabbed him. Otto turned from the driver's seat, bending into the back, and injected a needle into George's arm. Then he hit him sharply on the neck, knocking him out. Wally got out and walked slowly into George's house, as Otto drove around the block. Wally spread gasoline throughout the rooms of the small bungalow. He flipped a match on his way out, walked to the limo, and got into the back, beside the unconscious George.

The limo was miles away by the time the fire department arrived. They fought to extinguish the flames and save the house, but were unsuccessful.

George was regaining consciousness and heard Wally talking, but it sounded fuzzy. He was having trouble concentrating.

"Otto, how long before it works?"

"He'll be dead before he hits the water. Don't worry, Wally."

George couldn't figure out what he was hearing; 'water'? He was going to have plastic surgery. He'd better tell them. He couldn't move, but he heard Otto talking, "Okay, Wally. We can get out of here."

They were on a cliff behind a wooded area, overlooking a stream sixty feet below. Otto pulled a brick out from behind the driver's seat and handed it to Wally.

"Okay, Otto. The brick is tied to the accelerator," Wally was still half-bent under the steering wheel when Otto yanked a hidden rope, putting the limo into drive. The car leaped forward and over the cliff. Wally, George, and the limo flew into the water below. "Sorry, Wally," Otto said without emotion.

He walked through the brush for a mile until he heard the signal horn. He emerged from behind the trees. "Get in." Otto got into what had been George's car. Mary drove them back to Peter's house.

Chapter
14

Lisa was full of remorse for the way she'd behaved on her first day home from the hospital. She went into the kitchen, greeting her family with the warmth she should have shown the day before. They responded, happy to see her cheerful, by catering to her affectionately.

Early that afternoon she called her parents, reassuring them she was fine. She convinced them that there was no need for them to leave the resort and fly in. She called a few close friends, showered, put on a lounging outfit and light makeup. Feeling revitalized, she walked into the den to find Ronnie engrossed in conversation with Yale and David. Her greeting was nonchalant. Hoping her buoyancy seemed natural, she sat down and picked up the mail Ronnie had brought in earlier.

Marc and Steve sauntered in full of excitement and questions. The talk went from the limo in the driveway to the concert the boys were so excited about. It was only a day away. Yale offered the boys a limo for the concert, and gave each a hundred-dollar bill for spending money. The boys looked at Lisa to see if it was all right to accept Yale's generosity when the doorbell rang. Lisa, needing an excuse to leave the room, went to the door. She came back holding an express mail envelope.

"What's that, honey?"

"I don't know, Ronnie. It's postmarked Los Angeles. Maybe, it's my autographed picture of Neil Diamond, from the Friends of Neil Diamond Fan Club. You know how crazy I am about him," Lisa answered. She needed to rile Yale, but wasn't sure why.

"If that's not it, let me know. Neil is a friend of mine. I'll see what I can do to get you the picture," Yale rallied, feeling a need to needle her back.

"Thank you, Yale. You are so generous to us simple folks," she countered sarcastically, as she opened the envelope. She removed the paper, read the note, and began to feel ill. She tasted bile and a tremor went through her, which she tried to conceal. Turning to Marc and Steve, she said, "Boys, Mr. Frye has been really nice. You can accept his gift. Now, I'd like the two of you to ease up and take off for a while." It was hard for her to stay calm. "Go on, boys. Maybe you'd like to go over to the swim club for a while."

"It's okay, Lisa," Yale tried, "I'm enjoying talking to them."

"Please, Yale," Lisa said sharply.

"Come on, Mom. We wanted to show Yale our music collection. He said he wanted to see what we liked," Marc pleaded.

"Some other time," she said, looking to Ronnie for assistance.

Ronnie knew the look and said, "Later, boys."

Knowing when to quit, the boys left the room. When they were out of sight, Lisa handed Ronnie the note. He, in turn, handed it to Yale, while picking up the phone to call Sergeant Daly.

It only took Sergeant Daly thirty minutes to arrive at the Klein's residence, and two hours to turn their home upside down. Daly clearly felt that the threat needed to be taken seriously. He ordered surveillance near the house, and had telephone equipment installed to record and trace every call. Speakers were attached near the doors to monitor anyone coming in or near the house. An intercom system was set up and a special private line connected. The telephone company was running a computer check of calls that did not appear repeatedly on the Klein's monthly bill. The note was sent to the lab for analysis. Ronnie was asked for all the mail that had come to the house since the shooting.

While Lisa sat mortified, the boys returned to discover the upheaval. They began yelling at her for treating them like babies. They obviously felt that they should have been told what was going on instead of being sent away.

She felt thoroughly exhausted and subjugated. Her home had been seized by strangers, and her privacy violated again. She went into her bedroom and closed the door. She heard something like glass breaking, coming from another room. There was noise and raised voices. She turned on the same radio that had played all day when she was getting ready for Yale's concert, her special night. It seemed so long ago. Peter, Paul, and Mary were singing. Where have all the flowers gone? Long time passing... She tried to ignore the knocking on her door. Where have all the young girls gone? "Lisa." Long time ago... Yale stood in the doorway. Where have all the flowers gone? She sang along, as he walked toward the bed. Long time ago... "What can I do, Lisa? I'm sorry." Gone to graveyards... "Lisa."

She looked up at him. "You know what you can do? You can get me a signed picture from your friend, Neil Diamond. It seems it didn't come in my mail today," she spat the words at him, needing to vent her frustration on somebody.

"I'm just as upset as you are. Don't think you're the only one suffering. I never asked you to get involved," he responded angrily. The phone started ringing, cutting short his retaliation. She reached for the phone, having been instructed to answer as many calls as she could herself. "Hello." The recorder was on so that everyone could hear the conversation.

"Hello, I'm sorry to bother you. The hotel told me I could reach Yale Frye at this number. This is his mother calling."

Yale reached for the phone, feeling his privacy infringed upon, "Hi, Ma. Everything okay?"

"That's what I called to ask you, Yale. I didn't hear from you, and was getting very nervous. You know, the hotel gave me this number, but no name, nothing. Where are you?"

"I'm fine, Ma. I'm at Lisa Klein's house."

"Oh, so now I know why you didn't give the hotel a name. Is that who answered? I would have thanked her for everything she's done."

"I'll tell her, Ma. She's not feeling great today."

"What's wrong?"

"Ma, can I call you a little later?"

"Yale, what's going on? I know when something's wrong. What aren't you telling me?"

"There's nothing to worry about, Ma. There are a lot of people here right now. I'll call you a little later."

"If she's not feeling great, why are there a lot of people around?" She was persistent, and Yale was uncomfortable. But he knew she was too intuitive to be dismissed easily.

"Later, Ma."

"Yale, when are you coming home? Maybe I should fly to Canton today, and stay until you're ready to come home?"

"No, Ma. Stay there. I should be back in a day or two. I'm fine. Stop worrying. There are just endless questions to answer, and I'm, uh, tired." His voice was cracking, giving him away. He knew he had to get off the phone. His mother knew him too well, and she was adding to his difficulty in remaining composed.

"Honey, I love you. You're my reason for breathing. It's not easy at this end either. Okay? If you don't want me to come, I won't."

He couldn't talk. He was crumbling. She evoked emotions in him no one else could. She knew which buttons to push; she always had. He was afraid to speak.

Lisa understood and intervened. Taking the phone from Yale's hand, she said, "Mrs. Frye. Hi. This is Lisa Klein. You know, I always wanted to meet Yale personally, but this sure isn't how I wanted it to happen. Mrs. Frye, we've got a problem. I received a threatening letter in the mail today, meant for both Yale and me. The police don't want to take any chances, since they haven't caught this suspect yet. So they are going to trace and monitor my calls and go through my mail. It's been a zoo here for the last few hours. My kids are upset. I'm a wreck. And I'm concerned about what to do. My father isn't a well man, and my folks have gone through a lot. I'm not sure, just like Yale, what to say, what to tell them, and what not to, you know?" She stopped. There was a long silence.

"Thank you, Lisa. I'm sorry you were hurt. I'm just grateful it wasn't worse. Tell your parents the facts, honey. It'll be better coming from you than finding out another way. Honey, it's better to know than to be in the dark. I know you want to protect them, but they are your parents. If you can't tell them, who can you tell? I think I'll fly into Canton."

"Mrs. Frye, I know you're right, but I'm going to wait a day or two. I'm having a hard enough time keeping myself together. If they come in, I would have to try and hold back my feelings so I wouldn't upset them. It would be harder. I don't want to have to worry about them, or how they are handling things, on top of everything. I just think it would be too hard for me."

Another long silence. "Okay, Lisa. I'll stay put, too. Can I count on you keeping me informed?"

"Yes, you can. Hold on. I'll let you say good-bye to your son. We'll call you later. I promise."

She waited a second, then handed Yale the phone. He still couldn't talk, knowing he couldn't conceal the emotions piercing his heart. "Ma." Silence followed. His mother understood. She knew her son.

"It's okay, Yale. That's quite a lady. Call me later. I love you."

"Bye." They hung up at the same time. Lisa had taken Yale's hand in hers. He looked at her tenderly. "Thanks," he managed, regaining some composure.

"Come on," she said, getting off the bed. "Let's put something to eat on the table. Everybody's probably hungry."

They were comfortable with one another for the rest of the day. Yale helped set up a table with sandwiches, snacks, and drinks. Later he put dirty dishes in the dishwasher like a member of the family. He spent time with the boys, talking about rock stars, giving them tips about their stereos, listening attentively to their opinions, and answering question after question. He sent David and the boys to pick up pizza later in the evening, and tried to make sure Lisa wasn't exposed to anything else that might upset her. Yale listened to her conversations with friends who called, marveling at her ability to relate to everyone calmly. With genuine interest and a sense of humor, she dismissed comments about "how awful this whole thing was" with "Well, at least I got to know Yale Frye."

It was midnight when Yale and David returned to the hotel under police protection. At eight the next morning they were brought back to the Klein house.

This routine continued for three days without incident. The police were continuing their investigations. Late on the eighth day after the shooting at Diamond Coliseum, the Los Angeles Police Department called. They had a positive identification of one of two men found dead on the outskirts of Studio City California: George Benson, a local architect. He was twenty-eight, single, a loner, and was the individual in the video taken at the Coliseum. The information confirmed that he was in Canton the night of the shooting, and on a return flight to LA later the same night. He had been identified by a stewardess from a police photo. There was also a woman, as yet unidentified, with him. They had traveled under assumed names, with false picture identifications.

Yale and Lisa were listening intently when the other shoe dropped. They were told George Benson's house had burned down. Police could not determine if he had sent the death threat. They had not located, or identified, the woman who had been with Benson in Canton on the night of the shooting. Neighbors of George Benson had claimed that they'd witnessed nothing unusual. The limo found at the site where the bodies were discovered was from Nevada. There was a temporary Nevada plate on it, stolen from another vehicle. In addition to the body identified as George Benson, there was a second body, identified as Wally Burns, the twenty-three-year-old son of Barbara and Ted Burns. The wealthy parents owned Burns Markets throughout California.

Barbara and Ted Burns had not seen or talked to their only son in four years. He had refused to go into the family business, and had moved to an Indian reservation in Arizona. People on the reservation said that Wally had left the reservation over two years ago to work on social reform. They hadn't seen or heard from him since. They knew he was in a group called P.A.P. There was no listing for P.A.P. in the California Records, and for that matter, no one else seemed to have known Wally. There was no ID on him when the body was found, and no money. Police suspected the deaths of the two men were interrelated, and might well be connected to other individuals, possibly something to do with the P.A.P. group. George Benson was a freelance independent architect who worked from his home, while Wally, it appeared, was not employed in the area. Neither man had bank accounts, credit cards, or current employers.

"The investigation will continue in conjunction with the L.A.P.D.," Sergeant Daly told Lisa, Yale, and Ronnie. " I'd like to keep your phone tapped and continue the police protection.

"No, Sergeant," Lisa protested. "Everyone has gone through enough. We don't even know the note wasn't a prank. I can't live this way indefinitely. I want my life back. I refuse to live in fear when I don't know if there is anything left to be afraid of. I want Ronnie to go back to work, my boys to go on their camping trip as scheduled, and I want to heal, which is becoming increasingly difficult as we sit waiting. We don't even know if there is anything to wait for. It's time to go on with our lives. I can't go on this way."

She stopped to answer the ringing phone. It was Dr. Feld. She had forgotten about her appointment, and told him she'd be in his office within the hour. Yale accompanied Lisa and Ronnie to the doctor's office.

After Lisa was examined, the doctor requested she wait for him in his office. Ronnie and Yale were already in the oak paneled room. In order to provide privacy, they had been allowed to wait there, away from the curiosity of the people in the waiting room. Doctor Feld was sympathetic to the scrutiny that had revolved around them since the shooting. He entered, seating himself behind the massive desk. Opening Lisa's folder, he examined the medical records for a moment before speaking. "Lisa, I am going to be frank with you, and would like your husband to hear what I have to say, if you have no objection."

"Lisa, I'd like to stay, too," Yale added, hoping their bond was strong enough for him to be involved.

"Go on, doctor. They have a right to hear whatever you have to say. They were with me during the worst of it. So they're entitled to be here, now that I'm mending."

"That's part of the problem, Lisa. You are not mending as I anticipated you would. With all that has happened since you left the hospital, you haven't been able to get the rest you need. To be honest, I'm wondering if maybe it wouldn't be in your best interest to go back into the hospital for a few days."

"No way!" Lisa responded quickly.

"Your blood count is still low. You are bordering on anemia. You need plenty of rest, and to follow a proper diet. I will prescribe a vitamin with iron, but, the rest is up to you."

"What do you suggest?" Ronnie asked.

"For Lisa to act like she's on a vacation, and do as little as possible. She needs to relax."

Yale spoke up, "Lisa, you have been selfless in helping me. I'd like you to come to California with me and allow me to do something for you. I have help, so you won't have to do anything. You will have privacy, away from reporters and the scrutiny of the public. That way, Ronnie can return to work, fly out for weekends, and you won't be home alone. I need to go home, Lisa, but I don't want to leave knowing you haven't recovered. Will you consider this offer and come with me, and let me try to help?"

"I think it's a great idea," Ronnie said, adding, "I'll feel better going to work, knowing you're safe and being taken care of."

"Okay. Okay. Just remember, I don't do windows or floors. I'm a sick person," she answered, smiling at Yale warmly.

They left that evening in Yale's private plane. The pilot's voice over the speaker related, "Looks like a smooth flight all the way to Los Angeles, Mr. Frye. There's not a storm in sight."

Chapter
15

When the five remaining members of PEOPLE AGAINST PUPPETRY were assembled, they agreed to continue their efforts to eliminate the inferior from society in order to serve humanity.

"It saddens me," Peter began, "that two of our members had to leave our group. However, their personal perspectives became more important than fulfilling their responsibilities as agreed upon when we formed P.A.P. George became careless, as you have witnessed. Wally was considering leaving our organization. A treacherous choice for so young a person. He knew, as we all did, when we committed ourselves to P.A.P., it was for life.

"We vowed honesty. We vowed dedication. We vowed loyalty. We cannot compromise ourselves. Deception will not be tolerated. It makes us as superficial as those in power we deplore.

"We will choose the next person's name for elimination from the urn, and proceed with our work. This disruption will not interfere with our plans and goals. I request, however, that we all live together under this roof. Mary will continue to share my quarters. The rest of you will share the lower quarters, effective immediately. We will devise a foolproof plan for the next assignment. However, we must also finish what George left undone. Along with Yale Frye we must now bring about the earthly departure of Lisa Klein, to ensure our safety and Mary's."

Peter requested that Mary select the next name from the urn. She pulled out a slip of paper, reading aloud the name of Myra Sullivan.

"Excellent choice," Peter exclaimed with a crooked smile. He alone knew that Mary had just chosen the name he himself had placed in the container.

Myra Sullivan was the most powerful African American in television. Her daily talk show had a viewing audience larger than that of any other show of its kind in the history of television. She was an attractive woman who used her personality to captivate and endear herself into the hearts of many. Her ratings continued to soar weekly.

Peter had chosen Myra Sullivan because she was a black success story. He hated her, and felt it was time to halt her philanthropic activities, before more of the niggers thought about educating themselves, and trying to better themselves like this whore. He was glad she would be the next target. He was going to make sure that nothing would stop him from showing the world that blacks have a place, as long as it wasn't a place he was occupying.

Mary undressed before Peter in the bedroom. He unzipped his pants, saying, "Honey, I love watching you get naked. Come here. I want you to sit on my cock."

She walked seductively toward him, removed her red bikini panties, and straddled him. He grabbed her ass as she moved on him. "Slow and easy, baby. I want to fuck all night." She moved rhythmically, kissing him eagerly, cupping her breasts for his mouth. With one hand he pulled her hair back while his other hand squeezed her nipples. She kept moving, hoping to make him come. She pushed down hard on him, feeling her need for an orgasm growing nearer. "Stop!" He pushed her away. "On your knees. I want your mouth."

"Come on, Peter," she pleaded. "Fill me. You feel so good."

He pushed her backwards, until her back felt like it was breaking, pulling himself out. "Down! Suck!" He knew she was close to climaxing but didn't want her to.

She got on her knees and looked up at him. His face looked evil. She engulfed his dick. He grabbed her head and moved ferociously. He felt his urgency increase. His breathing intensified. Suddenly he pulled out and pushed her down on the floor. He got on her from behind, forcing himself into her. She screamed but he paid no heed. He pulled her up against his hardness so she was on all fours, pushing, pushing, pushing. He grabbed her neck with a violence she had not encountered before.

When he was done, he got up, left her on the floor, and went to bed. She wasn't sure she could move. He put his head on the pillow, pulling the blanket around himself. "Get in bed, Mary. You need extra rest if our baby is to develop properly."

She rose slowly, noticing blood on the floor, and went to lie beside him. She was just drifting off when Peter asked, "Do you think we'll have a boy or a girl?"

"What would you prefer, Peter?"

"A girl, I think. Maybe her mother can teach her to be as good a cocksucker as she is." He turned, then told her to put her fingers up his ass, and make him feel good again. She obliged. He stroked himself, while she pushed her fingers up higher into him. He squeezed his ass tightly around her fingers while he stroked his shaft vigorously, until he exploded again. Spent, he went to sleep with Mary beside him. She buried her face in the pillow, so he wouldn't know she was crying.

In the morning, Peter gathered the group together. He advised them of their next mission. "All individual accounts are to be closed, and living arrangements modified."

Peter kissed Mary gently on the cheek before she left the house. "You know, Mary, what I treasure most in our relationship is the candor between us. It is a wonderful thing when a man and woman can understand each other, and be open and honest about their needs, their feelings, their hopes and dreams. I am grateful you are a part of my life. Destiny has ordained we remain together, united, not only in flesh but spiritually as well. Try to come home early from the art studio. I'd like to offer you the same pleasure you gave me last night."

"Do you love me, Peter?"

"It's much more than love we share, Mary. We share loyalty, honesty, and commitment. Have a good day."

She left the house for the art studio, wondering at the complexity of the man who stood in the doorway. Getting behind the wheel of her car, she turned to wave to him. He was standing in the doorway, pissing on the driveway, as she drove off.

Chapter
16

Lisa slept for most of the four-hour flight to Los Angeles while David and Yale discussed business details that would require their immediate attention upon arrival. Yale said that his priority was to ensure that Lisa had every provision necessary to aid in her recovery.

After disembarking from Yale's private plane, the three joined Ruth Frye in Yale's chauffeur-driven Mercedes, and proceeded to his home. It was evident by the way Ruth and Yale embraced before getting into the car that there was a special bond between mother and son. The conversation in the Mercedes suggested there was not much they kept from one another.

Lisa and Ruth took to each other instantly. Conversing was easy, and Yale was pleased that they were all relaxed during the forty-minute ride to Beverly Hills. Ruth listened to everything her son related, asking questions like an attorney. Her fury was evident as she wished the worst for those who would dare to attempt to injure her child. She patted Lisa's hand affectionately several times, expressing appreciation for her intervention on her son's behalf.

Ruth was a tall brunette with an angular face. In spite of her large hands and a solid frame, everything about her personified femininity. She wore little makeup and not much jewelry. She was opinionated but a good listener. Lisa was comfortable in her company, feeling a security similar to that evoked by her parents' presence.

They approached the gate, which opened to allow the silver Mercedes to pass, and drove more than two miles to a sprawling, contemporary gray brick house with endless windows. The multi-level domain was surrounded by acres of manicured landscaping with tall trees, most of which were unfamiliar to Lisa. The Mercedes stopped at the front door and Lisa walked to the entrance, realizing that she could not see either end of the house from where she stood. As they walked into the marble tiled foyer, Yale took her hand and told her that their luggage would arrive shortly. He then introduced Lisa to his houseman, Victor.

Lisa had seen the inside of mansions on television, but actually being inside one was intimidating, especially when she remembered that only a few days ago Yale had been placing dishes in her dishwasher. Now she was in his house, where he had probably never seen the inside of his own dishwasher. For a moment she felt humbled by her spacious surroundings, and didn't like what she was feeling. She wasn't a jealous person, but when Yale turned on the light in the elegant coral chamber, she felt less his equal than when he had been on her turf.

The bedroom had a private bath adjoining the room, with a stall shower, sunken oversized tub, whirlpool, vanity, and bidet. There was a walk-in closet larger than Lisa's bedroom back home. On one of the mirrored dressers in the bedroom were a vase of colorful fresh flowers, a tray filled with crystal bowls of fresh fruit, nuts, and chocolates, and a crystal pitcher of iced tea. Another dresser was covered with current bestseller novels, magazines, a bottle of Lisa's favorite perfume, a silver comb and brush set, and a new stuffed koala bear holding a helium balloon that said 'WELCOME' in bright red letters.

In the bathroom were fresh towels, toothbrush, toothpaste, mouthwash, scented soaps, and a terrycloth robe for her convenience. On the dressing table, in front of a large mirror, was a tray of new cosmetics and a crystal bud vase with a single, long-stemmed white rose. She was overwhelmed and embarrassed by the care taken to welcome her. "Thank you, Yale. This is very special."

"If you need anything, Lisa, don't be shy about asking."

"Okay," was all she could manage to say. She followed Yale back to the others as Victor brought in trays of sandwiches, drinks, snacks, and pastries. She was just thinking what a lot of food it was for so few when the barrage began.

First to arrive was Yale's manager, Robert Bowman, followed by Yale's publicist. Then she was introduced to several business advisors and a few close friends who had been informed of his homecoming. They had stopped by to express how glad they were to see he was unharmed.

The phone calls were endless. Within an hour of their arrival, the house was filled with more than twenty people, all familiar with each other, all strangers to Lisa. There was no protection from the bombardment or from the anxiety Lisa felt, surrounded by so many strangers. She felt uncomfortably like an intruder. All the topics of conversation were foreign to her. Needing to escape, she got up and walked to the kitchen. Victor was busy getting coffee, tea, and several additional bowls of goodies ready, to bring into the family room. "Anything I can get for you, Miss Lisa?" he asked.

"No, thanks. Here, let me help you carry some of this," she said, picking up a couple of the bowls before Victor could point to the cart he was about to use. She carried the bowls to the visitors, oblivious of Victor, behind her with the cart.

As she placed the bowls on the octagon mahogany table, in the center of the conversation pit, a new arrival asked if she'd please get her an ashtray, evidently thinking that Lisa was part of the domestic staff. Yale heard the request and tried to intervene with an introduction. But Lisa, quick to please, said, "Sure." She turned and found Victor behind her, with a cart containing several ashtrays. Lisa picked one up and extended it to the woman, when Yale took it from her.

"Sit down, Lisa. You've had a long day," he instructed, placing the ashtray in front of the lady. Yale introduced Lisa, but it was clearly an extremely awkward moment for all of them.

He was called to the phone again. She sat, waiting for his return, feeling out of place. Ruth took the phone from Yale, whispering something into his ear. He glanced at Lisa, prepared a plate of food, and brought it to her. She accepted the plate as he was called away again.

Lisa was not hungry, but attempted to nibble at the food on her plate. She tried not to show how badly she felt about being an inconvenience, as one obviously needing supervision in order to prevent any further humiliating moments. Ruth came and sat beside her, but when she patted Lisa's hand this time, it didn't feel affectionate, but patronizing. Lisa glanced at Ruth's watch and excused herself, explaining that she was exhausted. Te tears in her eyes did not go unnoticed by Ruth, who was wise enough to know when to say nothing.

Lisa went to the bedroom, craving the familiarity of her bed back home. She waited for the lights on the phone to show they were not in use and dialed the operator. She placed a collect call to Ronnie, waking him since it was almost one a.m. in Canton. He accepted the call, frightened. "What's the matter, Lisa?"

"Nothing, Ronnie. Sorry I woke you. I didn't realize the time. It got hectic here. I didn't have a chance to call earlier."

"I called you, Lisa, but got disconnected. So I decided to wait and hear from you. I must have fallen asleep. How are you doing?"

"I don't know. I feel out of place and like a pain in the ass. Maybe this wasn't such a good idea. There's a lot of people, and a lot Yale has to do. I feel in the way."

"Lisa, you're not a pain. Just relax, don't overdo, and don't worry so much."

"You don't understand, Ronnie. I'm a fish out of water here." She heard him yawn into the receiver and got angry. "Never mind, Ronnie. I have to go. I'll talk to you tomorrow. Kiss the boys." She hung up before Ronnie knew what had hit him, got undressed, put on the terry robe, and plopped down on the bed.

She looked at the silk nightgown, wanting her own clothes. She picked up the ensemble to hang in the closet. When she opened the closet door, all her own clothes had been put on hangers. She took out a nightshirt of her own, got ready for bed, and went to sleep with the lamp on, holding onto her new koala bear. She didn't hear Yale knock and enter to check on her later that night. She didn't feel him tuck the blanket around her, nor did she feel the kiss he placed on her cheek before going to his own bedroom.

It was almost noon when Lisa climbed out of bed. She felt drugged and decided to shower to help get rid of the lethargy before getting a morning cup of coffee. She got into the shower, turned the water on, and passed out. When she came to, she was on the bed, wrapped in a towel, with Yale beside her.

He told her that he had gone to check on her, as he had several times that morning. When he'd opened the door, he had heard the shower running. He'd been standing outside the bathroom door, about to ask what she wanted for breakfast, when he'd heard a strange sound. Alarmed, he'd opened the door and found her unconscious on the floor of the shower stall. He had wrapped her with Victor's assistance, and put her on the bed. "Don't move, honey. I've called the hospital. An ambulance is on the way."

Paramedics were examining Lisa within minutes. She vehemently protested when it was suggested she be taken to the hospital for further examination. "I'm fine. I fainted. I've been under stress. I'll be fine. I am not going to any hospital. Nothing hurts. I'm okay now."

It was finally agreed that Yale would have his personal physician check her at the house and that someone would stay with her at all times until it was determined that she was medically fit.

Doctor Jack Weiner diagnosed Lisa as anemic and suffering from exhaustion. He prescribed bed rest, a high protein diet, and another, more potent, vitamin fortified with a higher dosage of iron. He gave her a vitamin complex injection and confined her to

bed for the remainder of the day, telling her to make an appointment to see him in a week. She agreed to follow his instructions,
but sulked behind the closed door for the rest of the day, feigning
sleep whenever someone came to check on her.

The next day she decided to make a conscious effort to be
more agreeable. Yale would be out for most of the day and Ruth
would be in charge of her care. Victor had the day off. Ruth pampered her all day until she wanted to vomit. She wore a path in the
plush carpeting, bringing soup, toast, cheeses, fruits, chopped
liver and crackers, and every imaginable juice in existence. She
felt Lisa's forehead every half hour, and followed her to the bathroom all day, standing just outside the door, "just in case." Lisa
went to sleep at six-thirty, after eating a spinach salad that Ruth
had prepared. She prayed Yale would be back when she woke.

She slept until ten the next morning, when Yale greeted her,
carrying a breakfast tray to the bed.

"Yale, I'm going home. This is bullshit. I'm disrupting everyone's life. I have to leave today."

"Grow up, Lisa. You can't always do, or have, what you want.
Stop fighting everyone. We want to help you."

"Go to hell! You think waiting on me is helping me? I want a
life back. My life. I don't want to be treated like some simpering
invalid. What you're doing isn't for me, Yale, it's for you, so you
can feel less guilt. Go away, big shot, and grow up yourself. My
condition is not your fault. When you can treat me as an equal,
instead of feeling beholden, let me know. Maybe, then, we can
communicate."

He left the tray on the bed and closed the door behind him.
Leaving the room, he realized what she said was true.

Obediently, Lisa ate most of the meal on her tray. Coming in
to see how she was, Ruth nodded approvingly. "Nourishment will
give you strength, dear."

She was depressed and kept the conversation short when Ronnie called. She plummeted even further, submerged in self-pity,
after their conversation. Ronnie had told her that the boys had left
for their camping trip, and that he had asked Yale not to wake her
earlier when they'd called to say good-bye.

Things were not going well. Lisa knew that, but what could
she do? Reaching for a cigarette on the nightstand, her hand accidentally hit a button on the intercom system of Yale's elaborate
telephone system.

"Ma, leave her alone. She's angry for good reason. By now,

she probably feels like a prisoner instead of a guest. Just stay out of it."

"Yale, you're wrong. You did the right thing not waking her to talk to her boys. Her sleep is important now. She can talk to them later. Ronnie said they would call back."

"Maybe. I don't know shit right now. Go on, Ma. You'll be late for your hair appointment."

"Yale, what are you going to do, just sit here all day? This is not doing you any good either. You're not eating. You check on her all night. I heard you get up a dozen times last night. I thought that if I stayed here, at least you'd rest easier. But it did no good. You're going to make yourself sick."

"I'll be fine. I just need to know she's okay. Go on, Ma."

"Yale, I think you feel more than you're saying about this girl."

"So what if I do? She's probably sorry she ever met me. Anyway, she's married. Remember?"

"I'll come back after I'm done at the salon to fix dinner. What a day for Victor to get sick, on top of everything!"

"No. You go on home. I'll order in. Go to your bridge game tonight. I'm going to lie down for a while."

"You know where I'll be. Call if you change your mind or need me."

"Okay, ma. I'll talk to you later."

Lisa turned the system off. She put on a lounging outfit and a little makeup, and fixed her hair, then walked to the family room where Yale was.

He glanced up from a novel, surprised, "Do you need something, Lisa?"

"Yes. I need some company. Can I join you?"

"Sure. Let me get you a pillow and quilt." He got up before she could stop him, and came back with two pillows and a comforter. He put one pillow behind her, and took the other for himself at the opposite end of the sofa. He placed the blanket between them.

She opened the blanket. "Here. We can share. It's big enough for both of us."

"Want the television on?"

"No."

"Hungry?"

"No."

"Some music?"

"Okay. Do you have anything by Elton John?" It was the first time he'd seen her smile since they arrived. "I'm sorry I've been such a pain, Yale. I'm just not used to being catered to, or feeling useless. I guess part of it is insecurity, too. I felt like part of a team in Canton and close to you. I forgot about who you were, and was comfortable there. When we got here, I felt... I don't know how to explain it, it just wasn't the same."

"I understand. It happens to me a lot. People act differently toward the 'celebrity' than toward the 'me'. It makes it hard to develop real relationships. Sometimes, you wonder if the person would be with you if you weren't famous, or if that's the only reason they hang around. I'm glad you were able to forget who I was. I wish you still could."

"It's not you, Yale. You're still the same. It's me. I feel out of place, like a guest at a fancy resort."

"I'm not going to apologize for being able to live like this, Lisa. I've worked long and hard for it. It seems I'm being judged by my trappings; it's a hazard of the trade."

"You don't understand. It's not just the way you live or where. It's a feeling of not being equal. I feel small and insignificant here."

"You're being a snob, Lisa, reacting to possessions rather than to me. Don't judge me by what's visible. Look at me, the individual. I accept you for the person you are. Why can't you do the same?"

"You're full of shit! That's easy to say from where you're sitting."

"I didn't always live like this. I know what it is to struggle. I may have a name that's known, and more money than you, but I've had to pay a big price and miss out on many things because of it."

"Yeah. Well, with your name and money, I'm sure you can buy whatever you've missed out on."

"Now you're full of shit! My money can't buy me happiness or children. My name can get me a good seat anywhere, and people who will suck up to me. But it can't make me feel complete, content, or at peace with myself. Fame and money cause doubts and fears, too. Feelings that some of what's been achieved and acquired isn't permanent. I'm a commodity, Lisa. I travel like a globetrotter, but can't enjoy it because of who I am. I'm hounded, watched, scrutinized and dissected, piece by piece. Your opinions are out of line. Try thinking more clearly."

She got up from the sofa. "Go back to your book, Yale. I'm not going to dispute lifestyles. If we can't speak harmoniously, it's a clear indication of how different we are. I don't want to argue."

"No, you'd rather judge than try to understand," he snapped.

Lisa walked back to the bedroom, unable to refute his logic. She was determined to remain calm, feeling that there was no way this discussion was going to end agreeably. She refused to be condescended to, although she didn't want to put stipulations on what they could discuss. She wanted to feel close, and recapture the bond they shared before coming to LA.

She returned to where Yale had been sitting, intending to apologize. He had left the room. She saw the book he had been reading on the table and went looking for him. She found him at the kitchen table with a cup of coffee in hand. He spoke before she had a chance to say anything.

"Here," he said, handing her a check. She looked at the check made out to her for one million dollars. "Now we are both rich. Maybe you'll feel equal."

Her fury was irrepressible. "Go to hell, you bastard!" She tore the check into pieces and threw them at him, running back to the bedroom.

He barged into the room without knocking. "Don't ever, ever, call me a bastard! Who gave you the right to sit in judgment of me? What the hell do you think I've been going through? This hasn't been a joy ride for me either!" He was yelling angrily, approaching her with unleashed emotion that had been repressed for too long. He grabbed her by the arms. "I didn't ask for any of this! I'm not responsible for the shooting, or your injuries! I never asked you to intervene! What do you want from me? You're not the only one suffering."

He stopped himself abruptly, realizing he was losing control. He still had her by the arms as she stood with tears running down her face. He let go of her, ashamed for his outburst. "I'm sorry. God, I'm losing it." She sat down on the bed, her head bent. "Are you all right, Lisa?" He sat beside her.

She turned and saw the anguish in his eyes. She understood his distress and torment, for they were the same intense feelings she was enduring. He touched her hand. The anger died as they were possessed by an immeasurable need for each other. She touched his face gently. He grabbed her, fiercely, with a passion kindled by her delicate fingers tracing his lips, and kissed her hard. She responded, opening her mouth to his tongue. She drew his mouth back to hers when he pulled away, trying to suppress the passion that was affecting his ability to restrain himself from her. They felt the volcanic tremors of their bodies as they clung to each other.

"I want you, Yale." She pulled him down, feeling his hardness against her through their clothes. She pushed against his erection, holding her hands on his behind, to press them closer together. "I want you. I want you, Yale," she repeated.

He moved off her, holding her away from him. "Let me just hold you, Lisa. I don't want to do anything you'll be sorry for later." She unzipped his pants, and started stroking his penis with her fingers. She kissed his face, while she continued to run her fingers up and down his shaft. He had a large penis and she wanted it inside of her. He put his hand inside her panties. She moaned, moving to his touch. His fingers probed inside of her as she closed her legs, pushing against his circling motion. He had to stop; he had to.

As if reading his mind, she whispered, "It's okay. I won't be sorry. I was sorry last time that I stopped. Make love to me. I'm sure, Yale. I want you."

He undressed her, while she slid his pants down. The urgency was increasing as they gave in to the needs of their bodies. As he mounted her, she spread her legs and felt him penetrate. He pushed deep inside of her and she closed her thighs tightly around him. She kissed his neck while he bent to suck her breasts.

Their bodies were soaked with perspiration. They continued moving, pushing against each other. She grabbed his ass and started moving faster, feeling herself getting close. He was kissing her hard and pumping even harder. They knew their bodies wouldn't allow them to stop now, even if they wanted to. He was groaning as she met each push of his penis. He was deep, filling her. His shaft was rubbing against her clitoris, and he heard her breathing peaking as she moaned, "now, now." He felt her coming as the muscles contracted in her vagina. She screamed as his semen poured into her.

"I love you. I love you," he repeated, over and over, as his body shuddered with the intensity of the climax. He stayed on top of her, his weight on his arms, as their panting subsided. He kissed her gently on the lips, the nose, and her cheeks. He finally moved off of her, cradling her close against him. They were content in each other's arms. He whispered as he kissed her head, "I meant it, Lisa. God help me, but I've fallen in love with you."

She snuggled even closer, not wanting this moment to pass. They fell asleep in each other's embrace. It was the first restful sleep for either of them since the shooting.

Chapter
17

Jeff and Peggy Rose did not need much time to get organized in their new surroundings. They had stored a few special items with Jeff's parents when they went to Canton. Now they retrieved them for the apartment in Los Angeles. Their plan was to save as much money as possible for the next two years. This would allow them to accumulate a substantial down payment for a house, then start a family.

They were glad to be back in California, in the apartment they had agreed to rent the same day they had arrived. It was cozy and clean. They had felt no need to spend days in search of something that might end up being less than their first choice.

Jeff and Peggy had made a list of priorities when they were first married and they coexisted agreeably, following their outlined plans and making all decisions together. They were comfortable, in and out of bed, always enjoying each other's company. Peggy had found a job as a medical assistant the first week back in Los Angeles. She would be working forty-five hours weekly, with Wednesdays and Sundays off. She would be earning four hundred dollars a week, with a guaranteed raise after ninety days if she worked out.

On Jeff's first day as an employed attorney for the law firm of Hall and Davis, he entered the outer office and heard the receptionist announce his arrival to John Hall, the senior partner of the firm. He was greeted warmly when he walked into Mr. Hall's office. Jeff had accepted this position as a training ground, feeling it best to work for a small firm, learning diversity before attempting to build a private practice.

John Hall was in his late fifties, with thirty years of experience as an attorney. He was even-tempered, sophisticated, and overworked. His partner, Herb Davis, had suffered a stroke less than a month earlier. John was impressed with Jeff, and being a confident judge of character, he offered Jeff a position with the firm.

He explained to Jeff that his partner would be in rehabilitation for months as a result of partial paralysis incurred by the stroke.

"Jeff, I need help and you appear eager and enthusiastic. I like both qualities. I realize you will have to work longer hours to compensate for Herb's absence. Therefore, I will offer you a new automobile and sixty thousand a year. You'll receive medical coverage for both you and your wife, and a bonus at the end of the year when we renegotiate terms regarding employment for the following year. You will receive a two-week paid vacation at the end of one year and a legal secretary to assist you. I will even offer you the option of hiring your own secretary," he added with humor.

Jeff accepted the position the following day, after discussing Mr. Hall's offer with Peggy. He took a few days to get organized and purchase proper attire for his new position.

Now, after shaking hands, John Hall took Jeff to what would be his office. The desk was piled with unfinished business from Mr. Davis' clients, and stacks of new mail were waiting. John Hall wished him luck, leaving to go to the 42nd District Court for a hearing.

Jeff didn't know where to start. He had just poured himself a cup of coffee when the receptionist knocked and came in with a stack of new mail. Telling her that the oldest correspondence should receive priority attention, he asked her to put the new mail in a tray while he tried to sort through the documents already opened on the desk. Placing the bundle in the tray, she picked up one that had fallen and added it, a bulky envelope postmarked "Canton", to the bottom of the pile of new mail. She returned to her desk to answer the ringing telephone.

The same day Jeff Rose began his new career, Mary Nelson signed for a certified letter at the art gallery she operated on another street in Los Angeles. She had been glad to get away from Peter after the abusiveness of the previous night. She was more than a little afraid of him. There were days she thought of packing her clothes and leaving the country. However, Peter had insisted on having only one account for P.A.P.; everyone had closed all individual savings and checking accounts, turning all their assets over to him. Mary couldn't leave because she had no money, no charges, and no life outside the one she shared with Peter. She was trapped.

Mary believed in white supremacy, but she had joined the group more because of her attraction to Peter than to change the world. In the beginning, Peter had showered her with attention and affection. Soon she was in love with him. But as soon as he was sure of her love, he began to manipulate her until she was totally dependent on him. She had no family and had terminated all friendships when she moved in with Peter.

Peter could still excite her, but more often of late she felt more like a convenience than a lover and companion. Mary was certain she, too, would have met with the same fate as Wally and George if she had not told Peter she was carrying his child. She prayed she would conceive, fearful of Peter's reaction if he ever discovered that she had lied to him. If she wasn't pregnant yet, she had to make sure she was soon.

Mary walked to her office carrying the certified letter. She sat down behind her desk, opening the envelope. She read the note: "If I'm a friend, I'll be one you defend. But if you pretend, we will all meet our end." Then, with trembling hands, she inserted the cassette and listened to George's taped message. She sat numbly. If she didn't tell Peter about this and he found out, he would never trust her again. She would be eliminated. If she did tell him, she would gain his trust, but lose the one thing she could use to free herself from him. Now that George was dead, this cassette could put Peter away for life while she vanished from sight.

She was still uncertain what to do when she locked the door of the gallery to go home. She had the envelope with her. She was considering placing it in a safety deposit box until she made a firm decision. Then she saw Peter, standing next to the Volkswagen in the parking lot, holding a dozen roses for her.

"What is this, Peter?"

"Just a little lift for the mother that carries my child within her womb."

"How sweet." She accepted the roses with shaking hands. Peter explained that Otto had dropped him off in order to surprise her. Now he was taking her to dinner to celebrate the conception of their child.

The envelope was in her portfolio. She decided, there and then, to tell Peter about it, reaffirming his trust in her. "Peter, I have something vital to share with you, too. I'd like to give it to you at home after dinner, when we are alone." She leaned over, kissing him gently after they were in the car. "Thank you for the roses, Peter."

When they returned to the house, Mary took his hand and Peter followed her to their bedroom. She opened the portfolio, handing him the envelope. He read the note, listened to the tape, and wondered with whom she had shared the contents. He wondered if she had made a copy. In fact, he wondered if she would have given him the envelope, had he not been at the studio to meet her with the flowers.

"My love, I'm sure you'll agree that we must destroy the note and cassette. Is anyone else aware of what we have?"

"Oh, no. I read the note and listened to the tape in my private office. No one was around. I'm certain, Peter."

He believed that part. But had she made a duplicate of the cassette? He couldn't be sure of her now. He couldn't let her out of his sight. "I'm pleased no one else heard the tape. I was right to rid the world of George. He was a poor choice for our mission to eliminate Yale Frye. He was unreliable, placing you in danger, as well. I misjudged George. I thought him trustworthy and loyal. I am grateful no harm came to you, my Mary, or our child. So, tomorrow morning, to ensure you remain safe, you will call your employer, and resign your position, my dear, indefinitely. Claim that an illness in the family commands your attention immediately."

As Peter spoke, Mary was aware that she, too, had misjudged. Now she would be Peter's hostage. She had played into his hands, and he held the trump card. Her only prayer was the baby. She had to be pregnant. She attempted to seduce him, but was only successful in arousing lust. When he was hard, he pushed her down, ordering her to suck him. When she tried to move up, to get him inside of her, he held her down as he turned her face down on the bed and jacked himself off on her. "Honey, I don't want to fuck you too often. I couldn't bear it if I harmed you or our baby. Go to sleep now. A pregnant woman needs extra rest."

She was awake all night, praying she was pregnant. In the morning, she watched Peter set fire to George's note and cassette. As the room filled with smoke, She heard Peter laugh. His evil laughter was what Mary imagined the devil would sound like.

Chapter
18

Yale tried to get out of the bed without waking Lisa. He had to pee so bad! It reminded him of younger days when he would party, knocking off a six-pack of beer, and the guys wore a path to the toilet. Many times, one of them would have to piss in the bushes, unable to wait for the bathroom to be vacated. He made it to the bathroom without a sound, then laughed at himself when he flushed the commode out of habit. With ten bathrooms in the house, he had barely made it to this one in time, and after all the caution not to wake Lisa, he flushed the thing with the door open.

He walked out, feeling guilty when he saw her sitting on the edge of the bed. "My turn." She got up wearing the sheet and went into the bathroom. He came back to the bedroom a few minutes later, still naked, carrying two glasses filled with fruit juice. He handed one to Lisa, already back in bed, and moved closer to her. While holding the other glass, he tried to fluff a pillow behind him with one hand. He tipped the glass in the other hand spilling cold juice on himself. "Shit!" he shouted. Lisa started giggling. "Go ahead and laugh while I have cold juice running down my stomach!"

"Let me help you." She put down her glass, and turned back to him, sliding down on the bed, licking the juice from his body with her tongue.

"Mmm, I think you missed some," he said, pushing the sheet off his body with his feet, and intentionally pouring more juice on himself. It slid down his groin.

"So I did." She moved lower on the bed. She ran her tongue down his body until she reached his erection, waiting for her. Teasingly, she licked his groin and upper thighs, moving gentle fingers all over his lower half, without touching his member. His body moved. He raised his hips off the bed, making it easy for Lisa to hold his ass as she continued exploring his body with her mouth. He was making beautiful sounds of desire. She heard him gasp as she finally covered his hardness with her mouth. She listened to his need mount.

"Come here," he begged, as she moved up to find his mouth hungry for hers. He kissed her until she was as hungry for the climax as he.

He moved his hands over her body, rubbing between her legs. Their hands moved over each other with desire. He was about to mount her when she grabbed his hands and moved on top of him. Holding his hands down over his head, she sat on his erection feeling the deep penetration slide up inside of her. She kissed his face, his hungry mouth. She continued holding his hands down, while moving and contracting her muscles as she pulled on his organ with her movements. She kissed his mouth repeatedly. He pulled his hands away to hold her buttocks. He pushed up hard, going deeper inside of her, and heard her pleasure as she climaxed. He pushed again and again, wanting to come too. She moved her legs between his and grabbing him like a vise, pushed and rubbed against him while he thrust, until he arched his back, exploding.

He rubbed his hands across her back. She stayed on him, listening to his heart pound, both ignoring the sound of the doorbell chiming. It was minutes before she moved off him and onto her back, pulling the sheet around her. She reached for his hand and squeezed it in her own. He turned to kiss her, seeing unshed tears in her eyes. She looked at him as the tears rolled down her cheeks, "I didn't think I could ever feel this much passion again." He cradled her to him, stroking her hair, and feeling a contentment he had forgotten existed.

They stayed in bed talking for the next hour. He found himself getting aroused again when they shared intimacies, while holding each other. Yale got out of bed, already concerned that Lisa had expended more energy during their lovemaking than she should have. He pulled on his jeans saying he would order dinner in.

"Okay, Yale. I'll be out in a minute." She lit a cigarette, inhaling deeply, feeling relaxed for the first time since the shooting. The nervous tension and rigidity were gone, replaced by restfulness.

She went into the kitchen feeling significantly better. Yale had ordered steak dinners, and was checking the answering machine for messages. There were several calls he needed to return and one she needed to place. Ronnie had left two messages while she had been in bed with Yale. Disconcerted, she left the room.

Yale returned calls while she attempted to fix her hair, which was in total disarray.

His behavior confused her when she sat at the kitchen table to have dinner with him. The serenity of the last few hours was vanishing. She was unable to ignore the effect he was having on her. She knew something was bothering him, and attempted to recapture their earlier mood with vivaciousness. He was virtually impenetrable. Her liveliness went unnoticed. She ate ravenously while he barely ate at all. He informed her that David was stopping by with some business papers and mail he needed to look over.

"You know, I feel really raunchy. I'm going to soak in the tub for a while."

"Did you feel raunchy before we were in bed together, or did the raunchiness develop when you heard Ronnie's messages on the answering machine, Lisa?"

"I'd be a liar if I told you his messages didn't bother me. I'm not interested in artificial relationships with deceit or evasiveness. I really believe the principle ingredient for good rapport between people is the ability to understand each other's emotions."

"I didn't feel raunchy in bed with you, Yale, or as a result of making love with you. I don't feel raunchy because I heard Ronnie's messages. I feel sad that I betrayed his trust in me, because we have been faithful to each other until now. Maybe I feel raunchy for not feeling guilty about being with you. I took what I wanted for myself, with no regard for anyone but myself, for the first time in my life. Maybe I feel raunchy because I still want you and am not willing to stop touching you or sharing myself with you. I know Ronnie would not do what I'm doing. Maybe I feel raunchy because it doesn't come easily to me to know I have settled for less than I wanted, for a very long time. Now, I don't want to. I'm not interested in entanglements, but for now I wanted to take from you what I needed, and in return give to you what you needed. I'm sorry, Yale, that you found it so difficult to tell me what was eating away at you. Maybe we should resist responding to our needs and settle for being friends."

She put her plate in the sink. He came up behind her. "Lisa, can we start over, one more time?"

"Yale, you can't start over once you've crossed the finish line." She left the room and went to the bedroom to call Ronnie. Her conversation with him was perfunctory. When she got off the phone, she collected the pills she had forgotten to take earlier, and headed to the kitchen for juice to wash them down with.

Yale and David were sitting at the table talking business when

Lisa asked where the glasses were stored. Yale got up to get her a glass and she snapped at him. "I didn't ask you to get it, just where you kept them. I'm not an invalid." She took the glass from him, asking sarcastically, "Can I pour myself some juice or do you want the honor?"

He opened the refrigerator and bowed to her. "Help yourself."

She poured some apple juice, put the container back, and sat down at the table. David was taking it all in but said nothing. Lisa continued, "You know, Yale, just because you crossed the finish line, and you can't start over, doesn't mean there's anything to stop you from entering a new race."

"I have one problem, Lisa. I hate to lose. Sometimes I don't enter a race because I'm afraid I'll lose."

"Well, Yale, seems to me you're a bigger loser if you don't try, than if you give it your best shot and don't succeed." David was watching curiously when she addressed him. "Tell me, David. You've been with Yale for a long time. Do you consider him a winner?"

"In my book, he's always been a winner," David answered.

"See, schmuck, you don't have enough confidence in yourself." She got up, walked to the family room, and turned on the TV. She switched the channels until she found a movie. She fell asleep with the television on, curled up on one of the oversized leather sofas.

It was late when she opened her eyes. She was covered with a blanket that Yale must have gotten for her. He was in the recliner reading. The television was still on. Sleepily she asked, "Do you always read with a TV on?"

"No, but I wake if I'm sleeping with it on, and someone turns it off. In case that happens to you, I left it on."

"Thanks."

"I'll send you your share of the electric bill."

"Putz."

"Thanks."

They both laughed. She sat up, smiling at him, "Did David leave a long time ago?"

"About half an hour ago. He said to say good-bye to you."

"Oh, Tell him I said good-bye."

"I can't; he already left."

"Schmuck."

"Thanks." He wanted to go hold her but restrained himself.

She got up. "I'm going to bathe. If I pass out, just ignore me. But if I drown, send flowers." She went to the bedroom.

He appeared a minute later, naked. "I'm going to bathe too.

Can I join you? If you pass out, I'll be there and I promise not to let you drown. I can't afford flowers."

"Well, asshole, start the water and don't forget, you'll have to wash my back."

"I'll wash yours only if you'll wash mine in return, Lisa."

"Boy, you drive a hard bargain, but I can handle it."

"That's what I was hoping."

"What?"

"That you'll handle it." He looked down at his dick.

He filled the tub and had to answer the phone, since he'd neglected to switch the machine back on for the night. When Lisa climbed in the tub, he got off the phone quickly and went to join her. He climbed in behind her and held her against his chest, immersed in the warm water. He took the liquid soap, poured some in his hands, then washed her body gently and slowly, rubbing until she moaned.

She turned, kissed him, and put soap in her hands. She rubbed her hands together until they were slippery and asked him to stand. The red heat lamp cast a warm glow in the room. When he rose to his feet, she appreciated again how well endowed he was. She took her slippery hands, washed his legs and his thighs, and finally ran her lathered hands around his shaft.

The satiny feeling of her touch was bringing him close and he didn't want to come yet. He sat down and pulled her against him again, kissing her back.

She took more soap, turned, and rubbed his chest with a circular motion. She kissed him, pushing her tongue against his. She reached down and squeezed his dick, then moved her hands up to his chest, and down again to grab his cock.

He was going to come if she didn't stop. But it felt so wonderful he didn't want her to stop. Again, she seemed to read his mind.

"Tell me, baby, do you want more, or should I stop?" She ran soapy hands across his groin and around his penis. She took his dick in both hands and rubbed, enthusiastically, both sides of his member. "Should I stop or not, baby?"

"No, no! I want to come now!"

She tightened her hold and seconds later he exploded, flooding the bathroom floor with water from his jolts. He came with an intensity that left him breathless. Eventually, they climbed out of the tub and rinsed off under the shower. She washed his hair and he washed hers. They washed each other's backs and dried each other off when they were through.

She slipped a nightshirt on and got into the bed, snuggling under the covers. He climbed in next to her and started to play between her legs, wanting to satisfy her. "I can't, Yale. I don't have the strength right now." The truth was that Ronnie had called to say he'd be arriving in the morning for the weekend. Yale had told her this as he was drying her off. Somehow she lost the feeling and now wanted only to sleep. Maybe Yale had been right. Maybe guilt had made her feel raunchy.

She slept fitfully all night. Lisa found herself alone in the bed when she woke. She went to the kitchen with the terry cloth robe on.

"Good morning, Miss Lisa," Victor, the houseman, greeted. "Can I get you some breakfast?"

"No, thank you. How are you feeling, Victor?"

"Much better, missy. Nothing will keep me down long. I won't stand for it. Even if I am sixty."

She poured herself a cup of coffee from the carafe and sat at the table. Victor didn't comment that he would be glad to serve her, because he knew this lady didn't take to being waited on.

"Where's Yale, Victor?"

"He had an early appointment. Said he'd be back around eleven. Mrs. Frye is coming around noon, and I'll be fixin' a nice lunch for when your husband gets here."

"Thank you, Victor." She took her cup of coffee to the bedroom with her and dressed.

Victor knocked at the door a few minutes later, announcing that Dr. Wiener's office was on the phone for her. She picked up the receiver. The woman's voice on the line explained that the doctor would be leaving town for a few days and that her appointment needed to be changed. The doctor wanted to see her this morning, before he left, rather than delaying the visit until he returned. Lisa wrote down the location and agreed to be there at eleven.

It was almost ten when she finished applying her makeup and called for a cab. She wasn't sure how long it would take her to get to the office. Nor did she feel like writing a lengthy explanation that might alarm someone. So she merely asked Victor to tell everyone she had to go out for a while, deciding against explaining her destination to him. She was unaware that the telephone intercom in the house had been activated after she woke in accordance with Mr. Frye's instructions. Yale had feared she might faint again, and this had seemed a logical course of action.

Victor pushed the button for the gates to open after the cab driver announced himself. It was ten-twenty when Lisa left the house for Dr. Wiener's office. She was early for her appointment and sat in the waiting room. She picked up the newspaper next to her, thinking it had been days since she read a paper.

On page two, she read:

> It is believed Lisa Klein is the only per-
> son able to identify the woman with George
> Benson at the time of the incident. Mrs. Klein
> has been unable to assist the police depart-
> ment with any additional information due to
> the severity of her injuries, sustained during
> the shooting at the Coliseum.

She was infuriated. Her first concern was the scare this would give her parents if they read this article. She had to call them as soon as she got back to the house. She flipped through the paper to see if there were any other articles regarding the shooting.

In the Entertainment section, bold print glared:

> Yale Frye is believed to be in seclusion
> following the attempt on his life. It is
> unknown whether he will resume his concert
> tour as originally planned. Friends close to
> Yale worry that his fear of crowds may inten-
> sify as a result of the incident. Sources
> interviewed confirmed that Yale has estab-
> lished a trust account for the college educa-
> tion of Lisa Klein's two sons, in appreciation
> of her intervention on his behalf. It is
> believed that he is also absorbing all of Mrs.
> Klein's medical expenses, including her psy-
> chiatric treatment. Knowing Yale, it is cer-
> tain he will do everything he can to show his
> gratitude to Lisa Klein.

She tore the two articles from the paper and followed a nurse into an examining room.

The results of her blood tests indicated some improvement, but she was far from well. Doctor Wiener recommended a local psychiatrist, noting her depressed state, and prescribed continued rest and proper diet. He asked her to set up another appointment, so she went to the desk to schedule another visit. When she extended her insurance card to the receptionist, she was told, "It's been taken care of, Mrs. Klein. See you next week."

Lisa left the office without calling for a cab, walking blocks in a daze. She was filled with ambivalence, wondering if Yale was merely expressing gratitude with his actions. Could she be so naive? She knew she wasn't very worldly. It would be easy for her to misconstrue his intentions. She walked on, confused, wondering if maybe he really thought her simple. But he seemed to genuinely care! Why hadn't he told her about the trust funds or about paying her medical bills? She had insurance. She didn't want anything from him. Maybe she was just a charity case for a famous, rich, personality to pity, and bestow on generously for all the inconvenience! He was getting good publicity besides! And what about her emotional stability? Did people think she was crazy? She thought she was handling everything pretty well, considering how much had happened.

She didn't know how far she'd walked or where she was. She was trying to understand, but her mind was cluttered with so much. She was concerned about the fact that the paper had said she was too ill to assist the police. Were people keeping things from her? Was it anemia or something worse? Everything that had been clear now seemed complicated. She was so engrossed in conjecture, she didn't seek shelter when it began to drizzle. Suddenly she was caught in a downpour, with the rain soaking through her. She had no idea where she was, and no energy left. She was standing in front of an art gallery. She entered, tired and nervous. Her body was cold and her head spun with dizziness.

A young woman came over and asked if she could help her. Lisa's lips were quivering. She needed to sit down. She started to sway. The woman took her arm. "I'm lost," Lisa said stuttering. "Do you have a phone I could use?"

"Sure. Why don't you hold onto my arm, and we'll go into my office. I have a phone there and coffee. You look like you could use a hot cup of coffee."

Lisa followed the attractive blonde into an office, noticing the artwork covering the walls for the first time. "You have a lot of serigraphs by Luongo, don't you?"

"Yes, quite a few. Do you like his work?"

"Very much." They entered a small office. Graciously, the woman pulled a chair away from the wall for Lisa, and poured her coffee.

"I hope you like it black. I haven't had a chance to pick up the things I like yet. I just started this job. The woman I'm replacing left unexpectedly for a family emergency."

"Black is fine. Thank you." She sipped the coffee, feeling exhausted and unsteady. "Excuse me, I'm not feeling great. Could I call for someone to pick me up?"

"Certainly. The phone is right here." She pulled the phone to the edge of the desk but it was still out of Lisa's reach. "I guess a longer cord is something else I'll have to get."

"It's okay." Lisa got up to call Yale's house. The woman guided her to the chair behind the desk, noticing how weak she was. "Shit! I can't find the phone number." Lisa thought she had placed it in her purse, but now she couldn't locate it.

"I'm sure directory assistance can help you."

"No. He has an unlisted number. Do you know the number of the nearest cab company?" The room was spinning, so she put her head down on the desk. "I'm sorry. I feel really lousy."

"Why don't I call 911? You look pale." She didn't wait for Lisa to reply. The paramedics were there in minutes.

"Miss? Can you hear me?" One of the paramedics asked. Lisa lifted her head. She saw a picture on the desk of a familiar face.

"Who's that?" she asked, pointing at the picture.

"Miss, how about letting us lay you down here," he pointed to a stretcher, "and we'll have a look at you. Okay?" They were lifting her out of the chair.

"Please, who is that?" She pointed to the picture again. She knew the face, but didn't know from where.

"Miss, what is your name? Do you know your name, Miss?"

She started crying. No one ever told her anything. She didn't even know where she was. The paramedic went into her purse looking for identification. He pulled out the contents of her purse and placed them on the desk. He opened her wallet, showing the driver's license to the other paramedic beside him. They exchanged looks.

"Mrs. Klein, can you answer a few questions?"

She started shaking. They put a blanket on her. She was going to be sick. "Please, call Yale Frye to pick me up. I can't find the phone number."

"Is this it?" The other paramedic held the paper with Yale's phone number and address on it.

"Yes." She was trembling. She held on to the desk for support. She continued looking at the picture of the familiar face. When they dialed, she heard someone say something about a hospital.

"They are going to meet us at the hospital, Mrs. Klein."

"No! No hospital. No!" She was trying to get up but couldn't. She tried again, swaying. She was strapped to the stretcher, screaming.

The woman who had brought her to the office tried to calm her. "Relax. You'll be fine. Just try to relax."

"Please," Lisa begged. "Who is the picture on your desk of?"

"I don't know her. It's the woman I'm replacing. All I know is her name. Mary Nelson."

"I want to go now. Please. Let me up." She was struggling against the straps, as they carried her out of the art gallery and placed her in the ambulance.

When Lisa woke, she was in a hospital room. It was after midnight. Ronnie and Yale were in the room with her. They both looked like someone had died. She remembered. She looked at them. "I'd like to go now." She sat up. "I got lost." She laughed deliriously. "Know what? You found me, but it's not enough. Know why? 'Cause I'm still lost." She went back to sleep with Ronnie and Yale beside her.

Chapter
19

Yale and Ronnie brought Lisa back to the Beverly Hills estate against the attending physician's advice. It was recommended that she remain in the hospital for a few days under observation. Lisa vehemently refused. She signed a waiver demanding to be released before the breakfast trays were delivered to the rooms.

She was silent in the car. Once they returned to the house, she rushed to the bedroom. Ronnie followed her to find out what had happened. The only information he and Yale had been given was from the paramedics the previous night. A woman operating an art studio had called for assistance after a soaked lady had come into the premises, lost, in need of a telephone, ill. Paramedics found Yale's phone number in Mrs. Klein's purse and called.

"Lisa, can we talk? I'm worried about you. Yale and I were going crazy yesterday. We thought something had happened related to the death threat. Talk to me. What happened, Lisa?"

"I got lost, Ronnie. I got caught in the rain and felt like shit. That's all. Okay?"

"Lisa, Yale's houseman heard the doctor's office call. You said you'd be there at eleven. I wasn't even told a doctor had been here to see you until yesterday. Why? After Yale filled me in, he called the doctor's office and was told you had left there around noon, and that you had appeared to be fine. Why didn't you come back here? Why didn't someone go with you to the doctor's office? Why didn't you at least call? God, Lisa, you knew I was arriving. Yale said he told you. Talk to me. What is going on? Lisa, did someone hurt or threaten you? Talk to me. Please!"

"I can't, Ronnie. I'm sorry. Yesterday I got lost, wet, and sick. Today I'm better. Please, Ronnie, I don't want to talk. Please."

"Lisa, did something happen between you and Yale? Is he the reason you didn't come back from the doctor's office? Did something happen? He said he had an appointment and didn't know you had gone to the doctor until he got back. He said he wouldn't have known where you went if Victor hadn't heard your conversation on the phone. Why didn't you tell Victor yourself, or leave a note? For God's sake, what happened? I know things have been difficult. The doctor called the hospital last night. I talked to Doctor Wiener. He said he had hoped for more improvement, but that you were no worse. He said he gave you the name of a therapist because you seemed depressed. But Yale said your spirits seemed fine to him. What am I supposed to think when you refuse to talk to me? I don't understand."

"Me either."

He waited, but she didn't elaborate. They had been through a lot together but this was different. She wouldn't let him in. His concern began to turn to anger and he spoke sharply. "It's time to go home, Lisa. We're leaving."

"Wrong, Ronnie. You're leaving but I'm staying. I have unfinished business here, and I'm not ready to leave. I'm asking you to go home tomorrow, as scheduled, and not to come back next weekend. I need to stay, and I need to stay alone. I'll call every day, but I'm asking you to do this for me, without any questions."

"I can't believe what I'm hearing. Lisa–"

She cut him off. "Ronnie, if you don't do this for me, I'll disappear until I'm ready to come home. Then you'll have no idea where I am. Ronnie, please go home without me."

"I lost you to him, didn't I?" She was silent. "I guess I just got my answer."

"Ronnie, you don't have an answer because I don't know what the answer is. I do know I need to be here, right now, more than I need to go home. Give me some slack, Ronnie, or you'll lose me for sure. Please, I need you to do this for me."

"Have you fallen in love with Yale, Lisa?"

"Ronnie, I am incapable of loving right now."

"Okay, Lisa. I'll leave tomorrow. I'll go home. I'll go and wait for you."

Yale sat in his bedroom with the intercom on, listening to the entire conversation between Ronnie and Lisa. He didn't care that he was eavesdropping. He knew something had transpired to disrupt the tranquility Lisa had displayed only a day before. There was a distinct incongruity in her behavior. One moment she seemed bold and full of aggression, then childlike and unruffled the next. Yale's thoughts were jumbled, trying to make sense of her present disposition and the reason for it.

Ruth arrived, invading his categorization of the events preceding Ronnie's arrival. They went into the kitchen, to sit over a cup of coffee.

"How is she, Yale?"

"I don't know. She hasn't spoken to me. She just told her husband to go home tomorrow, without her."

"Why?"

"I don't know, Ma. She's hurting but won't say why. She's angry but I have no idea why. She's afraid, but I'm not completely sure what of."

"Maybe it has more to do with heart than logic, Yale."

"She just told Ronnie she's incapable of loving right now. I think if she felt more than she wanted toward me, she wouldn't shut me out this way."

"Maybe she's afraid of her feelings, Yale, and is insulating herself. She's been married a long time. She doesn't take things lightly. You saw how she felt the night we arrived. She's fragile. Give her time. When she's ready, she'll talk."

"I think I'm in love with her. She's all I think about, night and day."

"Now, tell me something I don't already know."

"I don't think she's in love with me. Not really. I think she liked the image better than the person."

"Very good, Yale. You're absolutely right. After all, how could anyone fall for you? You are nothing, correct? Be honest, honey. You're afraid to admit she might love you, because it's safer not to."

"So what do you suggest, Ma? Do I take away another man's wife, so she can follow me around from city to city, living out of suitcases?"

"Yale, you can't take a woman away from a man if she doesn't want to go. And if she chose to leave, she'd know it was because she was going of her own volition. Honey, a person can't take another person. People are not for taking. People give themselves. They give love. They give caring. They give their heart. No one can take these things if a person doesn't want to give them."

Ronnie and Lisa heard the words between mother and son over the intercom in the bedroom. They sat looking at each other, knowing there was no argument for what Ruth said. Lisa turned the intercom off.

"Lisa, no matter what happens, I gave my heart to you a long time ago. I still want to go on giving it to you. I hope you'll want what I give, and soon you'll know what you can give, and who you want to give it to. I'm going home today. I can't stay. I can't force you to come with me either. I know that. Just know how much I love you, Lisa, and how important you are to me."

He picked up the phone and reserved a seat on the next available flight to Canton, then called for a cab. There was nothing to pack since he had never unpacked. Lisa walked with him to the front door and pushed the button for the gates to open. When the cab arrived minutes later, she watched him get in. They didn't kiss each other good-bye. Lisa stood on the step as the cab drove away. Ronnie didn't turn to look back. He couldn't. She turned, walked into the house, passed Yale and Ruth, and went to bed.

Yale walked into the bedroom to check on her less than thirty minutes later. She looked up at him with vacant eyes. "What hurts worse, knowing you are the cause of someone else's pain or being the one who is hurting?"

"Why did you run away yesterday? What was so horrible, Lisa?"

"Yesterday I thought knew why I was confused about so much. Today I'm not as sure. Maybe more was bothering me than I knew. Your mother is smart. Ask her what you're supposed to do if by nature you are a giving person, and all of a sudden you're not sure you'll ever be able to give again."

"Why did you turn the intercom on? Is that why Ronnie left?"

"Ronnie left because I asked him to. I turned the intercom on for the same reason you have been, to see if I could learn something that would help me understand things more clearly."

"Maybe we should try talking with each other instead."

"What for? When I told you I felt less your equal here, you wrote out a check for a million dollars. You didn't understand. When I wanted to give to you, when we were making love in the tub, you felt obliged to reciprocate when we got into bed. You couldn't accept what I was giving unconditionally. And when I woke, twice in the last few days, my bed was empty. You were gone and I had a baby-sitter watching me, with no way to reach you. What if I wanted or needed you? You couldn't even tell me you had somewhere to go. Why should we talk, Yale? Only one of us is being honest, and it's not you! Go away, I'm starting to nag."

"You think running away is communicating, Lisa? You think hiding your feelings is being honest? You think scaring the shit out of people is communication? Look in the mirror, honey, before you point a finger at someone else."

"Go away, Yale. Let's stick to the intercom. If I want to know anything else, I'll read a newspaper, okay? Just one favor. Before you release anything else to the media, remember one thing. If my parents or my children are hurt, in any way, by what you say, I'll retaliate. You'll wish you had been shot!"

"What the fuck are you talking about? I'd never hurt...I'd better leave. When you're well enough, maybe you should too." He stomped out of the room furiously, slamming the door behind him. He yelled to Ruth, "Watch her. I have to get out of here for a while." He got into his black Jaguar and drove off.

Half an hour after Yale ran out, Ruth went to the bedroom Lisa was occupying, carrying a tray of food. She found Lisa dressed and packing. "Maybe you should rest. When Yale gets back, he'll take you where you want to go."

"I've been enough trouble, Ruth. I think I've worn out my welcome."

"You're not going to let me talk you out of this, are you?"

"No."

"Okay, I'll help you pack. Eat something. I'll drive you wherever you're going myself."

She looked at Ruth skeptically. "Thanks." They finished packing. Ruth asked Victor to put the bags in the car, as Lisa sat on the paisley-covered chair in the bedroom. She wrote Yale a note, took the newspaper articles from her purse, signed a blank check, and placed the contents in a sealed envelope. She then handed everything to Ruth. "Please, give these to Yale for me."

"I'm not a messenger. Leave them on the kitchen table."

"Fine." She walked to the kitchen, placed everything on the table and asked Ruth if she knew where there was a reasonable motel.

"Reasonable? No, Lisa. I don't know of any around here. Most of the ones in this area are quite expensive. I'll lend you some money, if you want. I'd drive to a less expensive area, but without a reservation it might be a waste of time."

"Maybe I should call a cab."

"Go ahead. But it'll cost you as much looking for a cheap place, schlepping luggage, driving around in a cab, as going somewhere a little more expensive."

Lisa took out her wallet. She had stopped at the bank teller machine with Ronnie before she left Canton, taking out five hundred dollars. That was all the cash you could withdraw at one time by machine, and the bank had been closed. So at the time, she had had no alternative. She hadn't thought she'd need much anyway. "I have five hundred on me. That should be enough until tomorrow. I'll use my credit cards if I run short."

"Okay. Where do you want to go?"

"Any hotel that's not out of your way."

"I wasn't going anywhere, so anyplace is out of the way. Actually, there's a nice hotel about two miles from here."

"Good. That's fine."

"Victor, please tell Yale I'll be back soon. I'm taking Lisa to the Oak Plaza."

"Yes, Miss Ruth. I'll tell him."

Ruth made a mental note of the room number and gave Lisa a kiss as she got in the elevator. "I'm sorry we didn't have more time together. Thank you, again, for being so brave. Yale is all I've got, you know." The elevator closed and a tearful Lisa entered her room. Ruth went to the phone in the plush hotel lobby and called Yale's house. Victor answered, saying that Yale had not returned. She gave Victor Lisa's room number and said she'd be in the hotel lobby until she heard from Yale.

Yale arrived at the hotel an hour later, carrying the envelope Lisa had left for him on the kitchen table. He and Ruth went into the bar, talking over a drink.

"Did you see what she put in the envelope, Ma?"

"No."

He handed her the note:

Yale,
I'll never be sorry! Thanks for everything. I'm glad I heard you tell your mother you loved me. I think it was my doubts that made me want to run. I read the enclosed articles at the doctor's office and felt betrayed, upset, confused, and angry. You're right; I wasn't honest or able to aptly communicate my feelings either. I'll have to take your advice and take a better look in the mirror. The check is for a front row ticket to your next concert in Canton. You still owe me that! Be well. Be happy.
Love, Lisa

Then Yale handed the clippings to his mother, watching her brows furrow as she read. "No wonder she was upset. You come out smelling like a rose, while she sounds sick and unbalanced."

"I haven't been to the office. I didn't read the paper yesterday, and I didn't call David back last night or this morning. I had no idea!"

"What are you going to do?"

"First, I'm going to try and talk to her. A couple days ago, David said Myra Sullivan wants first shot at airtime. I'm going to do her television show and set the record straight publicly. I owe it to everybody, especially Lisa."

"Okay. Good idea. I'm going home now. Room 1122. I'll talk

to you later."

"Thanks, Ma."

"See if she'll eat something. She hasn't eaten all day." She kissed him and left.

Yale went to room 1122, after stopping in the gift shop to pick out another koala bear. He was hoping he wouldn't have to carry the stuffed animal back down with him. He knocked on the door. He couldn't believe how nervous he was.

"Room service for Lisa Klein." She opened the door and he held out the koala bear. She let him in.

Chapter
20

Mary found Peter without virtue. Her love turned to hatred as she became his prisoner. Provisions were made so that she rarely left the fortress, and when she was allowed to go anywhere, it was under someone's watch, with the understanding that close supervision must be provided for her best interest.

His recent changes in temperament frightened her. He seemed to derive pleasure from his ability to make her quake. She was his subordinate and completely dependent, living in isolation mandated by his prevailing attitude of the day. She was becoming submissive, conforming to his ways. He was in possession of her mind and body, displaying his influence to the other members of the group with delight.

To ensure her well-being, she performed for him like a trained animal upon request. She knew her life depended on it. Her attempts at cajoling were met with passivity, and she had recurring nightmares about dissected cadavers. Only references to their baby, growing within her, seemed to mitigate his vengeful disposition in front of the others. She tried to be alone with him as little as possible. Otto never seemed to work, so it was easy not to be alone with Peter during the day. The nights were different.

For the last few nights, Peter tied Mary to the brass frame of the bed they shared. He said he found it reassuring, knowing she was next to him all night, and it pleased him that she was agreeable. The truth was, she was too afraid to refuse anything he wanted when they were alone. So she disguised her disgust and capitulated to his every demand. She was nauseated by his body next to hers, finding sleep a reprieve from her repulsion.

Peter mocked Mary openly in front of Otto, Brian, and Barry. He told them that she would be the one to rid the world of Myra Sullivan. "After all, who better to get rid of one cunt than another cunt?"

He was the patriarch, and although he enjoyed being influential, it disturbed him how easily he controlled the others. He was the example; they weak imitators. He proposed; they complied. He initiated; they followed.

All monies were put in his care and disbursed by him. He had the only post office box key, and handled all correspondence for the group. If one of them received anything questionable in the mail, he examined and destroyed it without disclosure. He claimed to advocate majority rule, yet realized that not one of them would vote differently from him. Idiots. He was splendid in maintaining his hold on all of them, while they treated him like royalty.

Mary was a moron, too, but he still needed her. He made a mental note to act more kindly where she was concerned.

He went to the kitchen where Mary was preparing spinach pies for dinner. She looked tired. "Have you been getting enough sleep, honey? You look a little pale."

"I'm fine, Peter. Just restless since I haven't been working. I'm not used to being home all the time."

"Why don't you put on something pretty, Mary, and I'll take you shopping. Women love to shop, I'm sure you're no different."

"Peter, could I buy a new dress with an elastic waistband to accommodate my belly? It will soon begin expanding."

"Certainly, Mary. I think, perhaps, I'd like you to purchase a couple of wigs to change your appearance occasionally, too. I do so enjoy variety in women, and have been faithful to you for so long that a different look could enhance our sex lives."

"Should I finish baking the pies first, Peter?"

"No, Mary. Otto can watch them. He's very good in the kitchen, you know. He used to do all the cooking when we were roommates in college."

I didn't know you and Otto were friends in college. I thought you met him at the same time we all became acquainted."

"No, Otto and I have been like brothers since we were small, living with the same foster parents. He would go to hell and back for me. Most of the time we were growing up, we relied on each other for companionship, and only had each other to confide in. He's a quiet man, very private. Perhaps that is why our devotion to each other is not evident to others. There is an unspoken bond we share."

"Why doesn't he have a job, Peter?"

"He finds work mundane. He derives his income from the buying and selling of cocaine through outside sources. That is why it was so easy for him to inject the comedian with a lethal dose of cocaine. He has accumulated a great sum of money in the last five years, and knows many influential people. It was one of Otto's friends that obtained the limo for Wally's and George's misfortune. Of course, I handle all of Otto's finances, since I am the only person he has ever trusted completely."

Mary went to the bedroom and changed. When she returned, the pies were in the oven and Peter's dick was inside Otto's ass, while Otto held onto the counter grunting. "I'll be with you in a minute, Mary. I have to give Otto his 'fix' for the day."

Chapter
21

Lisa accepted the gray furry koala bear from Yale as he walked into the hotel room. "What's with the bears? This is the fourth one you've bought me."

"I don't know. They remind me of you. Cute, cuddly. A rare, beautiful, soft, unique species which, although strong, needs protection. You, too, can only be found in one place in all the world, and I was lucky enough to have the chance to admire and hold the creation with so many unusual qualities. I'm drawn to the distinctiveness that sets you apart from others, Lisa. Seldom have I been with someone who touches me as you have. I want to talk to you. I want to hold you and I want to make right all that is wrong. Will you give me that chance?"

"I'm afraid to be with you, Yale. One minute I feel like 'Queen for a Day', the next we're yelling at each other. I'm sick of the roller coaster, but I'm not sure I want to get off. I feel special when I'm in your arms, but afraid that it's not real. It's like I'm reading too much into what we are to each other, because I need more than I already have. Maybe we are drawn to each other to compensate for voids in our lives."

"Lisa, I didn't know about these articles," he said holding out the note and newspaper clippings. "I didn't read yesterday's papers and wasn't in touch with my staff all day. I know how they must have made you feel, and for that I'm sorry. Maybe we can rectify the situation."

"Rectify? How do you tell the world I'm as normal as anyone else would be under these circumstances, after what's been printed? How do I stop my parents from pain and worry, reading something like this? How can I trust you when I read you've set up educational trusts for my boys, when you didn't even tell me or ask me if it's okay? I feel deceived, Yale, and when I left the doctor's office I couldn't think straight. I started doubting everything.

Doubting what was happening between us. I was lost, Yale, physically and emotionally. I don't even remember how I got to the hospital. All I remember is hurt. A lot of hurt and confusion."

"Can I take you to dinner, Lisa, so we can talk? I haven't explained things that I probably should have. I'd like you to come back to the house with me."

"Not tonight, Yale. I'm tired, emotional, and feeling very badly about the way I treated Ronnie. He is a decent person. He deserves better than what I did to him. Our relationship has been far from perfect for a long time, but it's hard knowing you've hurt someone who has always been there for you. Don't misunderstand, Yale. I'm not sorry about us. I knew what I wanted, and take full responsibility for my actions. But it still hurts."

"I'll go if that's what you want. But I hurt too, Lisa, knowing you've gone through hell because of me. I do love you. More than I wish I did, because I like Ronnie and feel badly, too. But I'm selfish. I'm not ready to let go of you. I don't want to, although I know I should."

His eyes were pleading to be allowed to stay. He was being honest with her. She didn't want him to leave, not yet. But she was afraid of her feelings. She was so vulnerable. Even worse, she wasn't ready to let go of him either, and was unsure she ever would be. "How about ordering room service? We'll have more privacy to talk that way."

"Sounds good. Thanks, Lisa." They ordered dinner. Then he asked if she'd like him to explain to her parents that most of the articles in the paper weren't accurate. She gave him the phone number appreciatively, feeling her tenderness for him increase. Yale called them immediately, reassuring them that everything was under control. He offered to send his private plane for them anytime they'd like to come see Lisa. She felt better. At least she knew her parents would be less worried after the conversation.

He also apologized for establishing trust funds for Marc and Steve without her consent. He explained his need to do something special after all she had done, knowing she wouldn't accept anything for herself. His hope was that she wouldn't refuse something given to her children. He explained that he had intended to tell her, feeling angry the media had exposed his actions before he had a chance to relate them to her first.

They ate dinner, more comfortable with each other now that some of the issues had been addressed. They resisted touching, allowing friendship and trust to supersede the other elements of their relationship. There were some successions of clever retorts exchanged with light sparring, which had become an affectionate way of transmitting ideas without criticism. They were restoring their bond, able to speak candidly, tranquil and relaxed.

He recognized that she was tired and suggested she go to sleep. "Call me when you get up, Lisa. Okay? I don't want to wake you." He stood, looking at her loveliness, feeling a desire so strong he stammered, "I'd better go." Before he lost the ability to refrain from grabbing her, he opened the door. "Good night, Lisa."

She put her hand on his arm, looking into his eyes with the same rapture he was feeling. "Don't go."

He turned, unable to hold back his need to hold her another second, and swept her into his arms. He kissed her with all the passion he'd kept intact since he arrived. She kissed him back fiercely, holding him tight.

Carried away by their overwhelming emotion, they proceeded to ravish one another, greedily devouring each kiss. He positioned himself against the wall, running his hands over her body until the heat radiating from her possessed him with a need for immediate gratification. Unconsciously, he was pushing himself against her without sensitivity, savagely jabbing with quick movements, repeatedly, losing self-control, crazed by urgency.

He felt the palpitation of her heart against his. He took her hand, wanting her soft palm to caress that part of his body he could not halt from motion. She was wet with her own desire. He brought her down to the floor with him, unable to restrain or sub-due his lust. As excessively hungry for him as he was for her, she tore his trousers down while he pulled the blouse from her, push-ing the shoulder straps of her bra down, to expose her breasts. The protective clothing was cast aside as he pushed himself deep inside her.

They culminated their fierce desire with a simultaneous out-cry. They had only quelled the immediate need. They didn't quench the thirst or extinguish the fire. They wanted more. They walked to the bedroom and took refuge beneath the blanket and refueled. Holding each other contentedly, they were overcome again with desire. They snuggled while excitement built.

"Let's hold each other," he whispered, kissing her gently. He was afraid she was using more energy than she should. She ran her fingers up and down his arm softly, feeling intimate. The deli-cate fingers continued moving as she looked beneath the blanket, verifying her suspicions. She moved her fingers to his stomach, stroking there a while, then moved her fingers a little more, mov-ing closer to his hardness while feeling her own breathing quicken.

"Don't, Lisa." He took her hand in his. "You're not up to more."

"I see you are."

"Come on, let's get some rest."

"Let me please you, Yale."

"You already have."

"I want to hold it, touch it, and lick it," she said, moving her body over him, intent on arousing him further.

"Don't make me act selfishly, Lisa. You know I want you, but not at your expense. I can wait."

"But you don't have to."

"I want to."

"Being a superstar, I bet you've had a lot of women. How many do you think?"

"Over three thousand."

She looked up at him in shock. He burst into laughter. "Very funny! Come on, Yale, how often do you usually...oh, never mind."

He stopped laughing, seeing it was more than curiosity. "Lisa, fame makes everything accessible. But knowing you can have whatever you want for the asking spoils the fun of pursuit. There was a time I abused my fame, by my actions, and lack of sensitivity to others. I haven't always been this wonderful," he mocked himself.

"Have you been deeply in love with many women?"

"A few. One who I still sometimes think about that way, although we're close friends now. We make choices. Some we regret, others we know are right. I wanted this career more than I wanted other things. I chose."

"I felt lousy so yesterday when I read those newspaper articles. How can you stand it when people do that to you all the time, writing lies, picking you apart, making insinuations?"

"Some hurt more than others. A lot of people would say you get used to it, but you don't. Every time you think you're safe, someone comes along and finds something that gets to you. It comes with the package."

"What was written about you that hurt the most?"

"When I first received recognition, with a few hit songs, a Hollywood reporter wrote that my fame was due to my love affair with Jack, the president of the record company that signed me. Jack wanted to sue. I wanted to die. We did neither."

"Are you still with the same record company?"

"Yes, and Jack Stahl is still the president."

"Did you have an affair with him?"

"Would it matter?"

"Maybe to your mother."

"What about you, Lisa?"

"Maybe twenty years ago, when I needed everything to feel neat, and I lived by every rule. Today, some of the rules seem stupid. No, it wouldn't matter. I'm sorry I asked. It wasn't an appropriate question."

"It wouldn't matter to my mother either, Lisa. All she wants is for me to be happy."

"Are you?"

"Less than I want to be, more than many."

"What do you want that you don't have?"

"To understand."

"Understand what?"

"Everything I don't understand. What do you want, Lisa?"

"To make love again."

"Okay."

"You told me I wasn't up to it a minute ago."

"You weren't."

"Now I am?"

"You tell me, Lisa." Her body was calmer, her breathing even. She had stopped perspiring and her fingers were driving him crazy as they moved like silk over him.

"How much are you worth, Yale?"

"To whom?"

"To yourself."

"Depends what day you ask me."

"Do you believe in God?"

"More spiritually than religiously."

"Do you talk to God?"

"I thank God often. You?"

"I ask for help more often than giving thanks."

"I ask for help, too."

"Help for what?"

"Understanding."

"Understanding what?"

"All I don't understand."

"I'm serious, Yale."

"So am I."

"Who do you most admire?"

"Those who have learned how to give."

"Who do you hate the most?"

"Hate is a waste."

"You don't hate anyone?"

"I waste, hating."

"On who?"

"Dead or alive?"

"Dead?"

"Hitler."

"Alive?"

"The fucker who shot you."

"Do you believe in destiny?"

"Sometimes."

"What is our destiny?"

"To love."

"What would make you happier?"

"You, holding my dick."

"I'm serious."

"So am I."

"What has given you the most gratification?"

"Well, what we just did in the other room—" She stopped him.

"Come on, Yale, I need to really know you."

"Maybe you're better off thinking I am what you want me to be."

"Am I being too inquisitive?"

"I'm sorry. No, you can ask me whatever you want. Where were we? The most gratification, huh?" He tensed a little, feeling she was touching on topics he usually didn't talk about. He was afraid of where this might go. The question she had just asked brought back memories he wasn't fond of remembering. "Okay, this is the last question for tonight. What gratifies me most is the realization that because of my success, my mother has been able to live a part of her life the way I wish she could have lived all of her life."

They were quiet, side by side. "I'm crazy about you, Mr. Frye. Now go to sleep." She leaned over placing a kiss on his cheek. She noticed how difficult it was for him to be as honest as he had been with her. She turned the light off, then moved close to him again. They stayed, lying like two spoons, with tranquility surrounding them. "We're more alike than I would have thought, Yale. We both wear our heart on our sleeves. As a result, we're very vulnerable. I want you to feel safe talking to me, Yale. I'll never betray you."

"I know." He didn't say more. He put his arm over her and she took his hand. They stayed that way all night.

Chapter
22

Peter took Mary shopping. She rummaged through rack after rack looking for a dress. Finally, too impatient to watch her for another minute, he told her he'd be sitting on the bench outside the store, waiting. He picked up a newspaper and sat on a wooden form to wait for her. He hated shopping, always had, but he didn't trust her to go out alone. Anyway, he had to be nice. He still needed the bitch.

He turned his attention to the paper. There was an article detailing the L.A.P.D.'s investigation into the circumstances surrounding the deaths of George Benson and Wally Burns. According to the police, connections to gambling debts were being checked, since the limousine in which the bodies had been found had been registered to a company in Nevada previously associated with a syndicate known to many Las Vegas hotel managers. Dumb fucks, Peter thought, smirking. The article also said that no further details had surfaced regarding the attempt on Yale Frye's life. Ohio police were continuing their search for additional information. Numerous leads were being followed up. Peter felt satisfaction, knowing three states were actively involved in the continuing investigations. The five participants of P.A.P. would be able to work unimpaired as the police fought with themselves over territory.

Mary approached him carrying a package. He pretended to be pleased that she had found a dress. Quickly, he adjusted his demeanor, acting romantic, as she experimented with several wigs in another shop. Peter chose the wigs which most changed her appearance. He was excessively nice, permitting her to enjoy the day. She accepted his compliments, and agreed to wear the two wigs they had selected whenever he wanted. Showing further consideration, he allowed her to purchase shoes to match her new dress.

On the way back from the shopping mall, Peter stopped to

pick up the mail from the post office box. He sifted through the envelopes and stopped to examine the contents of one addressed to him. It was from the law office that handled the negotiations regarding the sale of the farmland bequeathed to Peter by the artist. He opened the letter and read the contents. He reread the pertinent paragraph:

> We therefore inform you, as a client of Hall and Davis, that you may experience a short delay in our correspondence, due to the sudden illness of Mr. Davis. We have, however acquired the expertise of Jeffrey Rose, attorney at law, P.C., as the newest member of our organization. Mr. Rose will be handling all legal matters formerly managed by Mr. Davis. If you require additional or alternate action, please contact our office at a suitable time. Handling your legal affairs effectively remains our top priority, as always.

Peter decided to stop at the office of Hall and Davis, to ensure that his business received prompt attention. He drove to the law firm with Mary beside him. They noticed a man locking the outer door as they approached. "I guess I'm too late." Peter glanced at Mary, adding, "We spent too much time in the mall." Mary apologized, fearing a scene.

"Can I help you?" the man asked, overhearing their exchange.

"I'm Peter Mann, a client of Mr. Davis'. He had been negotiating a contract for me. I received this letter in today's mail," he extended the letter, "and was hoping I could determine whether my case has been reassigned, abated, or processed."

"Well, I'm Jeff Rose." He extended his hand for a handshake. "I was going home, but I've got time to check and see. If you don't mind following me into my office, I'll see if I can locate your case. My receptionist was out today, and the secretary was gone for the afternoon. But I've begun working on much of what Mr. Davis did not complete when he took ill. I've only been with this firm for a week, so forgive me for not being familiar with all the remitted documents yet. You introduced yourself as Peter Mann, correct?"

"That's right." Peter didn't bother introducing Mary. They followed Jeff Rose to his office. Jeff checked the file cabinets but was unable to locate anything. He inquired about the nature of the case.

"Well, if it's not in the file, it is probably in one of these two trays," Jeff said, as he pointed at two stuffed trays of mail.

"I'd recognize the envelope," Peter suggested. "It's distinctive because I could only find a green marker to address it."

"Well then, Mr. Mann, see if you recognize it in this basket," he said, handing one tray to Peter. "I'll start looking through this one. Once we locate it, I will give it priority attention, I assure you."

The two men began going through the trays. Halfway into the tray on Peter's lap, he caught sight of a large envelope with George's name and address in the upper left corner. Surreptitiously, he pulled the envelope out, so it would fall on the floor. "Oops," he said picking it up and placing it back in his tray. He had felt what could be a cassette. He deemed it vital to somehow confiscate the envelope, and examine the contents.

"Oh, please, place it as close as possible to where it was, Mr. Mann," Jeff advised, when Peter placed the envelope on top. "Right now, I'm handling all the mail according to date of arrival."

"Sure," Peter said, squeezing the envelope. He was positive there was a tape inside. He placed it near the bottom of the tray.

"Is this it?" Jeff Rose pulled out Peter's envelope. "Yes. I found it, Mr. Mann."

"Good. As long as you've located it, if you wouldn't object, I'd like to recheck a couple things before processing the contents."

"No problem, Mr. Mann. I've got the time to answer any questions you might have, since you're already here."

Peter opened the envelope, asked a few questions, and then suggested returning in the next day or two, to discuss it further when they both had more time.

"That would be fine, Mr. Mann. Call the office in the morning, and let me know when you'd like to meet. I'll be happy to assist you any way I can."

"Thank you, Mr. Rose," Peter said, standing up, and shaking Jeff's hand. They walked out together, Peter carefully noting the double bolt on the outer door.

On the drive back to the house, Peter held the steering wheel so tightly his knuckles were white. Mary was aware that he was disgruntled, but she didn't know the reason. He was concealing something disturbing. His stillness frightened her, knowing she was often the object of his hostility. She walked into the house, going directly to the bedroom. She hoped to be out of his way when he unleashed the fury smoldering beneath the surface.

During dinner, Peter told the group that he had learned some disturbing news: a law firm was in possession of documents which could put them all in jeopardy. He continued, alternating between lies and truths. "It is imperative to destroy all files on George Benson in the law office of Hall and Davis, without delay." He claimed it would be necessary to destroy the entire building by explosion. Otherwise, the fireproof file cabinets would remain. Peter selected Brian and Barry to level the building by midnight; a natural gas explosion would be best, he said, since it would appear accidental, and leave no obvious proof of tampering.

The two men left on their mission after dinner. Brian and Barry parked the car blocks from the building, approaching inconspicuously as passers-by on foot. It was a small, one-story brick building, affording relatively easy entry. They located a window, partially opened, and managed to climb through. Brian located the storage room containing the gas tank, while Barry kept watch for any security. He covered the floor with a trail of lighter fluid from the small metal can he had kept in his jacket pocket. The noxious odor permeated the area. He emptied the remainder of the fluid in the file room. They were proud of how smoothly their endeavor was proceeding. They moved a chair near the window to ease their exit while the combustible mixture ominously filled the air.

As Brian climbed on the chair, a torch came flying at him through the open window, knocking him on top of Barry. They both fell near the yellow blaze already glowing on the floor. They jumped to their feet, watching as the fire spread.

The gas continued to leak from the other room. They climbed on top of a desk, near another window, away from the radiating heat. They tried hitting the window with a stapler to break the glass. They both slammed their fists against the window with desperate strength. Fervid flames continued to spread rapidly through the room.

They were coughing, having difficulty breathing. As their lungs filled with smoke, the glass on the window finally gave. Brian and Barry fought each other to escape, scrambling pathetically for fresh air. The flames reached the gas tank which exploded. Brian and Barry were buried as the building collapsed.

A few blocks away from the leveled structure, Otto tossed a book of matches into a storm drain. Returning to the house, he nodded to Peter. "Good," Peter said.

Totally ignoring Mary, Otto turned and went to the study to read. Mary passed the study with trepidation, on her way to the bedroom. Offensively, Peter called out, "How do you feel about a ménage a trios, my love?"

Chapter
23

Lisa was still snuggled against Yale in the hotel bed. Her eyes jolted open before sunrise. She was unsure what had interrupted the contentment of slumber. She remembered having dreams, without recalling what they were about.

Slowly, she left the bed to use the bathroom. She looked at the illuminated clock; it was only five-thirty. She took a glass of water back to the bedroom with her, putting it on the nightstand before climbing back into bed. She looked at Yale, sleeping on his side, noticing the stubble of hair on his peaceful face. He had high cheekbones and a large neck. His hair, shiny, admittedly dyed, was disheveled, its strands covering his forehead. She moved close to him and closed her eyes, seeking sleep.

After lying wakeful for half an hour, she again left the bed. She put on the robe and sat at the table in the dim room. Her heart and mind filled with sorrow for having hurt Ronnie the way she had. She picked up a note pad and pen. It was time to tell him what she hadn't been able to say aloud.

Dear Ronnie, I am finding it hard to be a modern, realistic woman with my bourgeois principles. They have created discomfort and guilt in me for following my instincts. I have tried to be a good wife, a good mother, and a good daughter. I think, for the most part, I succeeded. The one thing I have always been unable to do is seek fulfillment within, where I have felt an emptiness for a very long time. Perhaps I haven't expressed my needs enough. I had hoped you'd see, yourself, my need for more than what my life has become. The fault is mine for denying my needs, living from day to day, hoping I'd come to be a happier person. But I am not happy, Ronnie, and this shooting incident has forced me to reexamine many aspects of my life.

Ronnie, I don't know what I am searching for. I only know

that I need the chance to explore, until I can figure out what it is that will bring me contentment. I hurt, knowing the pain I caused you could have been avoided, and that I chose instead to be self-ish. I hope, one day, you will really be able to forgive me. We have shared a lifetime of experiences together; I am not saying good-bye now, or will I ever be able to say good-bye. The things we have brought to each other's lives are a permanent part of us. They remain forever even if events alter our coexistence. Don't hate me for sending you home alone. I couldn't leave filled with so much uncertainty.

Maybe there is a way we can try to rebuild our relationship. But that can happen only after we discover if our desires are similar, and if our future is filled with promise, rather than denial. Give me time, and take time yourself, to examine our feelings, and try to realize I never wanted to hurt you. I never doubted your love, and I never again want to see your eyes filled with pain because I put it there.

Love, Lisa

She folded the letter, which didn't say nearly enough. She still needed to be forgiven. She was unable to ease the searing pain in her heart for hurting the most decent person she'd ever known. She removed the robe and climbed back in bed beside Yale. Ultimately, she was unable to deny the feelings of desire that were filling her body again with heat and warmth. She moved against him.

It was only a little after seven, with light filtering in beneath the drapes, when she decided she was going to complete her journey. She had to determine what she wanted out of the rest of her life. Right now, what she wanted was to know more about the enigma of the man beside her. She wanted to uncover the mystery of who he was beneath the obscurity. She wanted to understand him, relate to him, and figure out why she was so drawn to him. Her marriage hadn't been what she wanted it to be for a long time. Maybe she just hadn't been able to face that before now.

Yale stirred beside her. She took advantage of his movements to push herself against him until her derriere was pressed against his genitals. His body was producing enormous fever between her legs. Boldly, she rubbed against his organ, hoping to connect with a sensitive area. Her pulse was quickening. It was becoming increasingly difficult to endure the closeness without further movement. She felt timid about initiating sex while he slept, but it was nearly impossible to resist her desire to touch him.

He felt her nestle against him, wanting her to abandon her reluctance and become more sexually aggressive with him. Inconspicuously, he moved away slightly, hoping to elicit a continuance of initiation from her. He wanted her to yield to the responses of her passion, and express her desire for him.

She slid, trying to touch his body again, and he turned over so his back was all she would feel. He lay still, wanting to see what her next move would be. His body was eager for her touch.

She thought he was still sleeping and started doubting how he would react to being awakened by a hand between his legs. She decided to wait for him to wake. By taking her hand and rubbing herself, she could alleviate the her body's craving.

He listened, hearing her sigh as she stroked herself. He turned over and she pulled her hand away from herself, still needing to be touched.

Boldly, she moved her hand beneath the blanket to touch him, finding him hard when she groped for him. She surrendered her inhibitions, longing for him. "Make love to me, Yale. I want you."

"I was hoping you'd ask," he said eagerly. Mounting her hungry body, he penetrated, pushing in deep, while she arched her body to meet him. She moaned. "Hard. Push hard," grabbing his ass. He pushed again, wanting to please her. She wrapped her legs around his waist. She was getting close. She thrust as he filled her completely.

"Slow down, baby," he gasped. "I'm too close."

"No. I'm ready! Push, push!" she yelled, climaxing a second before he did. They continued grinding, their bodies tingling from the ecstasy of orgasm. She rubbed his back, slid her hands to his behind, and continued rubbing, not wanting him to move off of her. She kissed him, "I can't seem to get enough of you." He kissed her back, pushing his tongue between her parted lips. She took her fingers, rubbing around the crack of his ass gently and felt his penis pulsating inside her. His erection returned. "Want more?" she asked, starting to rotate her hips.

"Maybe in a little while. Right now, you better stop and let me up. I have to pee so bad, I'm going to bust."

"Go ahead." She kept her legs wrapped around him, continuing to stroke his tush.

"Lisa, you're going to be sorry."

"I doubt it." She felt him squeeze around her finger, tightening his ass as he held his breath. "Go ahead," she repeated.

"Close your legs," he said, arching his back as she did. "Push in a little further," he asked. She pushed in with her finger. Her legs closed around him tightly.

"Does it feel good, Yale?" she whispered. "Tell me what you're feeling." She felt his semi-erect penis getting firmer, his body tensing to her pushing. The feeling was getting stronger and stronger.

"Are you sure, Lisa? I'm going to...I'm...oh...oh..." His body let go, shuddering. Relief had never felt better as he emptied himself inside her. He kissed her face, her nose, her neck, and came down hard on her mouth with his. Coming up for air a little later, he said, "You're full of surprises."

"I've never done that before, Yale. Somehow, I feel less inhibited with you than I've felt with Ronnie in all the years we've been married. I don't understand it myself."

"Maybe the real you just needed to come out, Lisa."

"Maybe," she replied, but wasn't certain that was it. Silently, she thought, perhaps it's because you're a famous star and I know you've seen and done it all, so I want to be open and liberal too. Her conjecture continued. She mused, when was the last time Ronnie made me feel desired? He was never spontaneous. He lacked initiative. He didn't make her feel beautiful or sexy.

Yale interrupted her thoughts, "Will you come back to the house with me now, Lisa?"

"Okay."

"One more thing. No, two things. First, don't ever be afraid to reach for me if you want me. I need to know you can be that open with me, Lisa. Second, it doesn't matter how many people I've been with, or who they were. No one has ever made me feel more or better than you. Now, get your sweet ass out of bed and fill the tub while I call down to have a tray left outside the door."

She felt like he just read her mind, but made light of it. "Boy," she chided, "give a guy a piece of ass in the morning and he thinks he's got the whole world in his hands."

"I did, Lisa," he said somberly. "I just had the whole world in my hands. Thank you."

Tears filled her eyes as she looked into his, seeing he meant what he said.

After breakfast, Yale called for her bags to be brought down. She accompanied him to the lobby. He took her hand when they began approaching the front desk. "Wait here, Lisa." She stopped near the sofas decorating the immense room, following his instructions. She waited until he came back a few minutes later. "All set. Let's go." She followed him to the outer doors where he waited until the door was held open. He put a hand on her back, guiding her out in front of him. His Jaguar was brought to him. He handed the parking attendant a twenty, then opened the door for her.

"Thank you, sir," the attendant remarked.

Yale handed another young man a hundred-dollar bill, then ordered, "See that Ms. Klein's bags are dropped off right away," and extended a business card with his address.

"I'll take care of it, sir," the young man replied.

Yale drove away from the hotel, stopping at the red light at the end of the street. "I have to make a stop, Lisa. You don't mind, do you?"

"No, it's okay," she answered, noticing how domineering he'd been since they left the room. The self-assured superiority he was projecting left her feeling disquieted. It was as if he became whatever the occasion called for. "Yale, what did you mean, in the room, when you said 'no matter how many people you were with, or who, that no one ever made you feel more or better'?"

"I was paying you a compliment, Toots."

Warning signals were going off in Lisa's head. She didn't want to spoil what had started as a beautiful morning. But he had been directing traffic since they got out of bed. She was questioning his compliment now, with the same feeling she remembered having had the first night they arrived at his estate. Those feelings were re-emerging, affecting her ability to perceive herself as his equal.

He stopped the car in front of a drugstore and got out. "Wait here. I'll be right back," he instructed, and was gone.

Now she was pissed. She turned off the ignition, took the keys out, locked the car, and went into the drugstore. "Bullshit! I don't take orders. Maybe I need to purchase something!"

He didn't notice her as she went through the aisles selecting several items. However, she noticed him talking to the pharmacist, then paying for something. He took what looked like a white prescription bag, then handed it back to the pharmacist. The pharmacist then put it in a regular drugstore bag, stapled the top shut, and returned it to Yale. He appeared to be thanking him.

She took her purchases to the counter at the front of the store as Yale reached her. "I needed a few things," she said, handing him the car keys. She put the items down, intent on paying the cashier.

He handed the clerk a fifty, with, "I've got it." He did, however, allow her the privilege of carrying her own bag to the car.

She wanted to interact rather than react, but her temper wouldn't allow it. She was furious, seething at his egotism. "Excuse me. I'd like to go back to the hotel, Yale." He didn't miss her tone, nor did her anger go unnoticed. "Please!" she added sharply.

"Lisa, there are some things I can't convey."

"Courtesy appears to be one of them. Please, take me back to the hotel, or I'll get out and call a cab."

He drove back to the Oak Plaza, and pulled the car in front of the lobby doors. He broke the silence, asking, "Will you reconsider?"

"No."

"Okay. You know my number. Just charge the bill to me. I'll call to authorize it. Let me know if you need anything, Lisa."

"And you'll pay someone to take care of it, right? By the way, you were not bad in the sack yourself, Toots!" She stormed out of the car and into the hotel. She went to the ladies room to regain her composure. She couldn't fathom what had provoked his present behavior, but did not appreciate his arrogance. He seemed more conceited than she had thought.

Yale realized this was about more than being left in the car at the drugstore. This was much more than a fit of anger he expected her to get over. He had the attendant take his car, and went after her. He didn't see her until he was at the desk. "There you are," he said, trying to spare them embarrassment. He saw the tissue in her hand, the teardrops that left spots on her blouse, and requested a suite for her.

She looked at him with fresh tears, "You really don't get it?"

"Please, Lisa," he said, as if speaking to a child, reaching for the keys to the suite.

"Excuse me, sir," she said to the desk clerk, "may I see the room before I decide if I'd like to stay?"

"Certainly. If you prefer a different room, or any other change in accommodation, I'm sure we can be of service to you. Mr. Frye has always been satisfied with our provisions. If for any reason you are unhappy..."

"No," she cut him off. "You misunderstand. The hotel is lovely. I have no complaints." She was on the verge of tears again. "Please, I'll be right back." She took the keys from a bewildered clerk, walking to the elevator. Yale shrugged to the clerk, then followed her.

She opened the door to the suite. He entered behind her. She turned, looked him in the eyes, and stomped her feet in frustration. "Don't, don't say a word until I'm done, okay? Then, if I'm full of crap, if I'm the one who's wrong, say so. Let me go through everything, so you'll know how I feel. Okay?"

"All right. I won't say a word until you're through."

She wiped her eyes, smudging her mascara. "Watch." She

walked to the bed repeating what he had said with emphasis on the first sentence. "It doesn't matter how many people, or who I've been with, no one ever made me feel more or better." Then she went to the phone, copying his request for her bags to be taken down. She pulled his hand, taking him out into the hall, and put her hand on his back, guiding him into the elevator, as he had done. When they got into the lobby, she stopped him, at the same spot he had stopped her, using his words, "Wait here, Lisa."

She walked to the clerk, who was watching with curiosity, completely mystified. She handed him the keys as Yale had done earlier, then walked back to Yale, putting her hand on his back, guiding him outside. "Should I continue, Yale?" She took money from her wallet, and said to Yale as if he were the attendant, "See that Ms. Klein's bags are dropped off. Right away." Then she forced all the bills in her wallet into his hand. "Should we get in the car for the rest, Yale? 'I have to make a stop. You don't mind, do you, Toots?' " She mimicked him, tears running down her face. She stood, hands on her hips looking at him. "Who the hell do you think you are?" Hysterical, she rushed into the hotel, and ran back into the ladies room.

He felt like someone had slapped him. In essence, she had. He knew there was no real way to justify his actions. Some were the result of being a celebrity; sometimes you treated others like an ass, but most of the time you were the ass. It came packaged. Part of the picture, went along with the territory. Lisa was right to be hurt. He was wrong. Now, he had to decide how candid he was willing to be. He either opened up completely or let it go. She was entitled to honesty. He went into the lobby, deciding to take a chance and ask her to hear him out. Maybe she'd understand how hard life in the limelight can be. How hard it was to be yourself. How hard it was to trust.

Lisa went into a stall, since voices indicated she was not going to be alone. She locked the door, reaching for more toilet paper from the dispenser. She overheard a woman say, "I'm sure that was Yale Frye. He doesn't look too good. It's no wonder, with what he's just gone through. You know, I heard someone at the salon talking, and it was said he'll be through for good now. He probably won't ever go on tour again."

Lisa listened, as the other woman's voice replied, "It's a shame. He always put on a good show. I've always liked him. I heard Myra Sullivan wanted an exclusive. She asked him to do her show, and he was supposed to be considering it. According to

Harry, he wanted to publicly acknowledge his gratitude to the woman who got shot, instead of him. But I heard he's barely holding it together. His career is down the toilet now. Speaking of toilets, hold on a minute while I use one."

Laughingly, the two voices left the bathroom, talking about some scene in a movie they had enjoyed. When they were gone, Lisa came out of the stall. She washed her face, applied lipstick, and left the ladies room. She had to get out of the hotel for some fresh air. It had never really entered her thoughts that there were ramifications the shooting might have on Yale's career. Her life would probably go on as before, but what about Yale's? He couldn't fall into obscurity. She walked through the lobby was lost in thought, until Yale stopped her.

"Are you all right?" Her face, pale and full of sadness, turned toward him. "I gave you the chance to explain why you were hurt, and you're not full of crap. I am. And I'm sorry. I'd like you to give me a chance to explain a few things. Will you hear me out, Lisa?"

"It's okay, Yale. Let's just drop it," she said, feeling that she had probably overreacted about everything.

He took her answer as an indication that she just didn't give a damn anymore. He felt badly, but his sensitive stomach was hurting and he wanted to get out of there. "Are you staying here? I have to leave. Will you come with me? I'd like to talk to you."

"Can we walk somewhere? I need some air, Yale."

"There's a park a couple of miles from here."

"Okay." She left with him and they drove to the park. She was quiet, thinking about how much trouble she'd caused since this whole thing had begun.

He took her silence as a barrier she was placing between them.

He was quiet because his stomach was acting up. He needed to lie down.

She thought he wasn't saying anything because he was sick of her and of all the things she kept making a big deal about.

He parked the car. They walked through a lush green lawn, surrounded by a woodland of magnificent trees. A gentle breeze blew the hair away from their faces. A path led to several hills encasing the area. They walked up a hill through an area enclosed by brush and dense looming trees, and came to a spot away from the recreational equipment, overlooking a brook. It was a private piece of ground away from traffic and people, like being in the country. Soft white clouds were floating through the blue of the sky. It was a picturesque, serene spot. "This is nice, Yale. Can we sit here for a few minutes?"

"Sure," he answered, his stomach aching. They sat on the grass watching the water, the small forest of trees rustling in the air. The pastoral feeling was nice and had a pleasing effect on Lisa. She felt the stress leaving her body, replaced with peace. The beauty and charm of this expanse of land filtered through the pores of her body.

Yale stretched out, on his side, next to her. "Here you are reminded of the beauty that exists. It's a place where you can be yourself, unafraid of emotions which often stifle you. You can feel suspended by the calm, allowing what you normally suppress to be released. I'm glad we came. I forget that there are places like this. I have the beauty of a place like this, behind my house, but I can't feel the same there. I have to put an iron gate around it, which spoils it. It's like the gate I put around myself. Sometimes to stop love. Sometimes to avoid pain. A gate that has separated me from being a complete person, for a long time, because I felt—still feel—I have to be what I'm expected to be. I became a star; I have to act like a star usually acts. I've got money, so I show I've got it. I flaunt it; I get kissed up to so often, I've come to expect it.

"You know, sometimes I think it would be nice to know, for sure, that it's okay to let my guard down. That there won't be someone waiting to use me for their own benefit, or to destroy me with what I allow them to see. It's hard. It's hard to have to hide so much. It's even harder to take a chance on letting in, what for so long you've kept out in order to protect yourself."

With a sigh, Lisa responded, "Maybe one day you'll be able to trust again, when you realize not everyone wants a piece of you for exploitation. Some people want you because you are you. A very special you, when you let yourself be the real you. Don't give up believing there are people like that. Try believing in yourself, aside from your career, as being special. People know what's real. You haven't been admired for so long because of an image, you're admired because you give yourself whenever you walk out in front of an audience; and if there are things you want for yourself, not to share, take them. Keep them. Allow yourself the things most important to you, Yale."

"Sometimes what was is lost, and you become what's been created, instead. Then fear of not being accepted in the original form prevents you from being anything other than the created version. We all need to feel safe, so we settle for what's safest, and sell ourselves. We lose ourselves, Lisa. Sometimes it gets you by, other times it doesn't."

"You're cheating yourself, Yale. There is no compensation for what you're giving up. You take chances with your career but not with your personal life, which is more important. When the career stops being the most important thing in your life—and it will— what will you be left with?"

She had touched a nerve. She watched his face; emotions were surfacing uncontrollably. His eyes filled with a pain he was usually able to conceal. She moved closer, stretching out beside him. "Hold me."

He came into her arms, letting his guard down. "Don't leave me, Lisa. Not now. Please. I need you, even if it's just for a little longer."

She held him. "I'm not going anywhere now, Yale. Just don't ask for more than I can offer. But accept what I can give, and let me do the same." A cramp in his stomach, gripping him severely, made him groan and bring up his knees. "What's wrong, Yale?"

"My stomach's acting up. I think I'm in trouble."

"Should I go for help?"

"Only if you can get a bathroom here fast." He was attempting to rise, in obvious discomfort. She got up quickly, trying to lend support. "Time out," he said, rushing into the brush-covered area behind them.

She waited minutes, worried about him. Then she approached the area where he had taken asylum. "Yale, are you okay?" Not hearing a reply, she took a few more steps and found him squatting next to a tree. She opened her purse, removed a packet of tissue, and walked closer. "Are you okay?"

She was extending her hand when he shouted, "Get the fuck out of here! God damn it!" She threw the Kleenex at him and went back to where they had been sitting, lighting a cigarette. He emerged several minutes later embarrassed and feeling bad about his outburst. "Close call," he said, sitting, without looking at her.

"I've had a few where I came close to having flies following me. Once from a reaction to a medication my system couldn't tolerate."

"Sorry I snapped at you," he said, his eyes still averted.

"I'm sorry I made it worse for you. I didn't mean to. Do you want to leave?"

He looked at her. "Can we wait a few minutes?"

"No problem, but I'm out of Kleenex. You'll have to use leaves if you get in trouble again."

"Great! I should know by now to carry my Boy Scout manual with me. With my luck, I'll wind up with poison ivy up my ass!"

"Be sure to let me know if you do. That's a story I could sell to the tabloids for big bucks."

They laughed, the tension broken. "Come on. I think I'll feel better at home." They walked to the car, passing a wooden structure clearly labeled RESTROOMS. "Where was this when I needed it?" he laughed. "Hold on, I want to wash my hands."

"That's probably not all that needs washing," she giggled, going into the lady's side.

"That's better," he said, approaching her minutes later.

"Fastidious, aren't you?"

"Yup, compulsively."

They drove back to Yale's estate, conversing easily. They were trying to get a better understanding of each other.

Each wondered, as they walked to Yale's bedroom, how long would they be able to hold on to what they were experiencing, and whether either of them would be able to let go, if they had to.

She looked around his magnificent bedroom, seeing it for the first time. "Quite impressive," she remarked.

"Yes, you are," he answered, covering her mouth with his.

Chapter
24

Myra Sullivan was arguing with her show's producers, trying to effectively express her conviction that the show was becoming too issue-oriented. It was time to interject lighter topics to keep their audience appeal. Since her instincts were good, and she was usually right, she got her way.

"Myra, what's the word on Frye doing the show? Did you hear anything new?" one of the producers asked. It was common knowledge that the two were friends, and had worked together on several projects to raise money for worthy causes. In fact, it was their mutual interest in lending support to an organization to help children afflicted with AIDS which had brought them together years ago.

Both Myra and Yale had grown up as only children, in homes without the traditional mother-father-children makeup. Myra and Yale had a strong kinship for another fundamental reason. Both came from nothing. They had worked their butts off to get somewhere; no one had paved the way for them. They had gone from poor to rich, but had never forgotten how it felt to be poor. They had gone from unknowns to household names. They had never forgotten how it hurt to be without.

She liked the way he sang, but told him her favorite was Luther Vandross.

He liked her style, but admitted his favorite talk show host was David Letterman.

Both loved jazz, fancy attire, and going to movies. They both hated superficiality, spiders, and being late for anything. Most of all, they shared a loathing for people who were prejudiced and openly discriminating.

Yale knew that any amount of change in the future could not alter the hate which had claimed more than six million, simply because they were Jewish. He openly vowed to persist in reminding people of the atrocity, to ensure that those who had been obliterated were remembered by the living.

Myra knew change in the future couldn't erase the way African Americans had once been treated. Nothing could alter the past or the fact that there were still disadvantaged African Americans throughout society.

Myra and Yale also shared pride in their own heritage, and supported legislation that fought against discrimination.

The producer asked about Yale again. She answered, "No, Al, I haven't heard anything yet. Yale hasn't been available. David Ross told me that Yale has promised I'll get first airtime. I should hear in a few days. But I have a feeling he'll do it."

Myra refrained from telling anyone about her private conversation with Yale. He was trying to keep it together, he'd said, adding that it wasn't easy, and that he'd like to talk to Lisa Klein. Perhaps she'd be willing to do the show with him, if it was okay? Myra remembered telling Yale she cared more about him than any ratings, and would like to help in any way she could. She'd hung up crying because he'd said, "You just did, honey. You just helped a lot."

When Myra spoke to Yale's assistant, David, she asked how Yale was doing. Since David knew they were good friends, he admitted his concern. He said he hoped Yale would get back on the road, because he had never been better and the response to the new show had been incredible.

"David, I'm calling as a friend, not a talk show host. I need to ask you something, confidentially. I'm concerned about how a show discussing attempts on the lives of celebrities might affect people, and whether it would be a good or bad thing. There are sick people out there. Could talking about trying to kill a famous person cause a negative reaction in a person watching, and incite some harmful act? Or are we serving a worthwhile purpose, allowing people to see it's not all glory and money? Many celebrities choose not to be friendly since they are continually harassed and victimized as individuals. Could a show like this provide people with a better understanding that everyone is entitled to privacy if they request it?"

"Myra, we could argue pros and cons forever. What concerns me more is, if Yale agrees to do your show, will he jeopardize his own safety? The police have no evidence to confirm that the attempt on Yale was the act of a single person; it could be part of something larger in scope. They can't say, positively, it was not conspired by a group of fanatics. I had hoped more evidence would have emerged by now."

"Well, if Yale agrees to do my show, we'll make sure there's additional security provided. I've done several risky shows with radicals, David. We've never had a serious problem. Fear not on that score. Listen, I've got to run, but you know, doing the show might help Yale make up his mind about going back on tour. You know how us famous people are; once we get applause from an audience, we keep coming back for more. Take care, David. I'll wait to hear the decision. Bye for now."

"Talk to you soon, Myra, or better yet, hope to see you soon."

Chapter
25

"I don't understand, Yale. The hundred dollars to have my bags brought from the hotel to the house, two miles away, was a tip? You already took care of the driver and the hotel clerk when you paid the bill? That's crazy."

"That's right. Money talks, Lisa. And in this town, it screams. Don't let anyone tell you differently because they'd be bullshitting."

Six hours after they had arrived, they were still in bed. "Yale, can we stay in here forever?"

"Sounds like a plan to me." He stroked her face, then leaned across her body for the telephone. He called David, asking him to handle everything for a couple of days. Before taking the phone off the hook, the only person they both spoke with was Ruth. Yale called her, saying, "Everything is fine, Ma. I gave Victor a few days off. Lisa and I are staying behind closed doors, trying to develop a better understanding of each other."

"When the two of you come up for air, let me know. I'm here if you need anything."

Lisa also spoke briefly and emotionally to Ruth, having a hard time expressing herself. "Ruth, I want to say, uh, thank you, and uh, I'm sorry I put you in an awkward position."

"Don't worry about it, Lisa. I'm glad you're better; that's what's important, honey. I'll see you soon."

"Bye, Ruth. Thank you." Yale stroked Lisa's hair after the conversation ended, feeling a lump in his throat.

The hours passed unnoticed from the time they climbed under the quilt in Yale's bedroom. They talked about their innermost feelings, stopping only to search each other's faces occasionally. They were unable to believe the relief they were experiencing in admitting things to each other that they never told anyone else. They were cleansing their hearts of all the fears they had always been afraid to admit. They shared fantasies, giggling at the outra-

geousness of some things they conjured up. They divulged ideas
that might be fun, without fear the other would become judgmen-
tal. At one point they had a silly pillow fight, teasing each other
about who got more hits. They talked about pains that never went
away, dreams they still hoped to achieve, and important people in
their lives, past and present. Both laughed and cried while revealing the most significant memories of their lives. Sometimes they
found their communication so intense, so absorbing, that when
one got emotional discussing a pertinent event or thought, the
other became as emotional. There was a connection of souls, a
merging, engulfing of one another's hearts. They confronted each
other on issues, colliding with opposition at times, and bravely
spoke about tormenting incidents which reproduced themselves in
dreams. They bonded. They were secure and establishing a permanent allegiance.

It was after ten when they showered, raiding the refrigerator
afterwards. By eleven, they were back in bed, side by side. They
had only kissed and embraced since arriving from the park, needing to cultivate their relationship, solidify their union. "Are you
going to resume the tour, Yale?" She wanted him to discuss his
fear of crowds.

"I'm not sure, Lisa. I still want to escape. I'm trying to
recover from what happened in Canton. But I'm sickened when I
think of going out on a stage right now. I've got very mixed feelings about the whole thing. I want a safety net, Lisa. Do you know
what I mean? Some guarantee that my fears are normal; that they
will pass, and that I can just move on without apprehension. Then
the other part of me says, listen Frye, you don't need this anymore. Stay out of the limelight; at least you'll know you're safe.
Realistically, however, I know that in the end, it would be detri-
mental both to my career and to my emotional stability. I don't
want to be sorry that I didn't accomplish what has taken me two
years to begin again. I'm angry, yet feel like going into hiding."

"It's okay to feel confused and troubled. I think it's great that
you don't deny your fear. Reconsider the notion of hibernating,
though, Yale Fight, really fight so you won't feel defeated. I think
if you surrender to your fears, it could destroy the most important
element of your life. You'll lose the thing for which you sacrificed
everything. Could you live with that, Yale?"

"You adjust. I'd learn to live with what I have to, if there was
no other choice."

"That's just it, Yale. In this instance, you do have a choice. I
just don't want to see you make the wrong one. Don't make a
choice you may always regret."

"I've been giving this a lot of thought, Lisa. Two years ago, surrounded with security, I was mobbed at an airport. I ended up with bruised ribs and torn ligaments. I honestly believed that I was going to end up dead. After that I became paranoid and reclusive. It's been a long hard road to revise my thinking, so I could restore my career. It took work to stop hiding. The corker is, I finally overcame the obstacles, and was targeted on my comeback tour. Go figure..."

"There's no correlation between then and now. The fact is, you succeeded! Don't give in; fight the fears with all the defiance you have. Don't become disillusioned by what happened, or you'll deteriorate and hate yourself."

"Lisa, I know you're right. I'm just sick of battling demons that don't go away permanently."

He was getting unnerved, wanting to change the subject. "I'll give it some thought. Come here and kiss me good night."

She gave him a kiss, turning onto her stomach. He evidently wasn't ready to confront this issue yet. It was sufficient, for now, that he could talk about it. She closed her eyes, but couldn't sleep. Yale seemed to be having difficulty finding a comfortable position. His body was moving fitfully, continually rocking the bed, unable to relax. She moved closer to him. "What's the matter, Yale?"

"Nothing. Sorry." He stayed with his back to her. Within a minute he was squirming again. She took her hand and began scratching his bare back. He stopped wiggling. She kept scratching until he purred with pleasure. She began to feel amorous with his skin so close to hers, while he made sounds of delight. She retracted her hand before she grew too excited, and he whimpered, "More."

She started scratching his back again, innocently asking, "Feel good?"

He purred again. Her hand moved down to his waist, rubbing gently. He felt a familiar throbbing in his groin and rhythmically started moving. What he needed was extraction from the rush of heat he was consumed with. He needed to purge, hastily, what had taken charge of his body. The demand was strong. He knew it was not making love he needed now, but the cathartic release from pent-up emotions. "Lisa, I need to let go."

She understood. She'd known, intuitively, that he needed to find a release for his sudden need.

She moved, placing her hand between his legs while his back was still to her. Reaching his groin from behind, she held him firmly. He started moving immediately, rubbing up against her arm with his legs tightly closed. She stroked him steadily. Some leakage made her fingers wet and slippery. She held him near the head of his penis, stroking with steady, quick motions, while he groaned, holding onto the bed. He started pumping faster. He urged her, "Hard, Lisa. Faster." She rubbed both sides of his shaft with quick persistent strokes. His legs tightened around her arm. He tensed his body and screamed. He found the release he needed. "Lisa," he said, but she interrupted, stopping him.

"It's okay, baby. I'm here. Go to sleep. Go to sleep. If you need me, tell me. I understand." She ran her hands over his back, then pulled up the comforter around them. He wasn't wiggling now. Shortly he was breathing deep in sleep.

While Yale had had trouble falling asleep, Lisa's unease manifested in her dreams. She was in a playground, sitting on a bench, while her sons were taking turns going down a slide. As soon as one slid down the shiny aluminum, he would run to the other side, climbing the ladder to go down again. She saw them, in the dream, taking turn after turn, laughing. One of them was at the top of the slide, getting ready to sit down. Suddenly, he began falling backwards until he hit the ground with a thud. Lisa ran and picked up her injured son, with the other beside her. She began screaming for help, while she ran through the street, which in the dream seemed endless. It started to rain hard, but she kept running. Then she was in front of a building.

She stood with one son in her arms, the other beside her. All of them were soaked from the downpour, when she realized they were lost. They went into the building, and she put her injured son on a desk. He started to move and she told him to lie still. She picked up the phone to call for help. She was screaming for help when the ambulance arrived. The boys were yelling, "Don't leave me! Don't leave me!"

She was crying and soaking wet. A picture on the desk kept getting bigger and bigger. She knew the face, but couldn't remember from where. The boys were calling her, over and over again. She picked up the picture and cut her hand. She was bleeding. Someone took the picture out of her hands. The blood was dripping, and the boys were calling her. She said, "I'm here, I'm here." She saw more blood. The picture was covered with blood. The boys were being taken away.

She saw the face on the picture. She knew that face! The boys called to her, "Don't leave!" She saw Ronnie pulling the boys away. Her blood was still dripping. "Don't leave, Mom, don't leave." She jumped and screamed.

"Lisa, it's okay. You were dreaming."

She looked at Yale, her body soaked with perspiration, her heart pounding. "Oh God. Hold me, Yale. Hold me."

He moved, cradling her in his arms, "Shh, shh. It was just a dream. I've got you. It was just a bad dream. Want to talk about it?"

"No. Just hold me, okay?"

"I won't let go until you tell me to."

She looked at him, with tears in her eyes, thinking to herself, what if I have to? What if I have to tell you to let me go? She nestled close and slept in his arms.

She stirred in his arms hours later, waking him. She went to the bathroom, half asleep, and walked back to the bed. Remembering she hadn't flushed the toilet, she went back to the bathroom, flushed, and returned again to the bed. Yale was on his side, head up, watching her with a smile. "How about a race around the track?" he asked.

"Have a good time," she answered, plopping back down.

"How about a game of tennis?" he asked.

"If you don't shut up, the only balls I'm going to swing at are the ones between your legs!"

He laughed, bending to plant a kiss on her cheek, "How about skinny-dipping?"

"You must be thinking about someone else's body," she answered.

"Well, I better take a closer look and let you know," he teased, pulling up her nightshirt, burying his head underneath. "No! This is the right body. Wow, what big knockers you have, my dear!"

"All the more to suck on, big boy," she retorted, wrapping her legs around his.

"How old were you when you got your first bra?" the muffled voice beneath her nightshirt questioned.

"Three and a half, putz. Any more questions?"

"Just one."

"Well?"

"Will you go pee for me?"

"If I could, I would. Come here, Yale. I want to kiss you."

"Can't I suck first?"

"Sure, but don't expect me to return the favor."

He cupped her breasts, licking her nipples with his tongue. He

sucked, squeezing gently, "You sure taste good." He kissed her
body, moving down between her legs. She spread her legs to his
touch, feeling his tongue slide against her. He flicked his tongue,
expertly, holding her thighs apart and tasting all of her, as she
raised her body to his mouth. Her movements were lascivious. Her
inhibitions deteriorated as she pushed against his tongue.

He savored the smooth softness of her. He felt the effects of
her unconstrained movements heighten his own desire. She was
drawing him up, "Come here, come here." But he continued to
manipulate his mouth between her spread legs, smothering the
sensitive spot with the pressure of his tongue. He heard her groan
as her body shuddered, braced against his mouth. Feeling that he
was near peaking, he moved to enter her. Brimming with passion,
he pushed. He was intoxicated by her. Suddenly she jolted, hearing the sound of a siren.

"Shit! It's the alarm." The moment spoiled, he got up and
went to shut it off. He returned and his disappointment was evident. She attempted to recapture the mood, but the alarm had sab-
otaged the feeling and ruined it for him. She didn't want the
moment spoiled or his hunger wrecked, when he had been so
heated a few minutes ago. She followed him to the bathroom,
"What are you going to do?"

"Pee. Do you mind?"

"No. I'll help." She stood behind him, holding his penis over
the toilet, moving it in circles.

"Cute. Real cute. Now get out of here."

"Nope." She sat on the toilet blocking him.

"Good. Then I'll pee on you."

She giggled. "It wouldn't be the first time." She touched him
and he looked at her, "Get up."

"No. You come down here." She pulled him down. As she slid
back, with him straddling her legs, she put his penis, facing down,
aimed in the toilet, "Go on." She stroked him softly, kissing his
mouth as he got firm. "Finish. I still want to play," she whispered.

"Then let go."

"No." She started making circling movements with his cock
again. He started laughing. He peed sitting astride her, finding it
somehow erotic. "So, want to go back to bed?"

"I kind of like it here, Lisa."

"Okay." She took him in her hands and started fondling him.
She rubbed the rim as he jerked to the sensitivity. Then she
stroked, slowly and steadily. He kissed her, hungry for more. He
needed to come but didn't want it to be over.

"Stop, Lisa. I don't want to come yet."

"Then don't," she said, only slowing the strokes, not stopping. His breathing was heavy. He pushed his mouth hard on hers. She let go of his penis. He pulled his mouth away.

"Okay. Now."

"What?" she teased. He took her hand and closed it around him, squeezing it. "Show me; do it with me." He kept his hand on hers as she stroked, guiding her to stroke faster. He felt the sensation taking over his body. She felt his urgency ready to spring. He wailed as all control was lost and he reached a shattering orgasm.

"Jesus," he said, still panting.

"Nice to meet you. I'm Lisa." She extended her hand for a handshake.

"You're something else," he laughed, getting up and helping her up. They went back to bed. "So what do we do next?" he joked.

She looked at him, trying to look serious, "Do you have whips and chains?"

He laughed, holding her to him affectionately. They rested quietly, comfortably. "Can I ask something of you, Lisa?"

"Sure. But this is as kinky as I get."

"Something important." She knew then that he was serious.

"What is it, Yale?"

"Will you go on television with me? I want to do the Myra Sullivan show and set the record straight."

"Are you sure?" She knew the show was done live, with a large audience.

"Yes, I'm sure."

"Okay, Yale. Arrange it." She smiled at him with assurance. He returned the smile.

Chapter
26

Sobbing, Lisa huddled in one of the chaise lounges around Yale's swimming pool. Earlier, she had been radiant but the day had ended in guilt. A remorse Lisa couldn't deny.

The nightmare she had experienced had left an unsettling feeling, prompting her to call home. Eerie flashbacks of the dream invaded her thoughts at the most curious times. She dialed Ronnie, beginning the conversation pleasantly, then inquiring if the boys had sent mail.

"Just the usual couple of postcards," Ronnie stated, adding sarcastically, "Nice of you to ask."

"I don't deserve that, Ronnie."

"No. You deserve worse."

"Look, Ronnie. I didn't call to argue."

"Oh, maybe it was to say Happy Birthday."

She gasped. She'd forgotten his birthday. She, who always remembered to send everyone cards for every occasion, forgot her husband's birthday! "Ronnie, I'm sorry. I guess I deserve whatever you want to hit me with. I feel awful."

"It's not my birthday I care about, although it would have been nice if we could have spent it together, as always. What I care about is us. How long am I going to sit, wondering what to do? Should I fight for you? Should I give you time? Should we discuss divorce? What do I tell the boys? What will you tell the boys? Your Mom called to wish me Happy Birthday, Lisa, asking when I thought you'd be coming home. I told her I wasn't sure. I guess that's what's bothering me most. I'm not sure of anything, and I need to know what to do."

"Ronnie, I need more time."

"Sorry, Lisa. That's not good enough. I love you, but I can't live like this."

"Okay. File for divorce."

"Well, look how easy that was. 'Happy Birthday, Ronnie, file for divorce.' Thanks, honey, nice present."

"Ronnie, I'm confused, too. You're forcing me to say things out of anger, as usual."

"Look. Set a deadline for coming home. Stick to the date and give us a chance. If you come home, and we can't work things out between us, so that we are happy together, we'll go from there. But, please, stop asking for time. I love you. Give me some time, Lisa. I deserve that much."

"I've given you over twenty years, Ronnie."

"I know. It says a lot. Can you throw it away so easily?"

"No, you know I can't, but..."

"But nothing. I want a date to pick you up at the airport. Now."

"August 21st."

"Okay, that will be fine. See you then."

"I'm sorry, Ronnie. I feel so bad about..."

"Lisa, I don't want to talk long distance with intercoms on. I'll see you August 21st, and if you want, we'll celebrate my birthday then. Bye, Lisa."

"Bye." She couldn't stop the tears of guilt. She needed to talk to a family member. Being so upset, she decided to call her parents in the Catskill Mountains; another bad move, she realized too late.

"Hi, Ma. How are you?"

"Better. And you?"

"What do you mean, better?"

"Nothing important. I fell on a step yesterday. No, the night before. It was dark. So I went to the hospital for x-rays."

"So what did they find, Ma?"

"A bad sprain. They wrapped it, and in a few days I'll start walking around."

"I'm sorry to hear that. I'm glad it's not more serious."

"And if it was, how would you know?"

"I just talked to you two days ago, Ma."

"At our ages, Pa and I should have a number where you are."

"I'll ask Yale if it's okay for me to give you his number. Okay?"

"Never mind, Lisa. I'll wait to call you when you're home. So, when are you going home anyway?"

"August 21st."

"You're gone a long time without Ronnie."

"He's a big boy."

"I know. He's also a good boy. A good husband. A good father."

"I know, Ma."

"I hope so, Lisa. I hope you're not going to ruin your life. You have kids, a job, a husband."

"Ma, I'm still recovering and will be home soon. How's Pa?"

"Fine. He's here. He says hello."

"Say hi for me."

"Okay. Lisa says hi."

"I'll call you tomorrow, Ma. I hope you feel better."

"Don't worry about me. Worry about yourself, being in a strange town. Nobody is normal in California anyway; who knows what could happen to you there."

"I'll be fine, Ma. Yale has a big house and security. Don't worry."

"It must look nice to the neighbors. A married woman, with children, staying there."

"The closest neighbor is the equivalent of two blocks away. It's a big lot with a lot of land."

"Good, so there's more room to run around in. It's not nice, even if no one sees."

"Ma, I'm a big girl."

"Too bad you're not a smarter one."

"I'll call you tomorrow, Ma."

"I'll be here. I can't go anywhere now with the leg."

"Bye, Ma. I love you."

"I love you, too."

Lisa hung up feeling even worse. She had no one to talk to. She felt isolated, and guilty. Fucking guilt. A whole lifetime of guilt. When does it end? She went out to a chaise lounge, where she remained, crying.

"Here, Lisa," Yale handed her the medication and juice, "you forgot to take them, again."

"Thanks." He sat on the foot of the chaise facing her. "You know I've devoted my life to being a good daughter, good wife, good mother. I've worked to help financially, taking jobs I didn't always like. And I did it all gladly. But there was a lot missing from my life. Inside, I haven't felt complete for a long time. Forget it, Yale. I'm just rambling. I guess I'm a dreamer, and I haven't learned to accept certain things."

She got up, went back to her favorite corner of the leather sofa, and curled up on her side. "Did you call David to tell him you're going to do Myra Sullivan's show?"

"Not yet. I haven't even checked the messages yet."

"Why don't you?"

"I'll take care of it."

"You know, I always wondered if you wanted to make movies?"

"So what if I did? I can't have, or do, everything I want, just like anyone else."

"What's with the attitude?"

"No attitude, Lisa. Just want you to know, we have been living a fantasy. Life wouldn't be all fun with me either. I travel nine out of twelve months, have projects going all the time, people around most of the time, and act the part, like what upset you at the hotel, often. As for the movies, the public likes what I'm doing, so that's what I keep doing. The crossover to another medium usually doesn't work anyway. Even if you're good, the critics, audiences, they box you in, and more often than not, you're a failure before you even start."

"Maybe you're boxing yourself in, Yale."

"Maybe. But I'm not complaining. I like what I do enough to keep doing it."

"What if you stop liking it?"

"I guess I'll take a good look in the mirror and evaluate my options."

"When you're loaded, you have more options, Yale."

"Yeah. It's terrific having a five million dollar house, that I get to live in for maybe a hundred days a year!"

"That's your choice."

"Yes, it is. I made a choice. I accept the ramifications, and live with the consequences."

"I'm not asking you for anything. I wouldn't marry you, even if I were free. I'm just not sure I choose to go on living as before."

"My mother always says 'you don't throw away dirty water, unless you're sure you have fresh water. Otherwise, you could end up with no water, all together!"

"That's crap. You don't feel clean washing with dirty water; it might as well be no water."

"Tell that to someone who is dying of thirst, Lisa, and see what they have to say."

"Can we turn the TV on?"

"Go ahead, Lisa. Avoidance is a good alternative to confronting important issues."

"You should know. I don't see you taking care of business."

"Now, who has an attitude?" He got up, going into the kitchen for a cup of coffee. He stood, sipping from the cup, listening to the messages on the machine.

Lisa sat in the other room counting the messages. She realized she only knew three of the fifteen people who had left messages. Suddenly, she was lonely for her friends, her home, and the boys. Something familiar. She started crying again.

Yale called David to have him set up Myra Sullivan's show for the next week. David asked if he'd made a decision about the tour, and Yale said he'd decide after Myra's show. When he got off the phone, he went to ask Lisa if she wanted to go shopping, and buy a new outfit for the show. He found her crying again and sat next to her. "Come on, sweetie. Things will fall into place. Somehow, they always do."

"Go away. If I want your advice, I'll ask for it."

"Want to go shopping with me tomorrow? Maybe we can find something nice for the TV show."

She started crying harder. "Don't patronize me, putz. I'm not some bimbo who needs a new dress to make her feel better."

"Lisa, that's not why I suggested it."

"Leave me alone! I feel like Scarlet O'Hara in Gone With The Wind. In every other frame of the movie she's blubbering about something."

"I like Scarlet, even if she blubbered a lot. She had spunk."

She got up. "I have to get a tissue. Shit. All that money, and you don't have Kleenex in every room. And no M&M's either!"

He covered his mouth to suppress the laughter. She came back carrying a box of Kleenex and her newest koala bear and sat down, looking like a very sad little girl.

"Come here, Lisa." He pulled her down beside him. She put her head on his chest, still clutching the bear. She listened to his heart beating, while he played with her hair. She heard an unfamiliar clicking sound.

"What's that sound?"

"The electronic alarm system. It's set to go on automatically at this time every night, and to be shut off whenever you want."

"Why did it go off this morning?" she giggled.

"I didn't turn it off. Someone must have been at the gate. I get people coming up to the gate, all the time, to look around."

"Why didn't someone respond to it going off?"

"If you shut it off within a certain amount of time, they don't have to drive over. They call. The guy on the phone was Jerry, from the alarm company. He asked if everything was okay."

"But he was talking to a machine. How could he..."

"He didn't. They probably sent a car."

"No one rang."

"They don't have to. There's a coded device outside. It tells them if someone got past the gate without the entry button being pushed from inside."

"Gee, too bad they didn't bust in; they could have seen a good show." Yale didn't mention that they had been under special drive-by surveillance since their arrival, because of the shooting. He was glad she was quieting when she asked, "Can we call your mom, Yale?"

"Sure. Push the top button. Never mind. Stay put, I've got it." He extended his arm, touched a button, and returned to play with her hair. "Hi, Ma," he responded to her greeting. "What are you doing?"

"Reading." She read even more than he did. "What about you?"

"Playing with Lisa's hair. I called David. I'm going to do Myra Sullivan's show, with Lisa, next week."

"Good. Thanks for telling me now. I'll have a whole week to make myself crazy, while you tell me not to worry." He smiled, grateful for her love.

"Ruth, it's Lisa. It was probably my big mouth that helped Yale decide to do the show."

"Don't worry, honey. Yale knows what he has to do and when. How are you feeling, any stronger?"

She started crying, "Oh, Ruth, you're the only one who's asked. I'm sorry. I'm upset, I don't know how I feel." Yale held her, stroking her hair gently.

"Want to talk, Lisa? I'm a good listener."

"I don't know..."

"My place or yours? Are you dressed?"

"Yea, in a nightshirt and slippers."

"Don't forget your koala bear." Yale interjected.

"Okay, I'll be there in twenty minutes."

"Ma, do you have M&M's in the house?"

"Plain or peanut?"

Yale laughed, "Bring both."

"That bad? I'll see you in a few minutes."

"Okay. Thanks, Ma."

"Just replace my M&M's! Bye."

He held Lisa, feeling as close to her that moment as he'd let anyone get in a very long time. He ran his hand over her with affection and tenderness. She snuggled closer, needing what he was offering.

Ruth arrived simultaneously with David Ross. Yale, figuring maybe Lisa needed to talk to another woman, explained he had a few things to go over with David, and preferred not to postpone them.

Ruth had brought two bags of M&M's and a cherry cheese-

cake. She knew Yale rarely kept sweets around. She kissed her
son, greeted David, and took Lisa's hand. "Come on. Let's sit outside. It's a beautiful night." She didn't miss Lisa's puffy eyes or
weariness. They sat, side by side, on chaise lounges, with the
beauty of the starlit sky above. The water from the pool glistened.
The air was warm and calm. "What did you and Yale do for dinner?"

"We barbecued steaks."

"It was a nice day for it."

"The day was wonderful. We laughed, swam, walked, talked,
barbecued. Afterwards, I called home to see if Ronnie had
received mail from the boys. I had a horrible dream last night, and
just needed to hear that everything was okay. Then, the whole day
was spoiled.

"Today is Ronnie's birthday and I forgot. I never forget birth-
days! He was hurt, not just that I forgot, but because I said I
needed more time. He kept pushing for a date, when I'd be home,
so I said August 21st. But I'm not going to go if I'm not ready for
a confrontation. I just picked a date so he'd stop badgering me.
But I felt guilty for making him feel so bad, and for forgetting his
birthday. God, I can't believe I forgot! Then I needed to feel better. So I called my folks. My mother said I'm ruining my life. I'm
indecent. I have obligations. All the things I didn't need to hear.
Nothing I ever do seems to be good enough for anyone! I'm sick of
it!"

"It's really a lousy feeling when you believe you're letting
someone down. Especially when it's people you love. It wouldn't
hurt as much if it was someone you cared less about. I always felt
responsible for the hurt Yale suffered because of me. I still feel
guilty for a lot. I always will. The problem is, you can't change
what's already happened. You can only try not to do the same
thing, make the same mistakes."

"I don't think I want to be married anymore. I'm not marriage material. I want to be free. I don't want to be responsible for
someone else's life."

"Really? Your boys too?"

"They're growing up. They don't need me as much as they did
before."

"They still need you. Maybe differently, that's all. You're
what, in your forties? But you called your folks today, because you
needed them. Okay, you didn't get what you needed; we don't
always. But you still turned to them, didn't you? I often wish I had
my parents to turn to, and they've been gone a long time. What
hurts is knowing they love you, and you're hurting them. Some-

times by not living up to their expectations. Other times, just by being different than they are."

"So, when do you stop making sacrifices?"

"When there's no one in your life worth making a sacrifice for. No one forces us to sacrifice, compromise, or rationalize; we do it because of our own needs. Most of the time it's to gain approval, respect, love, or just because it makes us feel good, or it fills a void we have. Yale has a need like yours. To protect. You're very protective of your parents. Yale is, always has been, protective of me."

"My parents have been through a lot, Ruth."

"Honey, you can't insulate them from things you have no control over. And you can't erase the pain they've had to endure."

"I want to make up for their suffering."

"How? By becoming someone who punishes herself, trying to suffer for them? Or to suffer more than they have? It doesn't work that way. You'd end up destroying yourself in the process, and as a result cause them more suffering. Live your life, Lisa. Live it the best way for you, and if you goof, try something else. Yale has adopted too much of my pain, for way too long. I'd like a nickel for every hour of psychiatric help he's needed because of me. He doesn't think I'm aware of it, because I don't come out and say it, but I know."

"He really loves you, Ruth. Probably more than anyone on earth."

"I know. He loves me too much. He's also hated me, for good reason. Lisa, we make mistakes as part of life. There are no absolutes, other than birth and death. All the things between, we learn as we go. Sometimes it's wonderful. Sometimes it's painful, but I don't know anybody who could say life is perfect. Do you?"

"Does that mean we should learn to settle? I'm not willing to do that. I want more. I like the way I feel with Yale. I like being in his arms. I like the talking and sharing. I like making love with him. He's a wonderful lover."

"So was his father. Too bad."

"Too bad, what?"

"I was just thinking about that mistake. I was a kid, so was his father. When I got pregnant, he ran off. But you know what is the worst part? I put Yale's father down. I made him sound like the devil. And because of me, because of my selfishness, and Yale's loyalty to me, he never got the opportunity to form his own opinion. I cheated him. I know it and he knows it."

"He grew up fine without him, didn't he?"

"Ask his psychiatrist."

"I'm crazy about him. He has so many special traits I admire."

"Tell him, not me. I already know. He's the one who can't be crazy about himself, consistently. You're the same way. That's why you both are so vulnerable. You both give more easily than you take. If you believed you deserved more, you could accept much more, without the guilt."

"So what do I do? Where do I go from here?"

"Into tomorrow, sweetheart. And you repeat the process, openly, hoping to achieve the one thing that is the most elusive to us all."

"What's that?"

"Better understanding."

David and Yale had accomplished very little in the way of business. They were absorbed, listening to the conversation between Yale's mother and Lisa over the intercom. Yale was having difficulty maintaining his composure after hearing the candid conversation. As Ruth and Lisa came into the kitchen, Yale's face was evidence of emotions contained, stirring fervently. Compassionately, Lisa used the pretext of exhaustion. She hoped to give Yale a momentary reprieve from his seat by requesting he get her a vitamin from the bedroom. But he didn't move.

"Yale," Ruth said, "maybe one day you will understand. I, too, have needed absolution for my mistakes. But it's hard to broach topics with someone who has been magnanimous in making allowances for you. I was always afraid of talking about things you might find hard to pardon me for. It's easier to justify with silence, that which may condemn you if discussed." She touched his face. "Forgive me." The tears fell, but words wouldn't come out. He looked at the floor, paralyzed by overwhelming emotions. "I'll call you tomorrow. I have to go," Ruth said, feeling his pain.

"No! Don't go, Ruth," Lisa spat at her. "You don't open a door and just leave it that way. Shut it or walk through it, Ruth."

"How do you tell your child things that could split the foundation you share? How do you admit errors, without fear of looking dishonorable, in the eyes of the one who has always meant the most to you?" Ruth cried.

"Yale, your mother is walking through the door. Are you going to welcome her, or close the door on her?" Lisa asked, turning away. "David, how about going for a walk with me? I need some air."

David got up. He and Lisa walked toward the foyer. Lisa,

looking back, watched as son put his arms around his mother's waist. Both were crying, holding each other, pardoning each other for the silence they had finally broken, and strengthening the bond they already shared. Mercifully, Lisa heard Yale say, "I love you, Ma. I'll always love you. I forgive you, Ma. Please, don't cry."

When Lisa and David returned, Ruth went over to Lisa, kissed her cheek, the tears still brimming, and with a hug said, "You did much more for me tonight than I was able to do for you."

As she and David were leaving, Lisa suggested, "Ruth, how about coming shopping with me and Yale tomorrow? I could use help finding something pretty to wear for Myra Sullivan's show next week."

"Okay, Lisa. Maybe you can persuade Yale to buy us lunch, too." Ruth winked affectionately at Yale and left.

Lisa took Yale's hand, walked to his bedroom with him, undressed him, and took off her own clothes. She moved her naked body close to his beneath the covers. This time she cradled him against her as they went to sleep.

Chapter
27

Lisa's body didn't want to move. She was drained and knew it. Her sleep had been plagued by nightmares. Fragments of the dreams nagged at her even after she woke. She couldn't understand it. Ronnie had teased her all the time that the house could fall around her and she'd sleep through it. She was tired of thinking. She left the bedroom, where Yale was sleeping with his head half buried beneath his pillow, and went to the kitchen. Opening the cupboard, she accidentally knocked over a pill bottle. Reaching to place it back on the shelf, she read the label. She was familiar with the medication, since it had once been prescribed for her, one of many attempts to counter the attacks of depression to which she was prone.

Replacing the container, she closed the cabinet and poured herself a glass of orange juice. Realizing that it was late enough for business in Canton, with the time difference, she placed a call to the florist she dealt with in Canton, ordering a jade plant for Ronnie with a note that read 'Just 'cause I forgot, doesn't mean I don't care. Just that my mind is not all there. Forgive me. Love, Lisa.'

The last call was to Sergeant Joe Daly at the Canton Police Department. He was glad to hear from her, saying he hoped she was well. They talked about the shooting at Diamond Coliseum. Although nothing new or substantial had been uncovered, he felt certain that it was just a matter of time until something popped. She requested a copy of the videotape for viewing. She hoped it would trigger a recollection of something. Sergeant Daly appreciated her willingness to help, and said he'd make sure the L.A.P.D. dropped off a copy. "If I notice anything new, I'll call you immediately," Lisa volunteered.

"Thanks. You've really handled yourself well after everything you've gone through. Thanks for calling and for your cooperation."

She was glad she'd placed all the calls but Sergeant Daly's words 'you've handled everything well' made her wince. She was not handling anything well. Anxiety, fatigue, sadness, apprehension, her marriage, Yale, her parents, her job, confusion, and dreams that kept repeating themselves. She dug out the number of the psychiatrist that Doctor Wiener had recommended. Since it was so early, only the answering service was there. She left no message, unsure about giving anyone Yale's unlisted number. "I'll call back later," she said, hanging up.

She went back to bed, still tired, and snuggled beneath the blanket next to Yale. She wasn't sure how long she'd been sleeping when she felt his hand on her arm. As he moved closer, she remembered dreaming about being lost, with a woman's face staring at her. His touch woke her. "I'm here, Yale. Are you okay?"

"Sorry. I needed you nearer!"

"Don't be sorry. Move closer and give me your hand."

He moved, putting his arm across her. She took his hand in hers. "I'm scared, Lisa." She squeezed his hand. It was a hard thing for him to verbalize. "I worked so hard to go back on tour. I know if I don't fight back again, now, I'll never be able to get up in front of an audience again."

"You can do it, Yale. I know you can and you know you can. You'll see once you do Myra Sullivan's show that it's not as bad as you fear. Keep fighting, Yale. I believe in you. Believe in yourself. You'll do it, you'll see."

"Lisa, I've suffered from depression so severe that I couldn't get out of bed. The day I left you in the car to go into the drugstore, I was picking up a new anti-depressant. On the mornings when you woke and didn't know where I was, I was in therapy."

"Usually David handles picking up prescriptions, but I felt pressed for time, and wanted it taken care of. It's something I keep quiet. Sometimes I get pissed, knowing I depend on a pill to feel in control. Other times I get frightened of being consumed with more than I can handle."

"I saw the prescription bottle earlier, Yale. It fell out of the cupboard when I reached for a glass. I wasn't going to mention it, but I'm glad you could tell me yourself. Thank you." They were connected, with no need for constant conversation, sharing tenderness and understanding. "Yale, did I trespass last night? Maybe I was wrong to open my mouth about private issues between you and your mother?"

"No, baby. You weren't wrong. I'm glad. I have a better understanding of things now, things I always wondered about, and couldn't ask."

She stroked his arm caressingly, taking his hand again. He kissed her neck, inhaling the fragrance of her body, pushing against her back with his genitals.

He wanted to climb inside her for protection. His need for security was producing a craving for shelter, for a place to encase himself, shutting out anything that could be harmful. He pushed against her with raging hunger born of the dread filling him.

"Don't be afraid to take what you need, Yale," she encouraged, moving and pushing her body against him.

He felt unstrung. He held her hand with force, alarmed by this awful stirring inside him. He was consumed by savage lust, fidgeting as flames raged through his body.

"I'm here, Yale. It's okay." She pushed against his rigid penis as his hunger intensified. He pulled her ruggedly to him for entry. He didn't conceal his need, as his solid organ stabbed into her like granite. He entered callously, pushing and pushing, while he held her positioned for deep penetration.

"Lisa! Lisa!" he shrieked, tearing at her while she held onto the bed so the violence of his thrusts wouldn't push her away. "Oh, God, Lisa," he moaned, his urgency mounting. He needed to thrust; he needed to come. He was pulling her harder against him, quickening his movement as he sought release. The grinding continued as his battering became piercing and painful.

"Yale, you're hurting me. Stop!"

He pulled out, unsatisfied. He was breathless. "Did I hurt you? I couldn't...I'm sorry."

"Come back. Just not so hard, Yale."

"Forget it. I can't anyway." He rolled on his back.

"Stop being a martyr, Yale. It's not becoming."

"Shut it!" He was seething with frustration, trying to suppress the rage. He couldn't even complete...for God's sake...and didn't know why he was taking it out on her. "I'm sorry," he sighed heavily.

"Sorry is not good enough. I have feelings and needs, too. Come here and make me feel good," she commanded. "Rub my body. I like it," she added dictatorially. He turned, and began running his hands over her.

She moaned, letting him know how good his touch was on her body. "I'm hot. I want you. Use your hand if you can't... Touch me all over, Yale." He gravitated to his former position, his hands still moving over her, feeling less aggression. His considerable size was penetrating like steel. She was excited again, too. "Oh, baby, touch me while you move." She kept moving, taking his hand and guiding it where she wanted to be stroked. "Faster, Yale! Move faster!" She increased her gyrations as he matched her rhythm. He was so close. She knew what he needed. She continued moving.

"Lisa, slow down." She obeyed.

"You want slow, I'll give you slow, baby. But what I want is to feel you fill me. I want to feel what you're holding back, Yale. I want it hard and I want you to do it now. Can you give me what I want, baby?" She quickened her motions, ramming hard. "Should I slow down, baby?" she teased, not slowing at all.

"Lisa, you better..."

"No. Push, baby, push. I want to feel..."

He jerked violently, the physical release flowing from his body. His groaning echoed through the room as the orgasm ruled. He held her with his fingers trying to please her. His body wet with perspiration against hers.

"I'm not ready now. I'm going skinny-dipping. Try me later, if you have the energy." She left the room without clothes or robe, ran out, and jumped in the pool.

He followed and grabbed her to him as she opened her mouth to his tongue. They pushed a raft out of the way, as he pinned her against the concrete of the pool.

She spread her legs while he played with her. She squeezed his ass and defiantly said, "Maybe I'm still not ready." He moved against her, hungry again, pushing into her. She closed her legs around him, kissing him fiercely. "I guess I am." She gave herself to the ecstasy.

After holding each other for awhile, he commanded, "Get dressed." With a loving squeeze on her behind, he teased, "It's time to go shopping, before you kill me!"

After picking up Ruth, They went to lunch at a cafe on Rodeo Drive, sitting outside at Lisa's insistence. It was a hot day and she wanted to people-watch. Ruth pointed out a few celebrities on the way to their seats, making Lisa wish she could go from table to table with an autograph book. A few people approached Yale before they were seated, asking for autographs. He was cordial. Lisa couldn't help feeling special, being with him.

They ordered salads and croissants. Lisa looked, but there was no meat on the menu. She watched people walking by, carrying bags from the exclusive shops, dressed in a variety of styles. She noticed there were only lithe, slender types passing. "I guess no one in Beverly Hills is larger than a size three." She suddenly lost her appetite.

They went to Giorgio's where Ruth tried on several pairs of slacks, trying to find a white tailored pair. She wanted white to go with a particular jacket she favored. She came out of the dressing room wearing linen pants with tapered legs and a pleated front. "I like that the best so far," Lisa stated. "It's just an inch or so too long." Yale was approaching with a red knit skirt and matching sweater, embroidered with white pearls, for Lisa. He'd remembered that red was her favorite color.

"What do you think of these, Yale? It's a nice fabric for the summer." Lisa knelt and turned the hem on Ruth's slacks under, to see how it would look after alterations.

A woman approached while Lisa was making the adjustment. "Honey, when you're done here, I need you to look at a few things I want shortened."

Lisa stood up, laughing, "I don't work here. I was just helping a friend."

"Sorry, dear," the woman said, walking away.

"Why don't you try this on, Lisa?" Yale asked, handing her the knit outfit. Lisa took the outfit, stopping at a sale rack before going into the dressing room.

She heard Yale, "Ma, don't let her make a fool of herself. Get someone from alterations over here so she'll stay off the floor."

Lisa found a pair of navy pants with a matching navy, short-sleeved blouse, trimmed with red and white stripes, on sale for ninety dollars. She took it and the knit Yale had selected into the dressing room. The red knit was gorgeous. It looked great. But the four hundred and fifty-dollar price tag ruled that one out. She tried on the bargain outfit, but it was tight. She decided to look elsewhere, walking out of the fitting room.

"So, did you like it?"

"Not especially. I'll keep looking."

A saleswoman interjected, "I thought it looked lovely on you. Very slenderizing too."

Well, she thought, I made a fool of myself turning up Ruth's hem, I was brought an outfit beyond my price range, and now I'm told, politely, that I'm fat. Also, the fucking salad was not what I wanted for lunch. She was trying not to show her discomposure, but she was perturbed.

Ruth bought the slacks, a jacket, and a Chanel leather purse before they left the store. The slacks were going to be delivered when the alterations were completed.

Yale and Ruth noticed Lisa's mood was changing. It was evident although she was trying hard to act cheerful. "Yale, I'll look another time. How about for yourself?"

"I've got plenty to choose from. Don't worry about me."

She was getting upset and didn't want to. "Well, I've got what I want to wear, too. Although it's a simple dress, I think I can wear it without embarrassing you."

Ruth intervened, "Honey, you wear whatever you like. Clothes don't make the person, they always say."

"Right, Ruth. Any more clichés for the dumb broad from Canton?"

"Stop it, Lisa! That was uncalled for!" Yale snapped.

"Sorry. Look, I need a little space. Can I meet you at the house?" She was close to tears, feeling out of place again. "I just want to walk around alone, okay?"

Before they could say anything, a reporter appeared, shoving a microphone in Yale's face. "Mr. Frye, Is it true you are canceling the remainder of your tour due to the attempt on your life in Canton?"

Yale remained composed. "I haven't made a decision yet."

"Mr. Frye, rumor has it you'll be on Myra Sullivan's show next week. Is that true? And will you have made a decision by that time?"

"Yes on both counts. Excuse me." He pushed past Ruth and Lisa, going into Armani's.

Ruth and Lisa waited for the reporter to leave. He turned to them asking, "Are you anybody?"

"Get fucked," Lisa retorted, walking away.

Ruth rushed to her, "See what he has to put up with?"

"It's his choice, Ruth. This is what he chose a long time ago."

"Did you ever pick something, a long time ago, that you regret, Lisa? Something you may have doubts about now?"

They looked at each other knowingly, then went to get Yale. He was inside the clothing store, holding a striped sport coat. "Lisa, how do you think this would look?" He tried it on. The red and black striped jacket looked great. He looked at the price tag, "Only five fifty." He mocked, raising his brows. "Hell, the red knit was less than that and much prettier." He looked at her pleadingly.

"Okay. You win. You get this and the red knit for me. We'll be a 'grand' sitting in front of millions. Get it?"

"Yeah, I get it, but you've got it wrong. You'll be a million, looking grand!"

"Thanks. I think you're grand too." She took his hand. They spent the rest of the afternoon having a nice time.

When they dropped Ruth off, she looked at her son with concern. "I'm worried about you, Yale. You've decided to go back on tour, haven't you?"

"I have to, Ma. You know it, and so do I."

Chapter
28

Peter went out for a while, Mary didn't know where. She was just relieved. She was sore, the welts on her arms still inflamed from the lashing Peter had inflicted last night. She was terrified all the time. She couldn't sleep. She was losing weight. But worse, she feared she was losing her mind as well.

Only the hope that, somehow, she could win his favor back enabled her to go from the hell of one day, to the hell of the next. She was isolated from the outside world, too terrified to even think of planning an escape.

The seven members of P.A.P. had dwindled to just three. Peter, Otto, and herself, under Peter's thumb. She had to laugh at the hypocrisy of it all. Peter, the one who formed the original bond, and instituted the principles they would follow, was pulling the strings. They all danced to his tune.

Mary was prostituting herself, trying to avoid pain. She remained passive when his temper flared. She used her body to quiet him, repulsed by the depths to which she had stooped in order to survive.

Totally debased, she decided to take another shower, hoping for some feeling of rejuvenation before having to face another day of horror. As she dried off, she gasped, realizing the fresh blood on the towel was from the onset of her period.

She wasn't pregnant! She hadn't conceived! Her lethargy was not because she was carrying a fetus in her womb. The gravity of the situation compounded her terror. She had to think of something. A sudden miscarriage! Yes, that would be it. She must sound convincing. They would try again soon. They would plan her insemination so she could give him a child. She would act heartbroken, playing on his emotions, pretending remorse for disappointing him. She had to concentrate. She had to make him believe her.

Her mouth was dry when he entered the bedroom, Otto

beside him. He looked at her disconcertingly. He approached. "My sweet, you appear distraught. I hope I have done nothing to make you feel beleaguered? You have been in this room all morning. What warrants such actions?"

"I lost our baby, Peter," she wailed. "I have been bleeding all morning." She sobbed, "Oh, Peter, I feel awful. Tell me we can try again, once I've recuperated." She produced more tears, continuing, "I am worthless, nothing. I have let you down. Let me fulfill our hopes, and validate our love by giving you a child. Tell me you want to try again." She held her stomach, rocking, sobbing, and praying.

Peter's face was calm. Controlled, without animation, he stood staring at her. "Otto," he said, still eying Mary, "Remember, as children, what a severe case of mumps I had? I was bedridden for over a week with swollen glands. Remember when, years later, it was determined I was sterile? Remember how glad I was, since I have never had the slightest thought of increasing the population of the human race? I was glad I would remain incapable of producing another life form. Remember, Otto, how grateful I was, knowing I could fornicate without concern?"

Mary's body stiffened as she listened to his speech. He continued, watching her blanch. "Copulation has been so much better, knowing I had no reason to fear, since I could not become a parent as a result." She was speechless. "Poor, poor Mary," he uttered, cold bitter eyes condemning her. He slapped her, watching her head reel from the sharp blow. Blood dripped from her nostrils. "Poor, poor Mary," he repeated menacingly. "Either you have been promiscuous, or you thought me a fool. Either way, my sweet," he added with venom, "it appears that our current three-some will be revised to only two. Otto, we began together. Evidently, we are destined to remain together. Just the two of us."

Mary suppressed her pain, shrinking away from his reach, engulfed by frantic horror.

She had underestimated Peter. She had played right into his hands. He had simply been toying with her, listening to her, knowing all along that she had been lying. Now she was going to die.

The oxygen was leaving her body. She was gasping for air. She was trapped. There was no hope, no salvation. She looked at Peter. Real tears racked her body as she sobbed. "Dear God, Peter, I loved you. I really loved you."

He looked at her with pity. "Get dressed, whore. Maybe you can redeem yourself. I have a plan. Just one thing: don't ever try fucking with me again! Be in the kitchen in ten minutes. And Mary, bring the new wigs."

Chapter
29

On the way to Yale's office, Lisa listened to him sing. He was singing an old Elvis song, trying to emulate the style. She was poking fun at him, laughing.

"Sure know how to ruin an Elvis song," she accused, giggling.

"Yeah? Well, let me hear you do better," he tossed back at her.

"Forget it, honey. If you heard me sing, you'd pull over to the curb and barf."

"That bad?"

"Worse. When I sing in the shower even the water stops flowing."

"Well, we can't all be gifted," he teased.

"Too bad. But it's the truth, Yale."

"Hey, I was just joking, Lisa."

"I know. Sometimes I get defensive because I wish I excelled at something. Anything."

"You do," he offered, raising his eyebrows with a gleam in his eyes.

"Are we almost there? You're making me nuts. Stop with the Elvis, already."

"Yup," he pointed, pulling his car into a lot and handing the keys to the attendant who was opening the door for him. "Thanks, Joe. Lisa, say hi to Joe. Joe, meet Lisa." They walked to a suite of offices, and after countless introductions, she forgot everyone's name. She followed him to David's office. David seemed glad to see her, giving her a hug.

"Anything major?" Yale inquired.

"Nothing that won't hold." Yale had asked to deal with as little as possible for the next few days. He was tense about the television show and tour.

"Okay, David. We have to be at the studio by two. Myra is

taking care of her end. You'll meet me at the house around noon. We'll take the limo and get there at one-thirty. I don't want extra time. Just to do it and leave. Everything else taken care of?"

"Yes, Yale. Extra security, everything."

Myra Sullivan had scheduled his appearance as soon as she could, before Yale had a chance change his mind. He was Monday's guest star, only three days from today.

"Okay. Have a good weekend. See you Monday."

"You know where to find me, Yale."

"Thanks, David. I'll be fine."

They were both quiet on the ride back to the house, lost in thought. Victor had been given a few extra days off to visit with out-of-town relatives. Yale didn't mind, wanting time alone with Lisa.

There were several messages waiting. Two were from Ruth, a couple from friends of Yale's, and one from Yale's psychiatrist's office asking him to call back. The salon had also called, verifying that Pierre would take care of Yale at the end of the day, as previously requested. And Ronnie had left word for Lisa to get back to him.

Yale set up an appointment with his doctor for forty-five minutes later, since there was an opening due to a cancellation, and decided to have his hair cut afterwards. "Lisa, want to come with me? Usually I have makeup applied at the studio before a show, but I'm nervous about this one. I want to arrive at the studio ready to go on. I wanted it to be special for you, but I'm too uptight to do it any other way. Why don't you come to the salon and get a facial and manicure? I'll see who can get here Monday morning to give us a hand before we go to the studio. Okay?"

"That's fine. Do I have time to make a quick call or two?"

"If you hurry."

While Yale showered quickly, she dialed the L.A.P.D. and asked for the tape to be delivered after eight. Then she placed a call to Ronnie, but no one was home. She hung up, planning to try again later.

They went to the office of Yale's psychiatrist. Lisa browsed through the little shops on the main level until he was done. She looked through a newspaper, finding an article that caught her attention, about the explosion of a law office, where two unidentified bodies had been discovered among the ruins. She saw an advertisement for stereo equipment, covering several pages, and thought about her boys. She glanced at the fashions, stopping to read her horoscope for the day:

SOMEONE SPECIAL WILL ADD NEW MEANING TO YOUR LIFE. STRIVE TO BE ACCOMMODATING TO FRIENDS IN NEED.

Yale found her and they left for the salon. She could tell he'd been crying, but said nothing. Bob Seeger was singing We've got tonight, who needs tomorrow... Yale flicked the radio off in the car. "Lisa, will you put your cigarette out? My eyes are burning."

"Sorry." She tossed it out the window.

When they reached the salon, Yale made sure she was well taken care of. She had a facial, manicure, pedicure, haircut and styling. Afterwards, she was brought coffee and pastries while Yale was getting his massage. She had declined the massage, figuring he had spent enough on her already. She sat in front of a mirror, where a woman was having her makeup applied professionally. There were several different colored wigs on a stand, next to the mirror. Pierre, the owner of the salon, went over to her. "Did you ever want to be a blonde?" He put a blonde wig on her head, changed her makeup, and she became another person.

"I suppose if I wanted to travel incognito I could, couldn't I?"

"Probably, but not to someone who pays close attention to details."

"What do you mean, Pierre?"

"Watch." He changed her appearance three different times. He snapped a close-up with a Polaroid camera of each look. "Point out what gives away that the picture is of the same person."

"I can't, Pierre."

"Look, Lisa. The arch of the brow line is identical, even with different shading and penciling. See how, essentially, the effect is more from all the makeup around the eyes? People don't usually alter their brows. Next, look at the nose. A close look will show distinct characteristics that could give a person away. Now, look at the laugh lines and compare. Some things, even makeup can't change. Teeth are another way to recognize a person; a very good way for an observant eye, unless a mouthpiece is being used. People generally just make superficial changes, and quite successfully alter their appearance."

Yale came out, surprised that she was ready. He arranged for Pierre to come to the house Monday morning and they left.

"Yale, I didn't know what I was supposed to do about tipping. I handed the manicurist a ten, and she wouldn't take it. Should I have offered more or what?"

"Don't worry about it, okay?"

"Well, thanks for being so helpful."

She got out of the car and lit a cigarette. He opened the door to the house waiting. "I'll be there in a minute."

"Lisa, are you going to start..."

"Excuse me, but I'd like to have a cigarette. I'm being fucking polite so I don't make your eyes burn!"

"How considerate!" He went in, before he took his frustrations out on her again. It seemed she hadn't had much fun. She wouldn't even accept pampering at the salon. She certainly was different from the majority of women he'd known. He felt an ache in his heart for all she'd been through because of him. How would he ever be able to tell her how much she had taught him about people? He wanted to tell her how it hurt, his new awareness that his life could have been much more if he'd been less absorbed with himself. She challenged his life. She made him want to share himself. She knew the insides of people, while he didn't even pay much attention to the outside. He just waited for people to be attentive to him. All those scars on her body were evidence of the pain she'd endured. Yet she never complained of it. Never.

Lisa came in, going to her spot on the leather sofa. He brought her the vitamins and juice she always forgot to take. "Why don't I call my mother, and I'll take my two special ladies to dinner? I feel like Chinese."

"Fine."

He called and arranged to get Ruth in half an hour. "I'm going to change, Lisa. Are you going like that?"

"No, I'll change. I wouldn't want to embarrass you." She got up, perturbed, and went to her bedroom. He was behaving peculiarly.

He didn't want to fight. He went to his room. He heard through the intercom that she was calling someone. "Hi, Ronnie. Sorry I didn't get back to you sooner. I called, but when the machine answered, I hung up. What's going on?"

"Thanks for the plant and note, Lis'. We keep missing each other, it seems. It's nice that you sent it, a nice jade. I'll have to make sure you stay away from it. Maybe that way, it'll live!"

"Well, Ronnie, how many other people do you know that have the ability to kill a cactus in only three days?" They both laughed.

"Lis', I wanted to say thanks, but the main reason I called, was because of a cassette the boys mailed. It's priceless. Do you want to hear it?"

"Of course! Put it on loud enough, okay?"

Hi Mom, Hi Pops,
We were going to write but are too wiped out. We can't remember how to spell, and didn't want you to find out we're not as smart as you keep telling us we are. The trip has been great. Going through Canada was sorta boring, but Alaska is neat. We met great people and great girls. Oops! We know girls are people. You know what we mean, Mom. Right? We're eating the same boring stuff a lot. Hope Mom has our favorite brownies and spaghetti ready when we get home. Tomorrow we are going to a place where they breed Huskies. Hey, if we bring one home, can we keep it? Just kidding! Well, gotta go cause there's some girls climbing the wall and maybe they want help. Ha, ha. We miss our beds—especially me, Steve—and we miss our friends. But most of all, we miss you. If we don't write anymore, it's 'cause we lost the pencils. We love you. Bye for now.

"Isn't that great, Lis'? I love the harmony at the end the best," Ronnie laughed.

"I'm glad they're having a good time. I can't wait to see them."

"Me, too," Ronnie added.

"I better go now. I hate to think what the phone bill is going to be." She was close to tears. "I told you that the folks are staying an extra two weeks in the mountains, didn't I?"

"No, you must have forgotten. They always have a good time there. You're on Myra Sullivan's show with Yale on Monday, right? That's what your last message said."

"Right."

"I'll tape it for you, Lisa. Want me to call anyone and tell them?"

"No, Ronnie. I wish I hadn't agreed to do it now. You know how I hate being center stage. I can't stand worrying about what people are saying or thinking about me."

"Don't worry, Lisa. You'll do fine. I'll even call to tell you how you looked after I see it, okay?"

"Sure, but you always say that I look good."

"To me, you always do. You always have. Always will."

"Okay. I'll call you tomorrow." Her eyes were filling.

"Bye. I love you."

She wiped her eyes and put on fresh lipstick. She had to blow her nose again. She sat on the bed for a minute, trying to regain control. It was hopeless. She couldn't stop the tears. She lit a cigarette.

When Yale knocked, she went into the bathroom so he

wouldn't see her crying. He came into the room and understood. "Lisa, don't hide from me." She didn't answer. He picked up the phone in her room and dialed. "Ma, we'll be a little late, like a day. Something's come up. Can we have dinner tomorrow instead?"

"Can I help, Yale?"

"No, Ma. No one can help with this. I'll call you tomorrow."

"Okay, honey. You know where I am."

"Yeah, Ma. Thanks."

Lisa opened the bathroom door and looked at him with tears streaming down her cheeks. She picked up one of her koala bears, hugging it. "Everybody knows who they are, except me."

He wiped her face tenderly. She went into his arms, "Hold me, Yale."

"Until you tell me to let go, Lisa."

Chapter
30

Late Saturday morning, Dr. Wiener gave Lisa great news during her visit. "Can we go to your office, Doctor? I want you to say this in front of Yale." They went to the office where Yale had been waiting for her. She looked at him smiling. "Congratulations! It's twins."

"Okay, doctor. I know she's not all there, so what's this all about?"

"I think she's just happy, Yale. Her blood pressure is good, all the tests are normal, and I'm pleased her blood count is up. She's doing just fine. I'm going to keep her on vitamins, but she can resume normal activities."

"Don't tell anyone, doctor, but I think my activities are the reason I'm normal."

He put a reassuring hand on Lisa's shoulder. "Well, then continue to do whatever you've been doing."

When they got outside, she looked at Yale happily, "So, mister, what's on the agenda?"

"How about lunch? Then we can check your twins," his eyes fixed admiringly on her breasts.

"Well, feed me, while I think about the rest," she joked.

He looked at her warmly, relieved that she was doing well. "You'd better get in," he motioned, holding the door open for her, "Or I will embarrass you, right here, on the streets of California."

She got in, sliding over on the seat, "Promises, promises."

They drove, heading toward a restaurant Yale often frequented, when Lisa yelled, "Stop."

Reacting, he put his foot on the brakes. "What's wrong?"

"Sorry, Yale. Can you pull around the block and stop at the art gallery we just passed? That's where I sought shelter from the rain, when the women called the paramedics. I never thanked her. I don't even know her name. I want to go in for a minute. Okay?"

"Sure, honey."

He found a parking space across the street from the art gallery. They walked across and went in. A saleswoman approached; Lisa didn't remember having seen her the last time she'd been in the gallery. "Can I help you?"

"I hope so. I'm looking for the blonde-haired woman who operates the gallery," Lisa remarked.

"Oh, Marilyn. She's in the back, in her office. Hold on. I'll see if she's busy. Can I give her your name?"

"Yes. Thanks. Tell her Lisa Klein is here, with Yale Frye, to say thank you. I think she might understand."

The saleswoman returned a minute later. "She's on a long distance call. She asked if you could come to the office. She'd like to see you."

They followed the woman to the private office near the back of the gallery. "Hi, Lisa. You sure look a lot better than the last time we met. Come on in, sit down. I'll be with you in a second. I have a rep checking on an Erté litho. Mr. Frye, please, take a seat." Lisa looked around the office, seeing it clearly now, while the phone conversation was concluded.

"I'm sorry," the woman said, replacing the receiver. "I'm Marilyn Wicks," she extended her hand to Yale. "You know, I wondered how you were, Lisa, but the hospital wouldn't release any information when I called. I wasn't sure how, or if, I should try locating you. I didn't want any publicity since I just acquired this position. So I decided to do nothing. I hope you understand."

"Oh, I understand, honest. That's not why I'm here. I wanted to thank you, that's all. You were so nice to me, when I was such a wreck, and I never had the chance to say how grateful I was."

"That's okay. I'm glad to see you looking so well. As you see, I'm not any more organized than when you were here last." She waved her hand across the room, "But I did buy creamer and sugar for my coffee. How about a cup?"

"No, thank you. We won't take up any more of your time. I saw several people looking around on our way back here. I just want to say, you really helped me when I needed it. I won't forget it. I'm just glad the place I took cover in had someone so charitable running it that day."

"I'm glad it turned out okay. I'll tell you, I was really frightened that day. I almost wished she was still here, instead of me," Marilyn Wicks said, pointing at the picture Lisa remembered. She turned it toward Lisa, "See, I haven't even replaced the pictures in here yet."

"Well, it's a pretty enough face." Lisa looked at the photograph, feeling disquieted and nervous. There was a stigma attached to the picture. It made her feel uncomfortable. She rose, extended her hand, "Well, thank you again."

"No problem. Nice to meet you, Mr. Frye. I'm taping the Myra Sullivan show Monday, so I can watch it when I get home. I've always been a fan. And Lisa, if Mary Nelson ever comes back for her things, I'll tell her you thought she had a nice face, although I think she would have been prettier if she'd worn braces as a child. The way her front teeth overlap ruins the photo for me." Marilyn walked them to the door. "Thanks for coming by."

They stopped for lunch before going back to the house. Lisa had been chain smoking since they left the art gallery, and Yale noticed that she left most of her lunch untouched. "Something bothering you, Lisa?"

"I don't know. I just feel edgy for some reason."

"Want to go for a swim?"

"Sounds good."

They checked the messages and changed into swimsuits. Yale picked up the package from Sergeant Daly. "You still haven't opened this. What is it, anyway?"

"Just something I asked to have dropped off a few days ago. I'll do it later. Come on, I could use some color before I become a famous television star. After all, I may soon be too busy signing autographs to bask in the sun." She didn't want Yale to look at the tape before doing Myra Sullivan's show. Fortunately, he had been showering when the officer from the L.A.P.D. had dropped the tape off.

They jumped into the pool, feeling revitalized by the cold, refreshing water. Yale never kept the pool heated.

Soon he was holding her, his hands caressing her. "I like your twins," he teased, rubbing her breasts.

She kissed him, creating their own heat in the water. "I like your twins too," she retaliated, grabbing his balls, inside his suit.

They had a water fight until Lisa begged for mercy. He pulled rafts over for them, while the rays were still strong. For an hour they floated, oblivious to everything but the kaleidoscope of color from the sun. She smiled, thinking about her desire to cover his body with her own, as the sparkling water slithered over them. The blaze she felt could not be attributed to the sun alone.

He moved his raft beside hers, reaching for her hand. Their eyes held, and the fire was evident. The smoldering persisted until they were pawing each other, on the way to his bedroom. Caught by fervor, they dropped their swimsuits on the floor, wrapping their arms around each other. Their lips merged enthusiastically, savoring each kiss exchanged. She entrusted her body to his hands, murmuring endearments, bewitched by the skilled prying fingers torridly exploring her flesh. He unleashed unbridled hunger. She groped for him eagerly, craving his hardness. She gave herself to the rapture of paradise, as she bathed in the heat of his embrace. He moved over her, as she drew his mouth to her waiting tongue, anchoring him to her. His eyes reflected his passion. "Take me, Yale. Take me."

He penetrated deeply, straining for control as she absorbed him, savagely thrusting against him. He tried slowing the tempo, with his hands holding her hips. She rubbed his torso, rotating her hips, unable to suppress the fire. He kissed her. His threshold surged to an increasingly high level, and he knew his excitement was rising to the crest. She grabbed his behind avariciously, holding hard. Demanding immediate satisfaction. She gasped as her body met his climatically. They remained horizontal, like magnets, held by a force that would not allow them to separate.

"I love you, Yale," she whispered, still clinging to him, as he remained over her.

"Thank you."

"What?"

"Lisa, this is the first time you've said those words to me. It's the first time you didn't use words like 'I'm crazy about you'. You, finally, said, 'I love you.' I needed to hear you tell me. I love you, too."

"You knew what I felt for you was love, didn't you? I didn't know if I had the right to tell you, Yale. That's all."

"What made you change your thinking? Why did you say it now?"

"I'm not sure. Maybe I feel safer. Maybe I'm less inhibited, or maybe I don't believe I was wrong to take what was offered me. I don't feel guilty for my desire. I feel the desire is a result of my love for you. It is you I love, not the image you create on stage, or what I once thought you might be like. It's the man I've come to know, Yale, that I love."

He pushed the hair from her face, engulfed by her beauty. He kissed her tenderly. "Lisa, I'm going to resume the concert tour. It's being rescheduled. I'll probably start the return here in Los Angeles, within a week."

Her eyes held his. For a long time she didn't move. Neither did he. There were no words exchanged. There was no need. Affectionately, she touched his face, still looking at him. His eyes glistened but did not leave hers. She ran her hand over his back, stroking gently. He felt himself growing firm again. "I love you. Do you hear me, Yale? I love you." He swallowed hard, unable to say anything. He kissed her and she knew what he was feeling. She ran her hands all over his body, closing her legs around him. Afterwards, she held him close. "You still owe me a front row seat at your next concert."

"My next concert belongs to you, Lisa. I'll be singing only for you."

"I'll be there, Yale. I'll be there."

He was beside her, but she turned on her side, not facing him. She didn't want him to see her tears or the fear she was feeling.

Chapter
31

Mary knew she was as good as dead. Peter had suggested that there was a possibility of redemption, but she was skeptical. She did not trust him to keep his word on any subject. He had evoked hatred she hadn't known she was capable of feeling. He repulsed her. But even worse, he was in control. There was no conceivable way for her to escape. She felt abandoned, alone, defeated. Her mind plotted several imaginative schemes to lure him into taking her someplace public. Somewhere—anywhere—as long as there were people. She surmised that then, she might be able to run away from him. But each idea came to a dead end. She remained a captive, enslaved by Peter to meet any fate he masterminded.

She dressed and went to the kitchen as ordered, afraid of what he planned next. Her body was aching. Her nose was still swollen and tender from the previous violence she'd endured. He had said to bring the wigs, so she gathered them on the way.

It was impossible for her to control the trembling as she approached the room. She heard the evil laughter of the two. The laughing ceased when she walked in. "Sit down, sweet Mary," Peter ordered.

She obeyed swiftly, sitting down to wait. He looked her over, then walked toward her, evoking the response he wanted: terror. She recoiled as if slapped when he suddenly stopped in front of the chair, staring at her with venom. He kicked her leg, enjoying her flinch. He took his hand and rubbed her stomach, inquiring, "Does Mary still hurt from losing the baby?"

When she didn't answer, he pulled her head back by forcefully grabbing her hair and yanking it. "Well, does she?" He tugged again at the mane in his hand, until she cried out. "And now, sweet Mary, would you like to begin repenting for your sins? You know telling lies is sinful, don't you?"

"Yes, Peter. I'll do whatever you say."

"Otto needs a fix, Mary. He likes being fucked, and having

his cock sucked. Right, Otto?" Otto stood in front of her, pulled his pants down, and shoved himself in her face.

"Go ahead, Mary. Make Otto grin," Peter snarled. "I'll watch, just to make sure Otto likes what you're doing." He let go of her hair, moving off to the side, with folded arms.

She put her mouth over Otto's flaccid dick, sucking. The limpness remained. She continued, but he stayed soft. "Poor, poor Mary. She can't even get Otto hard. You can do better than that, sweet Mary. Show Otto you're good for something. Some enthusiasm, Mary! If you can't get him to rise pleasurably, he may get angry, and Otto is not very nice when he's angry."

She cupped his balls in one hand, and stroked with the other until he started to firm. He pulled away, stepping back. "No, no, sweet Mary! He can jerk himself off; he doesn't need you for that. Suck!"

Otto stepped up, flaccid again. She put him in her mouth and began running her tongue around, as she moved him in and out. She moved over his dick with gentle teeth, increasing her movements as his flaccid dick grew hard. "That's good, sweet Mary. I see Otto starting to smile. I knew you could do better if you tried harder."

She wanted to vomit. She concentrated, pretending she was with someone she loved. She kept sucking. Finally, she heard a groan and prayed she was getting him close, so it could be over soon. She heard another groan. He put his hands on her head. Good, he must be close. She tongued him and put her hands on his ass, waiting for the end, waiting for it to be over.

"Stop, Mary!" Peter ordered. "I'm enjoying the show, but feel neglected. I think I deserve a little attention now. Don't you?"

Otto moved to the side as Peter undressed and approached her. "My turn, sweet Mary. Show me what you just did to Otto." She started sucking Peter, engulfing his dick with fervor. Aggressively, she ran her lips over the shaft. He started pummeling as she continued her movements. She inhaled his cock as far as she could, finally hearing him grunt. She knew him and knew he was close. She increased her speed. Violently, he pulled out. "Pull your clothes off, sweet Mary. Quickly! Otto wants your ass." She was beginning to undress when Peter said, "Okay, Otto, help the cunt speed it up." Savagely, Otto tore the clothes from her body. "Bend over, sweet Mary. Otto doesn't have all day." He put her hands on the seat of the chair. "Go on, Otto. Fuck the bitch."

She screamed when he forced himself in. She held tightly to the chair to keep from falling. He pounded hard, pursuing greedily. Peter stood in front of the chair and grabbed her hair. "Now

suck, this, bitch, until both Otto and I are happy." He pulled her
hair until she moved at a better speed. Otto was getting noisy.
Peter yelled, "Faster, bitch! I want to come when Otto does." Otto
rammed harder. She thought the agony would never stop when
Otto jerked, horrendously grunting. Peter pushed, feeling ready.
He still had her hair in his hand and a second before exploding,
tugged, coming all over her face.

"Get dressed, sweet Mary," Peter ordered. "Now, we'll talk
business."

Peter explained what she would have to do in order to live. As
he related the outlined plans, his words and features made clear
that she would have no alternative, other than death. He repeated
several times that her existence depended on the competent elimination of Yale Frye, Myra Sullivan, and Lisa Klein. Either they
were dead Monday, or she would be.

"Otto has connections which enabled him to get you in as one
of the security guards for the show where Yale Frye and Lisa
Klein will be guests. You will be uniformed accordingly, with
nothing to distinguish you from the others. You will wear a wig,
the blonde one, and you will be stationed near the stage. The timing and coordination I leave to your discretion. However, before
the show is over, you will have accomplished the mission by
shooting them at point blank range. By that, you will have performed a service for humanity and saved yourself. They die. You
live. It's as simple as that."

He continued, "I've determined that the best time to conduct
your business would be near the end of the broadcast. By then
everyone is more relaxed and less guarded. Simply win their confidence, establish an ideal location, and proceed. When you are
through, you will go to a bathroom, remove your wig, take off
your makeup, change into street attire, and blend in with the people exiting the area. You will not run, which would arouse suspicion, and you will abstain from speaking, so your voice will not
give you away. If you successfully complete the task, Otto and I
will set you free. I have procured an airline ticket to South America, on a secured private plane. There will be five thousand dollars
to start you off, until you obtain a proper source of employment.
That should be easy enough for a woman of your talents. Fail and
I will arrange for a wreath of weeds to be delivered to your
funeral."

Mary agreed. She went to bed, mindful of how vital the success of this mission was to her freedom. She would manage it; she
had to. Her life depended on it.

Chapter
32

John Hall had accurately assessed Jeff Rose. He took initiative, was organized, did his work thoroughly, and was not a clock-watcher. He was professional and pleasant. John Hall was pleased with his decision to hire Jeff, expressing his confidence openly more than once.

Jeff came home late the evening he met Peter Mann and the woman to whom he had never been introduced. He felt challenged by his work, and his enthusiasm prompted him to stay late most days. He hadn't hired a legal secretary yet. He wanted to evaluate what required immediate attention before offering someone a position. He wasn't sure what to delegate until a complete review of the mail and documents in his office was concluded.

Peggy began hurling accusations at him the moment he walked into their apartment that evening. She claimed he cared more about his work than he cared about her. He was tired, overworked, and unprepared for her sudden attack. Irately he countered, "I don't need this shit the second I open the door! So I'll come back in a while and we can start over."

He didn't know what had precipitated the outburst, but was angry that Peggy had decided to be less supportive than he'd hoped. She knew the strain he was under, and how consuming the job was. There was no reason for her to welcome him home with such hostility. He didn't need her fury and didn't want to argue. It was best to back off and cool down.

He got back in his car and drove around aimlessly, eventually ending up back to the law office, where he decided to take several wire baskets of work home with him. He felt annoyed that Peggy was so inconsiderate of his feelings, lashing out at him the minute he opened the door, for absolutely no reason. She knew he was going to have to put in extra hours until he was organized, and she really should be more accommodating. "Well, Peggy, see how you like all the work I'll do at home, if I feel like it," he said to himself, driving back home with the baskets from the office.

He arrived ready to do battle. He stomped back to his apartment door. He wasn't going to acquiesce to her mood, if she failed to consider his feelings. He barged in carrying the baskets of work, barking, "Are you going to bitch some more, or can I eat dinner now?"

Instead of the forceful retort he'd anticipated, there was Peggy on the floor. She was sitting on the carpeting, in the middle of the living room, crying while she rocked back and forth.

"What's the matter, Peggy?" Taken aback, he put down the baskets. He felt ashamed that he had resorted to running out. Feeling he was responsible for how upset she was, he muttered, "I'm sorry, Peg. Don't cry. I shouldn't have left. I guess I can be a jerk sometimes." He bent, trying to comfort her, but she only cried harder. "Peggy, come on, calm down. We'll start the night all over again. Okay?" She was trying to say something, but was crying so hard that he didn't understand a word. He tried soothing her, afraid to admit he didn't get what she said. He tried again, "Peggy, don't cry. I'll be more attentive. Okay? I won't stay late as often anymore. Don't cry, okay?"

She mumbled something again, but, for the life of him, he couldn't distinguish a single word. "Jeez, Peg. I can't understand what you're saying when you're crying like this." Well, he'd been right. It made matters worse. She cried even harder. He couldn't figure it out. This wasn't like Peggy.

What to do now was the question. He knew whatever he decided would be wrong, so what difference did it make? "Peggy, get up from the floor and calm down. I'm not clairvoyant. If I did something that awful, I'm sorry. But to tell you the truth, I don't know what the fuck I did to get you this upset, and until you talk to me, I don't know what the hell to do, either."

He waited, prepared for another mumble he wouldn't be able to interpret. But she fooled him again. She stopped crying and just sat there rocking, with a funny look on her face. Okay, wait it out, Jeff thought to himself. Leave the ball in her court, because you're screwed no matter what you do. Oh, oh, she was looking at him. Think, Jeff, you're supposed to do something. Something. Think! What is it? Shit. You should know. If she sees you don't know, you might have to start all over with the crying. Think!

"Jeff!" Too late! She addressed him. Now he was in for it, for sure. "Jeff, will you help the expecting mother up?"

"Sure, Peggy." He stood there a moment, stunned, then sat down next to her. "I'll help you up as soon as I think I can stand again." He hugged her, kissing her wet face. "Really?"

Libbie Richman

"Yup. In about six months."

"Well. Well. Wow, Peg!" He got up and helped her to her feet, forgetting about dinner, and took her into the bedroom. He made love to her. Then he lay beside her with his head on her belly. They'd both wanted a family. Their lives were full, with more than he imagined. Gosh! He was going to be a father. A daddy! Peggy was going to be a mother. Wow!

It was three in the morning when the telephone rang. He grabbed the phone. It was his employer, John Hall, and he came right to the point. "Jeff, the law office has exploded; it's a total ruin."

Chapter 33

Lisa's restlessness was worse than Yale's. She left the bed for the third time. She was nervous about the television show tomorrow. She'd never been on TV before. Now, she was going on Myra Sullivan's talk show, which had the largest viewing audience of any show on the air. She poured juice into a glass and went to her own bedroom instead of Yale's, until she felt she'd be able to fall asleep. She didn't want to wake Yale. He had squirmed long enough before finally drifting off, and she knew he wasn't sleeping soundly.

She turned the light on, picked up a magazine, and sat on the bed. Noticing the package she'd asked Sergeant Daly to have delivered, she picked up the tape, put it in the VCR and pushed the play button. Sitting back, Lisa watched the events which had led to her meeting Yale.

She felt detached, not wanting to be reminded of the ugliness that had preceded their current relationship. It was hard to watch herself struggling with the man they had determined was George Benson. She jumped at the point on the tape where the gun went off, feeling her heart pounding. She stopped the tape, suddenly feeling queasy. Her mouth felt dry, although she just finished a glass of juice. Walking back to the kitchen, she asked herself, "Do I really need to see this?"

Sitting at the kitchen table with another glass of juice, she answered her own question. "Yes, I have to see the damn tape. If I don't come to terms with this it may never go away."

Dr. Feld had intervened on her behalf when the police had wanted Lisa to view the tape before. He had felt that she needed time to recuperate first. Sergeant Daly had reluctantly agreed, seeing how fragile she was. Trauma often caused memory loss, but buried memories could cause trouble later. Better to know what happened.

She went back to her bedroom, pushed play on the VCR. She

watched the events following her injury, when she'd been unconscious, studying the faces of the people filmed by the camcorder. She saw a flurry of activity, and what appeared to be a row not far from where she and Ronnie had been sitting.

She gasped. She recognized the face of the woman with George Benson. She got up, pushed rewind, then played that portion of the tape again. Unbelieving, she replayed the section one more time. "Oh God, now I know why the face was familiar! Oh God, what do I do?" She was talking to herself, nervous, excited, and in total disbelief. Her hands were trembling.

Very quietly, Lisa went and turned the intercom system off on the phone, so Yale wouldn't be disturbed by her call. She placed a call to Sergeant Joe Daly at the Canton Police Department. She said it was an emergency. Daly would advise her what to do next, she thought, her hands shaking. The voice said Daly would be in after seven, asking if someone else could help her. She asked them to contact him, and tell him Lisa Klein called with an emergency. She explained it was a confidential matter, but she couldn't have him call her. They asked her to hold on. Shortly, a connection was made, and she was connected to Daly.

"What is it, Lisa?" Sergeant Daly asked, answering the call at his home.

"I know the woman who was with George Benson. I saw her picture in an art gallery." She was talking fast, her voice almost a shrill. "I know her face, Joe. She left the job, but her picture was on the desk, holding a sculpture, or statue, or something. I know it was her, I'm sure of it! Joe, it was only on the tape for an instant, but I swear, I know the face..."

"Slow down, Lisa," Daly repeated, several times. "Start at the beginning. How did you come to see her photograph? Wait a second; I'm going to record our conversation. Bring me up-to-date. Tell me as much as you remember. Okay?"

She recounted the events and answered questions until Sergeant Daly felt he had all the information she possessed.

"One more time, Lisa, what was her name, as told to you by the new operations manager of that art gallery?"

"Mary Nelson. I was told that her name is Mary Nelson!"

"Lisa. Do nothing. I will call the L.A.P.D., play your conversation, and we'll take it from there. Tell no one. Just wait for me to get back to you."

"Sergeant, should I wake Yale? I don't want to. We're doing the Myra Sullivan show tomorrow, and I don't want to make him more nervous than he already is."

"Cancel the show. You can reschedule it, Lisa."

"No! No!" she interrupted. "You don't understand. We have to do it. I can't say more than that, but we have to do the show, Sergeant. We can't reschedule. We just can't! If you interfere, I'll cause trouble. Please. Please."

She knew if Yale backed out now, he might never be able to go before a live audience again. They had to go ahead with it. "I should have waited to call you. I should have known better."

"Okay, Lisa. You've always been honest and played fair with me. If it's that important, go ahead and do the show. I'm calling the L.A.P.D.; I'm getting on the next flight out. I'll see you tomorrow. And Lisa, thanks."

"Thank you, too, Sergeant."

She put the phone down and went to Yale's room. She wasn't sure she'd be able to sleep, but she desperately needed to be next to him. She climbed under the blanket, moving near Yale. She thought about the sequence of events that had finally resulted in her being able to identify Mary Nelson. It wasn't surprising that it had taken so long. The fleeting seconds during which she could be seen on the tape were insufficient for a conclusive identification. She was barely visible long enough to be seen clearly. Even Sergeant Daly had said the lab couldn't get good stills off the tape. It was only because she had sat next to George Benson at the concert that somehow, something had triggered Lisa's memory. She would probably never have known who the woman was if she hadn't been in the office of the art gallery and seen the framed picture of Mary Nelson on the desk. Maybe now they'd be able to locate Mary Nelson, and tie the loose ends together. Finally, they would be able to go on with their lives, without any further apprehension. Yale stirred, "Come here, Lisa. I want to hold you."

She moved against him. Her heart was still racing from what she had just seen. "Go back to sleep, Yale. I'm right here."

"Lisa, I don't want to go back to sleep. I want you." She pushed her back into him coquettishly, wiggling around playfully.

"You got me, honey. Now tell me what you want to do with me."

"Do I have a choice about what I'd like to do with you, Lisa?" he asked seriously, surprising her. "Because if I have a choice, I'd ask how you'd feel traveling around with a singer from city to city, state to state, country to country, indefinitely."

She was quiet, not sure what to say. She wasn't prepared for the question, and not sure of her answer.

"Well, big fella, I guess I'll have to think, really hard, before I answer. But meanwhile, I want you to know that you really do have me. You have had me for a while, not just in body, but with all my heart, Yale." She answered with tears running down her face. It was the only answer she could give him at the moment. She didn't move. She couldn't let him see her crying. She had tried keeping it light while still telling him, truthfully, how she felt. She was afraid to say more. She finally managed, "Yale, you know how much I love you, don't you?"

He put his hand across her and she took it. "Yes, I know, Lisa."

She finally composed herself and turned over. "Hold me, Yale. Just hold me."

"I'm holding you, Lisa. I'll hold you until you tell me to let go." She stayed in his arms, their hearts and bodies joined. They didn't say any more; they didn't have to.

The morning was hectic, with Yale and Lisa both frenzied. They showered, dressed, and took turns on the phone. Ronnie called to wish her luck, and to tell her not to be nervous. It didn't help. She was beyond nervous; she was petrified. Ruth called three times. Yale told her, during the first conversation, that he'd asked Lisa to travel with him. In the second conversation, Lisa told Ruth how nervous she was. During the third call, they both found themselves reassuring Ruth that they were fine; a lie. Ruth told them both she loved them, before hanging up.

Robert Bowman, Yale's manager, called to see if he could do anything. He told Yale that the tickets for the opening show of Yale's return to the concert tour were going on sale after the airing of The Myra Sullivan show. Everything was arranged to bring him back into the arena. They wanted a big splash. Yale's opening concert was scheduled for Wednesday night, two days from today. A big one-night show, in Los Angeles, at the Aquarius Theater, then back to the east coast on Thursday. Yale told him to take care of business, and that he couldn't think of anything else he needed now. As he ended that conversation, Yale silently prayed for all their plans to go smoothly.

Pierre arrived to style Yale's and Lisa's hair and apply their makeup. David arrived at noon, punctual as always.

As they were leaving, Lisa ran back to her bedroom, and grabbed one of the koala bears for security. Then she ran to join Yale in the limo. They drove to the studio holding hands.

Chapter
34

Peter and Otto were on the way to an airfield; they had arranged to have a helicopter waiting. There would be a quick airlift to Mexico, where the private plane would be waiting for the commissioned flight to South America. They were only a few miles away from the studio, with Peter behind the wheel of his rented Oldsmobile. He was determined to be out of the country before Mary knew they were gone.

A police siren brought him back to reality, and he pulled over to the side of the road. "What's the problem, officer?" Peter casually inquired, after being asked for his driver's license and car registration.

"Are you aware you were going sixty in a fifty zone?" The officer questioned.

"I'm sorry, officer. I wasn't aware I was speeding, being unfamiliar with the feel of this rented automobile. I'll have to be more mindful."

The officer took his license back to the squad car. He called the Bureau of Motor Vehicles to run a check on Peter's driver license, and the car registration. Peter was annoyed by the unnecessary delay. He tried to remain calm, waiting.

In the studio, Myra Sullivan had completed the final review of her notes and questions prior to going on the air. She made a quick check of her appearance, and consulted with her personal assistant. Then she walked over to greet Yale, to reassure him that everything was all set, and that it was going to be a great show. She was bubbly and eager when she approached him, and her zeal was contagious. "Hi, Yale, David. This must be Lisa," she said warmly. She gave Yale a hug, and Lisa a reassuring squeeze of the hand. "Anything you don't want brought up, Yale?"

As Yale spoke to Myra, the monitor in the room, showing the

stage area she'd soon be occupying, caught Lisa's attention. She hugged the koala bear, feeling her anxiety increase. Myra noticed her nervousness. "Lisa, want to explore back here? Go ahead. Look around. We've got a few minutes yet, and if you prefer, you can wait until the show gets going. I'll have someone bring you out after the first commercial break. You'll have a chance to relax and adjust to what you'll be hearing and seeing on the monitor. Maybe it will feel less intimidating, doing it that way." Myra wanted Yale on the stage alone first anyway, for effect, knowing the audience would be carrying on as they always did for Yale Frye.

"Okay. That's a good idea," Lisa agreed, getting up. "I'll walk around for a minute."

"Would you like to be escorted?" Myra asked, noticing that Lisa was a little shaky.

"No, thank you. I just need a minute." She took her purse and left the room. She was sure she was going to throw up and make a real ass of herself. She walked around, noticing people all over the place. There were technical advisors conferring, someone running past her with a paper flying in his hand, a security guard near the stage, and another security guard across the stage, on the other side. There was noise, lots of commotion, as the audience was being seated.

She walked up to a security guard. "I just want to peek out for a minute." The guard didn't say anything. Lisa stepped forward, noticing how large the audience was. "Boy, I never realized there was such a big audience for this show. It's deceiving when you watch it on TV, isn't it?" She turned and looked at the female guard, questioning.

"Yes, it's deceptive," the woman answered flatly.

"Anyone ever pass out before going on, that you know of?"

"Not that I can recall," she responded.

"Well, I may just be the first. Just ignore me if I do," she laughed nervously.

"Don't worry. You'll be fine," the guard said, smiling at her.

"I hope you're right or I'm going to look like a real fool. Not that it would be the first time," Lisa added, noticing something familiar about the guard. "Can I smoke back here?" Lisa asked.

"I won't tell if you don't," the guard remarked.

Lisa lit a cigarette and looked out, again, at the audience. She saw Sergeant Daly sitting down, near the front. She had almost missed him, since she was used to seeing him with his badge hanging from his lapel pocket. If she remembered correctly, he was wearing the same bright green shirt today that he'd worn the day he'd been to her house. It was the only other time she'd seen him in street clothes; the last time she had seen him. Otherwise, she might not have noticed him at all. "Is there a bathroom back here?" she inquired of the female guard.

The guard laughed, looking at Lisa. "You know, I can't remember."

Lightning shot through Lisa's heart as she stared at the security guard with the overlapped teeth and familiar eyes. Suddenly, she knew this was Mary Nelson. Trying to remain calm, she said, "I'm sure I'll find it."

She walked back toward the room where Yale was, just as the audience was told the show was about to begin.

She was stopped by a male security guard on the way, "Hey, there's no smoking allowed back here."

"Sorry," Lisa said, handing the cigarette to the guard. "The other guard, next to the stage, didn't tell me." She pointed at the woman she believed was Mary Nelson.

"Oh, she's a sub. Someone got her a special assignment. I haven't worked with her before, and I've been with the company for ten years. They said she's tight with Yale Frye, and to place her close to him so he'd be more comfortable. You know how particular some stars are."

"Do you know her name?" Lisa stammered. "It's important. Please. I have to know."

"Sure. We check out all names, from drivers' licenses, before we put someone on." He pulled a paper from his pocket. "Well, she's the only woman sub today. Twelve extras, but she's the only woman. It's on here. Let me see."

"What's her name? Who is she?" Lisa urgently repeated.

"Oh yeah. Mary Nelson. Hey, I gotta go now. They're bringing out Yale Frye."

Frantic, Lisa rushed to the green room. She had to tell David to get help right away. She grabbed the handle, swiftly opening the door. The room was empty.

Chapter 35

Peggy had been vomiting all morning. She called in sick to work, then took asylum under an afghan on the sofa, with a box of crackers and the TV on.

Jeff was in the kitchen with John Hall. He'd told John after the explosion about the work he'd taken home, and asked if he should continue working on what he had for now. John had explained that most of the clients' files had been transferred onto discs as a backup procedure. However, the discs wouldn't be available to him until the investigation of the explosion had been concluded. John told Jeff how glad he was that Jeff had brought work home that hadn't been documented by the office yet. He suggested that they work on the baskets of mail together.

Jeff had inquired, "John, could I ask a big favor of you?"

"What is it, Jeff?"

"Peggy told me yesterday that we're going to become parents in about six months. She's feeling sick, so would you mind coming to my apartment? That way I can be close to her while we work."

"Congratulations, Jeff, and no, I wouldn't mind at all."

They set up quarters in the dining room and kitchen. Without a permanent office, they continued working steadily in Jeff and Peggy's apartment every day. The explosion was still under investigation. John wouldn't even begin looking for another location until the insurance claim was settled.

Working out of the apartment proved convenient for Jeff, since Peggy continued feel ill. Eventually, Peggy gave in to Jeff, and took a leave of absence from work. She hated giving up her job. She liked the position and knew they could use the extra money, but she was having a difficult time with this pregnancy, and her doctor had directed her to stay off her feet as much as possible.

With the new restrictions, Peggy had two men mollycoddling her all day long. John had grown fond of her quickly, and was like a watchful guardian. Jeff was the protective husband and father-to-be, and worried they might lose the baby. Although their attentiveness was excessive at times, it was a new experience for Peggy, and she was beginning to enjoy being pampered and indulged.

She was on the couch when Jeff came to check on her, "Do you need anything, Peg?"

"No, I'm fine. I'm going to watch the Myra Sullivan show in a while. Yale Frye is supposed to be on the program today. It's his first public appearance since the shooting."

"Call me in when it starts. I want to hear what he has to say. I'm glad we sent the tape to the police, aren't you?"

"Yes, Jeff, I am. But sometimes I wish we had identified ourselves. I feel you should have been credited with the assistance you provided, and because of me, you were cheated out of it."

"I don't care about getting credit for anything. I'm glad we could help. That's enough for me, Peggy."

"I love you, Jeff Rose. Now, get back to work. I'll call you in when the show starts," she said, feeling very lucky to have him for her husband.

He went back into the kitchen grinning. John was opening a large brown envelope. He read the contents of the note, holding the cassette that had been in the envelope in his hand.

"Jeff, isn't George Benson the man you said was identified as the person involved in the Frye shooting incident weeks ago?"

"Yes. He was the one found dead at the bottom of that cliff, near Studio City. Wally Burns was dead beside him, and the limo with a Nevada license plate smashed at the scene. Remember?"

"You have a hell of a memory, Jeff. Hand me the cassette player, and read this," John directed, feeling a sense of urgency precipitated by the note he'd just read.

John put the cassette in the cassette player. They listened, astonished by the story George unfolded on the tape. George had evidently realized too late that Peter was his adversary. "John," Jeff said, "I think Peter may also be in some way responsible for the destruction of your building. He was at the office, with a woman, the afternoon before the explosion occurred."

Pieces were falling into place. One thing was certain, a catastrophe could occur at any moment if what Peggy had said was accurate. They dialed the L.A.P.D., declaring that it was an emergency. They related to an officer of the police department the evidence they had in their possession. They added their concern for Yale Frye, who was scheduled appear on the Myra Sullivan show in five minutes.

They were directed to sit tight. Two officers were being sent over, to examine the evidence immediately.

As they were concluding their telephone conversation in the kitchen, Peggy called out, "Jeff. Come here. Jeff. Myra Sullivan is on. She's bringing Yale Frye out now."

Chapter
36

The officer returned Peter's drivers license and papers to him, issuing a traffic citation as well. "Watch your speed, Mr. Mann. Better to arrive at your destination a few minutes late than not at all."

"Thank you, officer. I'll be more careful." Peter was suppressing his anger, eager to get going. "Mother fucker," he shouted, after the cop was out of range. He pulled out, fuming, and headed to the farmland.

"Otto, do you think sweet Mary is going to pull it off?"

"Doesn't matter, Pete. She's dead either way."

"I don't know about that. She's not dumb. If she gets out of there without a hitch, she's smart enough to lose herself for a while."

"Won't happen, Pete. I gave her real name and driver's license to get her in as a guard. Even if she gets out, I fixed it so she'd be picked up for dealing. There's enough crack in her car to put her away permanently."

"Why the fuck did you give her real identity away?"

"Had to. I owed someone a name to lay a rap on."

"Terrific. Now they can trace her name to my post office box, too. We are going to have to stay away longer than I thought."

"Sure are, Pete."

Peter looked at Otto's face, aware that Otto had arranged it intentionally so that he would have Peter to himself. As far back as he could remember, Otto never had liked sharing.

They were approaching the airfield. Peter saw the chopper with the rotors moving. He felt relief, knowing that soon he would be enjoying the good life. He had arranged for the sale of the farmland, and told his attorney to mail the check to him. He'd just have to call to have the check mailed to his new location, once he got to South America. Otto had fixed it so he wouldn't be able to get back as soon as he had hoped. Otto was causing more trouble than he needed lately, dumb bastard!

Peter parked the rented car in front of a storage barn. "Okay, Otto, open it. We've wasted too much time already." Otto got out, opening the barn doors for Peter to hide the car. Peter pulled in and got out of the car. "You have some good people, Otto. Who got the chopper here?"

"One of my best people."

"Okay. Get the bags out of the trunk. That baby has wasted enough fuel waiting for us to get here." Peter tossed the keys to Otto.

"You know, Pete, I've never asked for much since we were small. I let you go first in all the games, from the time we met. I did everything to please you, because I loved you, Pete."

"I know, Otto. Come on, we're wasting time. We'll talk later. I'll give you a nice 'fix'. Come on. Open the trunk."

"I've done okay for myself, Pete." Otto opened the trunk with the keys, still muttering, "Did I mention to you that I figured out I was worth a great deal of money?"

"Stop gabbing, Otto. We have to get going." Peter went to the trunk of the car, to help get the bags out. "Otto, where in the hell is my big suitcase?"

"You mean the one you buried all my money in, Pete? Oh, I forgot to tell you, I put my money in my suitcase, the gray one here. I left yours in Mary's car, with the crack in it." Otto's face was crimson. "You know, Pete, I got a call at the house, asking if I had decided how reinvest the large sum of money I'd withdrawn. Of course, they thought they were talking to you.

"You should have talked to me about it. I always watched out for you, because I loved you. Why didn't you love me enough to talk to me? I would have let you have whatever you wanted, Pete."

"Okay, Otto. I was wrong. I erred. I'm sure I haven't been advising you adequately of certain things. We'll have to remedy the situation. We'll discuss how we can appropriately handle everything. My mistake, Otto. I never meant to deceive you." Peter was rambling on, afraid of the face before him.

"I let you order me around all this time because I loved you. I did everything you asked. I never kept secrets from you. I have to say, I'm very sad you didn't love me like I thought you did. I don't want anyone else to be hurt like me, so I'm going to make sure."

"Don't, Otto! We can talk now. I do love you. Listen, Otto..."

Otto fired the pistol he had removed from the trunk. Four shots into Peter's face spread the insides of his head all over the floor of the barn.

Otto picked up the gray suitcase and two others, then headed for the helicopter. He put everything in the chopper, threw a kiss to Peter, and lifted off.

He had only been in the air five minutes when a police chopper approached. When he couldn't get away, he fired his gun. The police had no choice but to shoot back. The fuel tank was hit, and Otto's chopper turned into a ball of fire.

Otto was dead before the chopper hit the ground.

The police put their chopper down, and went to the squad car that was waiting for them. They put in a call to the station. "Everything is under control here. Tell John Hall and Jeff Rose thanks. They were a big help."

"Too bad we couldn't personally thank Peter Mann for speeding today. It appears the traffic violation was the least of his problems," one officer commented.

The other officer answered, "Seems some people are just in the wrong place at the wrong time. Or is it the other way around?"

"Either way, it worked to our advantage, telling the cop in the patrol car to let him go, then following unnoticed at a safe distance. Peter was pretty stupid to have overlooked paying so many parking tickets."

Chapter
37

Lisa was in a panic. Yale was on stage with Myra Sullivan, being uproariously applauded. The woman who had been with George Benson the night Benson attempted to shoot Yale stood in the wings posing as a security guard. Totally frenzied, she realized she had to do something fast.

She picked up the phone in the room and dialed 911, only to hear an operator tell her to dial seven for an outside line. She quickly hung up, and was about to dial seven when the door to the green room opened. Standing before her were David Ross and Mary Nelson.

"Lisa, I went looking for you. Come on. Myra Sullivan is about to introduce you."

"Okay, David. Just let me run into the bathroom for a second. I'm more nervous than I thought I'd be."

She ran into the restroom provided for guests, carrying her purse. She considered yelling out for help, but thought that might cause harm to David and herself.

"Hurry, Lisa. We have to go." She grabbed a gum wrapper and pen from her purse, scribbling quickly on the tiny piece of paper, and came out. She had to slip the paper to David without Mary noticing.

"I really am nervous, David. I don't know about this." The door opened again. The executive producer approached Lisa.

"Ready, Lisa? The people out there are anxious to meet the brave lady who saved Yale Frye's life." He took her arm. "Leave the purse here, honey. No one will touch it."

She crumpled the paper in her hand as she put down her purse, and quickly grabbed her koala bear. "I need my security blanket," Lisa said, clutching the stuffed animal to her.

"Okay, honey. Come on. You and the bear are going to be a big hit..."

Oh, God! Lisa thought, if you only knew, mister. That's what

I'm afraid of: being a 'hit' for this woman. She was led to the wings, and Myra Sullivan was given a signal. Lisa's heart was racing. She had no idea what to do.

"Well, Yale, I think it's time we brought out that courageous woman who risked her life saving you from possible injury. Ladies and gentlemen, help me give a warm welcome to Lisa Klein." Myra stood, extending her hand for Lisa to come out. The producer touched her arm, "Go on, Lisa. They're waiting for you." He pushed her out to deafening applause. She saw people rising from their seats.

Oh, no! Yale was standing, too. Everyone was standing up! Lisa glanced back, to the wings, for a second. David was right next to Mary Nelson. He was giving her the OK sign with his hand. David winked at her. She didn't know what to do. Shit. What now? Think, Lisa, think!

Myra came over, still clapping, and stood right next to her. She guided her to a seat. She still had the koala bear. Yale came and kissed her cheek. She was sitting. What now? What now? Think, Lisa. You have to do something...

"Lisa, it's so nice having you on the show with us today. I wonder if you could tell us what was going through your mind the night you prevented Yale Frye from being injured? You jumped out of your seat and struggled with a stranger, which resulted in the firing of the gun and you being shot. Is that correct?"

"You know, it all happened so fast, I'm not sure anything was really going through my mind." Lisa looked at Yale. Beautiful Yale, smiling at her tenderly, wearing the red and black striped blazer he had bought the day they went shopping together. Sweet Yale, who had only purchased the jacket so he could persuade her into letting him buy her this pretty red knit. Wonderful Yale. Oh, God. Focus, Lisa; stay focused.

"Lisa," Myra continued, "I understand that at first, after the shooting, it wasn't known if you were the person attempting to shoot Yale, or the person trying to save him from injury. Is that also correct?"

She glanced toward the wing. David was gone. Mary Nelson was standing there alone, looking around. God, she had to do something. What if there were other people with her? What if someone else was going to try to injure Yale? God! Think. Think. "I was, uh, under suspicion, uh, at first," she stammered.

She looked out at the audience and saw Sergeant Joe Daly sitting near the front.

"But, uh," tears were starting to fall as she spoke, "But, things are not always what they appear to be."

She looked at Sergeant Daly, took the crumpled paper in her hand, and surreptitiously tucked it under the red ribbon, around the neck of the koala bear. "I would like to say, right now, publicly, that the police did exactly what they had to do at the time, not knowing anything other than that I was shot in the struggle, and, uh, Myra, if you don't mind," Lisa stood up, walking toward the audience, "Myra, I'd like everyone here to meet a very special person. Joe, come here, please. Myra, this is my friend, the policeman who first interrogated me, and then helped me, the night of the shooting."

Joe stood to the audience applause. "Come here, Sergeant, I want to say thank you, again, for the wonderful way you, and the entire Canton Police Department, did their job." Tears were falling down Lisa's face as Sergeant Joe Daly went to her. She kissed his cheek, whispering, "Help! Read," and handed Joe her koala bear.

Myra Sullivan was watching, thinking. What is she doing? First, she won't talk. Now, she's taking over.

Lisa turned, walking back to her seat. "Sorry. Sergeant Daly has become a good friend, and I trust him completely, and wanted to tell him how much his assistance has meant." Lisa's tears were falling. She kept her eyes fixed on Joe. "You know, Myra, things are not always what they appear to be." She looked briefly to the side again. Her hands were clammy. She was having trouble concentrating on the questions Myra was asking.

Sergeant Daly looked at the bear, saw the piece of paper tucked inside the collar, and took it out. He read:

S.O.S.
BLONDE GUARD PHONY
NELSON
HELP!

Lisa continued her conversation with Myra, "...when the police realized I was a victim, they proceeded on to other avenues." Daly was standing. Lisa looked to the wing again, noticing that Mary Nelson was putting her hand inside her shirtfront.

"Joe," Lisa hollered, "maybe you should come up here, really fast, and say something!"

Joe took the cue and jumped onto the stage, "I'd just like to say thanks." He rushed to the wing, following Lisa's eyes. He grabbed Mary Nelson just as she pulled a pistol from under her shirt. The gun fell to the floor.

Myra saw trouble, but wasn't sure what was going on. Yale

looked at Lisa. He understood completely. She had done something to help him, again.

Myra finally realized what was happening and said, "We'll pause here, and talk some more with Yale Frye and Lisa Klein right after these commercial announcements."

Sergeant Joe Daly had pushed Mary Nelson to the ground. The commercials were airing. Lisa, Myra, and Yale rushed over to him. Mary Nelson began vehemently screaming. Lisa kicked the gun aside.

People were rushing toward Joe: police, security guards, TV crewmembers, David, Myra's assistant, the executive producer.

Mary Nelson went out of control, yelling, "I have to! I have to! Peter will kill me if I don't finish the mission."

Police officers held her down. One grabbed both of her hands and cuffed her. Another officer patted Joe on the back and said, "Thanks, Sergeant Daly. Good thing you were here." He then directed his words at Mary. "You should know that the world's been rid of Peter Mann. Come on. You're under arrest. Read her her rights."

A television executive asked, "Myra, do you want to cancel the rest of the show? We can reschedule."

"Are we safe now?" Myra inquired of the officers nearby.

When the officers assented, Lisa quickly implored, "Please, I'd like to finish the show with Yale, if we could." She looked at Yale, tears still falling.

"Ten seconds," someone shouted.

"Yale," Myra asked, "want to continue?"

"Five seconds," the announcers voice bellowed.

"Yale," Myra asked again, "should we halt it here or do we go on?"

He looked at Lisa, his eyes holding hers. "Yes, let's do it. I'm going to go on."

Lisa looked at him, understanding the double entendre.

Chapter
38

Following the show, Lisa, David, Yale, Myra, and the sergeant were escorted to the Los Angeles Police Department headquarters. They listened to the cassette tape George Benson had dictated. It cleared up the comments Mary Nelson made when she was taken into custody.

It was incomprehensible to all of them that seemingly intelligent people could be obsessively consumed with hate, venom, and bigotry. There was no way to understand such thinking, since rational people could not conceive the workings of minds filled by depravity. Lucid people don't conjure evil acts of lunacy against others. These people were mad, insane, totally unbalanced. It was frightening, realizing such people really did exist. Society, somehow, had to suppress these outrageous violations. People had to learn to live harmoniously, respecting each person's identity as equal inhabitants.

"All the pieces fit. We learned the names of the two bodies discovered under the rubble of a building that toppled last week. They were members of a group calling themselves P.A.P. Mary Nelson had been terrorized savagely. She has requested police protection, in exchange for complete compliance and disclosure. "It's all over" Sergeant Cox of the L.A.P.D. assured them.

"Lisa," Sergeant Daly interrupted, "you are one hell of a lady, if you don't mind the language. And a smart one! You were quick and observant. Thank you for your help and cooperation. I know you've been through an awful lot."

"Can I ask you something, Sergeant Daly?"

"Sure, Lisa, what is it?"

"What made you think that the attempt on Yale's life wasn't the act of one person? Was it the death threat I received in the mail?"

"Actually, Lisa, the anonymous video tape, showing the struggle, gave me a feeling more than one person was involved. I still have a gut feeling about something else that I want to substantiate."

"What's that?"

"Sergeant Cox received George's cassette from two attorneys. A quick check showed that one was the owner of the building where the explosion occurred. But the other attorney just moved to L.A., weeks ago, from Canton. I think he's assisted with this case before today. After all, how many people are astute enough to recall events, and to act as quickly as Jeff Rose did, unless there's a reason he remembered so much, so soon? Just a hunch. I want to check it out."

"You know, Lisa," Myra Sullivan began, "I didn't know what you were doing on that stage. I was thinking, she's going to be a quiet one, and it's going to be tough to get her to talk. Then, the next minute, you're walking around like you own the place!"

"Sorry. I didn't know what to do. I just knew I had to do something fast."

"Well, girl, I'm glad you did," Myra added. "I've got a five-year contract, and wouldn't want to renege on it!"

They hugged each other; glad no one was hurt.

Sergeant Daly called to Lisa, as he was leaving, "Lisa, can I keep the koala bear as a present?"

"Sure, Sergeant. I have a supplier who keeps me well stocked in koalas. He'll just have to replace this one." She smiled at Yale. "Another thing, Sergeant, thanks for the plant you sent me in the hospital. But do me a favor; next time, sign the card."

He smiled at her, "You've got a deal, Lisa. Talk to you later."

Myra said good-bye, too. "Lisa, I'm glad to know you. I hope I'll see you again."

"You will, Myra, if you come to Yale's opening concert, Wednesday night."

"I'll be there. Yale, come give me a hug and I'll call you later."

The rest of the party traveled to Yale's home in the limo, ignoring the reporters outside the gates. Ruth was already inside, ready to offer comfort. David decided to stay for a while, although Yale protested he was fine. He had been mellow and calm, almost too calm, and had refrained from saying much since the end of the television show. He held Lisa's hand tightly, but otherwise he seemed very reserved, very composed. He wasn't sulking, nor did he appear to be stifling bitterness. Merely reticent.

"Oh, gosh! I'm so glad you're back," Ruth started, before they were in the house. "This is unbelievable! But at least, now, it's over. Once and for all. The television just flashed a special report. Mary Nelson named all the 'meshugganahs' and they're all accounted for. They are worse than crazy! They...I don't have words for what they are! Yale, Lisa, are you both okay?"

"We're fine, Ma. Take it easy." Yale went to the kitchen. "Any calls, Victor?"

"Here are all the messages. Sure am glad I came back to see this whole thing end on a good note!"

"Thanks, Victor," Yale answered, looking through the messages. "Why don't you fix a bite to eat? None of us have had anything all day."

"Right away, sir."

Lisa took a cup and poured herself some coffee. She took it to the table and sat down. "Yale, I only looked at the tape last night. I couldn't sleep. That's when I made the connection and called Sergeant Daly. If I was wrong not to wake you, to tell you, say so. I never thought anything would happen. I'd die before I'd let you be endangered, Yale. I wanted today to be a success. I knew you needed to feel victorious, so that you could move forward. Yale, do you hear me? I was trying to help you. Yale, talk to me. I don't like the way you're acting, Yale. Please..."

"Ronnie called an hour ago," he said, handing her the message. "Why don't you call him back? He must be worried sick."

She took the message, looking at him, "Do you think you're being fair with me? Do you know, do you have any idea what I went through today, Yale?"

"Yes, Lisa. I do." He looked at her; his eyes filled with unshed tears. "Excuse me a minute, I need to be alone." He left the room, leaving a trail of confusion behind.

"Don't worry, honey. Give him a little time to let everything sink in. Come on, bring your coffee, we'll see what it's like outside. A little fresh air will do you a world of good."

Lisa smiled affectionately at her. Ruth had a cliché for every occasion. "I'll be out in a few minutes, okay? I want to change, and make a couple of calls."

She went to the bedroom, changing into a pair of jeans and a t-shirt. She then placed her first call. "Hi, Ma. How are you?"

"I'm okay. What about you? You weren't hurt again, were you?"

"I'm okay. Nothing happened to me or to Yale. And we'll all sleep better, knowing it's over. How's Pa?"

"Worried about you, like me, what do you think?"

"Tell him everything's fine, Ma," Lisa said.

"Wait. He's coming to the phone."

"Lisa, how's my girl?" her father asked affectionately. "You looked pretty good on television. Maybe you should try to get your own show."

"Thanks, Pa. I'll think about it," she said, laughing. "How are you feeling?"

"Better now. Just take care of yourself, Lisa. I don't need anything else to worry about."

"Okay, Pa. I'll take care, don't worry. I love you."

"I love you, too. I'll talk to you tomorrow. Bye. Wait, Ma still wants to talk."

"Lisa, maybe you better give me the phone number where you are. I don't like not knowing how to reach you." She gave her mother the number and reassured her that she was fine. Before she hung up, her mother said, "I'm proud you're my daughter. You showed everybody what it means to be brave, honey."

Lisa had to blow her nose and dry her eyes before placing the next call.

"Hi, Ronnie, it's me and I'm fine," she started.

"Are you sure? I've been going crazy. The phone hasn't stopped. I cut everyone short. I was too nervous to talk."

"Yes, really. We're all okay; glad it will be behind us. I'm glad the boys are away."

"Lisa, they know. They called collect, very worried about you. I gave them Yale's phone number, but they may have to call collect from where they are. They want to talk to you. You know, Alaska is a state. They get the news there, too." He laughed, relieved she was safe.

"Oh, be quiet! So, how did I look?"

"You're going to kill me. I taped over your "Dirty Dancing" video by accident, but I'll buy you a new one or tape it again."

"Well, are you going to tell me I looked good or not?"

"I don't have to. You know you looked great. You had that 'I look good' look."

"When? Before I started crying, or after?"

"At the end. But you made me cry watching you, during the first part. By the way, how did Sergeant Daly know what was going on, and why was he there?"

She spent the next twenty minutes filling him in. Ruth and David listened in the den, leaning against the back of the leather sofas. Yale sat listening in his bedroom, unable to stop his tears.

"Lisa, I'll get a flight out tonight. I don't want to sit here worrying—"

"Please, Ronnie," she cut him off. "I'm fine and I don't want you to come out. I'm doing what I have to. Please, try to understand—"

Now, he cut her off. "Understand what? That you could have been killed while I was sitting here? This is bullshit! I'm not made of stone! Why don't you try being understanding, for a change?"

She started crying. "Just a little longer, please. I can't handle dealing with anything else now. Ronnie, don't back me into a corner. Just once, let me do what I have to, for me, just one fucking, God-damn time, without feeling guilty!"

"Okay, Lisa. I'll let you go. You've been through enough today. You know, once you used to come to me, lean on me, when things were bad. I wish you could still do that. I wish you still needed me. I'll be here if you want to call later. I love you, Lisa. I'm glad—God, I'm glad—it's over, and you're okay. Bye."

"Bye, Ronnie." She sat consumed with guilt, sobbing. As she went to blow her nose again, Ruth knocked on the bedroom door.

"Lisa, come have something to eat. Victor made a salad and lasagna."

"I'll be right there."

"You know what they say, a happy stomach is a full stomach."

Lisa couldn't help laughing. "No, Ruth. That's a new one on me." She opened the door, and went to the kitchen with Ruth.

Ruth gathered everyone around the kitchen table. She started by passing the salad bowl. She noticed Yale's puffy eyes. "So, what do we call this: lunch, dinner, or a mid-day snack? Now we'll be hungry at bedtime, when it's time to go to sleep." Her attempt to remedy their personal bruises wasn't working.

"Ruth," Lisa replied, "I love you, but I can't sit here pretending I'm okay. I feel crucified for being human. I'm not sure I can repress my feelings. I'm going out back, to walk for a while." Lisa stood, knocking over a glass of water. She tried to steady herself. "I guess I'm tired." She tried to stop the water from spreading with a few napkins. Victor came over with a towel to assist her. "Thank you, Victor." She was fighting against tears as she left the table.

"Lisa," Yale yelled with a sob, "It's not you. Don't go!" He was crying openly now. "Lisa, it's just hard."

"I know about hard, Yale," she roared back at him. "I know all about hard!"

He followed her back to her bedroom. "You don't understand. Until today, I didn't believe anyone could love me like you do. I didn't know there was a person, other than my mother, who would risk everything for me, who loved me enough, to repeatedly do that. Lisa, I thought that kind of love was only found in romance novels. Don't you understand? I can't believe it. I don't know how to handle it. I didn't know it really existed." He sat on the bed and put his face in his hands. She went to him.

"Hey, music man, what do you think I've been giving you all these weeks?" He lifted his eyes to her, "Yale, if you wanted a body, you could find a better one than mine. What you needed was heart, which I gave you completely. The love has always been there. You were just afraid of it."

"The first time, when you were hurt instead of me, I felt it was partially due to an automatic reaction. You see something going wrong, you try to stop it. Today, I understood how wrong I've been. I knew you loved me, Lisa, but your capacity for loving is so much more than mine. For the first time, I felt the impact of your kind of love. Do you understand how overwhelming that is?"

"Maybe your kind of love is safer, Yale, and I should learn from you. My kind of love makes you too vulnerable. I'm not sure it's any better. But it's me, Yale. It's who I am, and I can't change that. Give me a hug, Yale. I need you to hold me."

He moved, enfolding her, "Until you tell me to let go."

They went back to the kitchen, listening to Ruth jabber, "Sure. Now, it's not lunch for sure. It's dinner. Sit down, before Victor has a nervous breakdown from reheating the reheated food."

Before they finished the meal, Sergeant Daly called and asked for Yale. The conversation was brief. He informed Yale that in an hour there would be a special report, with the details compiled so far. He asked if they were alright, and said he'd call again in the morning.

David left shortly after dinner to meet with Robert Bowman for the final outline of Yale's tour. Yale pulled Lisa down beside him on one of the oversized sofas, wrapping his legs around hers. Ruth stretched out on the other sofa, turning on the television. Yale kissed Lisa's cheek, then her nose, while she stroked his face. Ruth swallowed hard, keeping her emotions in check. Silently, she thanked God they had come out of this horror unharmed. She felt comforted watching them, then focused on the TV special about to begin.

After the program, over coffee, Lisa asked, "Can we please not talk about this anymore tonight? I can't take another word."

"She's right, Yale. We have to try and put it behind us now."

"I know it's not easy, Ruth." Lisa responded. "I just feel tense and edgy. I can't explain it. Want to go shopping with me tomorrow?"

"Sure, honey. What do you want to buy?"

"I want a pretty new dress for Yale's opening show Wednesday night. You know, he's singing this one just for me."

"Sure. All of a sudden I have to take a back seat," she teased. "Good idea, Lisa. Maybe I'll buy a dress too."

"Why do I have the feeling this is going to cost me?" Yale asked jokingly.

"Well, new dresses for new beginnings are expensive, honey. But I'll make it up to you," Lisa quipped, running her hand across his chest.

"I think I'll go home," Ruth said, standing. "I've heard enough. I'll talk to you in the morning." She bowed, kissing Lisa's cheek.

"Hey, I always get kissed first, remember?" Yale said to Ruth, pretending jealousy. "Come on, my turn."

"Lisa, he's spoiled. I think it's partly my fault. I have always let him have his way, since he was little. Now the big shot takes advantage of it. Try to set him straight, if it's not too late."

"Oh, Ruth, I can set him straight, quite easily," Lisa giggled.

"Okay. Enough, I'm out of here."

They walked her to the door and said goodnight. Victor was also leaving, at Yale's suggestion.

Hand in hand, Lisa and Yale headed for Yale's bedroom.

"Ruth is so special. I'm crazy about her, Yale," Lisa said, while getting ready for bed.

"She's taken to you, too. You're very much alike, in many ways."

"I hope that doesn't play a part in the way you feel about me, Yale."

"I'd be lying if I said it didn't make me happy. It does. Lisa, I've got to make a few calls. I'll be in soon. Don't forget to take your pills." He turned the speaker off on his bedroom phone.

"Okay. I'm going to soak in the tub. I feel wired."

After she dried off and slipped on a nightshirt, she went to the kitchen for some juice. She heard Yale, still on the phone, over the speaker in the kitchen, as she walked to the cupboard for a glass.

"I'm glad I didn't wake you, Ronnie. I just wanted to reassure you Lisa is okay."

"I appreciate it, Yale. So, Wednesday is the first show of tour?"

"Yes, that's right. Lisa will get her promise for a front row seat and, hopefully, a whole show this time."

"Did she talk to Marc and Steve tonight?"

"No. They haven't called yet."

"They were backpacking and probably couldn't get to a phone."

"You've got two wonderful sons, Ronnie."

"I had a wonderful wife too, Yale."

"I think you still do. Sometimes people have a curiosity, wondering if the life they're leading is all there is, or are they missing out on something. I've gone through that. A lot of people do. Some never do. They're content."

"Maybe people who are really happy with their lives don't search, or need to question if there's more. I've been doing a lot of soul searching. I probably should have tried harder to make Lisa happy. To make sure she felt complete. I think, if I've learned anything, Yale, it's not to take what you have for granted."

"You know, Ronnie, I'm just learning that, too. I'm grateful you didn't hang up on me. I just need to tell you one more thing. You have no reason to believe me, but I never meant to hurt you. I know what I did was wrong, as far as you're concerned, but I feel bad, very bad, that you suffered because of me."

"Listen, Yale, I've really got to go." Yale heard anger mixed with anguish in Ronnie's voice. "I'll just have to learn, uh, to accept or adjust. Thanks for the call."

"Good-bye, Ronnie." The line went dead in Yale's hand.

Lisa ran back to Yale's bedroom, pulled her nightshirt off, and turned on the water in the shower stall. She got in quickly, and let the room fill with steam, so she could weep in solitude.

Chapter 39

Yale and Lisa had come too far to hide their aching hearts from one another. They went to bed quietly, close to each other. Unable to speak, they clasped hands.

In the morning, Yale talked about the many things requiring his attention during the day. Lisa smiled, saying she would be picked up by Ruth soon to go shopping. They didn't embrace before going their separate ways. Both were subdued, afraid of sharing their thoughts.

While shopping, Lisa selected a black silk dress. It was simple, elegant, and understated. She bought several t-shirts of famous rock stars for Marc and Steve, and a white lace wrap she admired.

Ruth, fond of wearing vibrant colors, purchased a crimson floral dress, and another pair of white slacks. They had lunch together, enjoying each other's company. They stopped at Ruth's apartment before going back to Yale's estate, so Ruth could pick up a few books he'd asked for.

Almost every wall in Ruth's apartment displayed a picture of Yale. There were a few pencil drawings, and two exceptional oil paintings. Most of the glass tables were cluttered with books and magazines. She laughingly admitted to Lisa, "I subscribe to everything, although everything doesn't always get read." She put her purchases in the bedroom before they left the apartment.

When they got to the house, Yale wasn't home yet. They went outside, only to dash in a few minutes later when it started drizzling. Lisa said she wanted to change, and Ruth sat down with a newspaper, reading articles about yesterday's events. She was still unable to comprehend there were people so deranged in the world.

The phone was ringing when Yale walked in. Victor pushed the intercom button, telling Lisa there was a collect call from her sons.

"I'll accept the call, operator. Thank you."

"Hi, Mom," Marc and Steve yelled into her ear simultaneously. "Sorry we had to call collect. How are you?" Marc asked first.

"I'm fine. How about the two of you? Are you having a good time?"

"It's been great! Wait until you see the pictures of everything we've done. Did they get everybody in the 'nut' group? We were worried about you."

"Don't worry. All of them are dead, except the woman. She's in police custody."

"Why isn't Dad there with you? You shouldn't be alone."

"One of us has to work, and I picked Dad."

"Very funny, Mom. If I was there, I'd kill that woman. She's scum. I can't believe she hurt other people just because she loved that Peter guy, like it said in the newspaper. She's an idiot. I hope she dies."

"Don't talk like that, Marc. Sometimes people do some crazy things because of love. It doesn't mean it's right. She's a sick woman, but don't ever wish someone dead. I've told you that before."

"I know. But, Mom, love is supposed to be caring about the other person. How can it be love, if you hurt people for someone else? Seems if you love somebody, you'd want good stuff for them, know what I mean?"

"Maybe it gets mixed up sometimes, Marc."

"That's crap! That Mary Nelson doesn't have a conscience, and if Peter really loved her, he wouldn't have asked her to hurt anybody to begin with. Hold on, Steve wants to talk now, we have to go soon."

"Mom, it's Steve, as if you didn't know. I miss you. Are we still going on our yearly trip to Cedar Point, when we get home next week? If you're not strong enough, it's okay if we don't go."

"We'll see. Let me think about it. I'm fine and strong enough, I just don't want to make any promises, okay?"

"Okay. Oh, I have to tell you one neat thing, then we have to go. We saw this beautiful Alaskan Husky giving birth. At first, Marc and I thought it was going to be gross. But when the Mom started to clean those little puppies... They were, like, almost under her, being protected. We were feeling...like we knew how a mom must feel about having a baby. It was so unbelievable, really amazing."

"You started to cry!" Marc yelled in the background.

"So did you, asshole! I saw you!" Steve yelled back. "We gotta go, Mom. I'm glad you're okay. Make lots of brownies, okay?"

"...and chocolate chip cookies, too." Marc added. "Bye."

"Bye, Mom. Love you, bye, see you soon."

"Bye, boys." She hung up and just sat there. Alone, desolate, knowing there was no way to avoid, or escape, additional pain for herself or for others.

She went back out to Ruth, and to her corner of the sofa, carrying one of her koala bears. Ruth pretended to be engrossed in a newspaper article, giving no clue that she'd heard the conversation between Lisa and her sons.

"Lisa, you know Yale's concert for tomorrow night sold out in three hours. It says so, right here in the paper."

"I'm not surprised, are you?"

"No, but I'm glad. You know what else, I'm going to make an appointment at the salon for tomorrow. Should I make one for you, too?"

"Make one what?" Yale asked, walking in, and pretending he'd just arrived.

"Your mother thinks I need to go to the beauty parlor to improve my appearance," Lisa said, getting up to kiss him.

"What are you talking about, Lisa? They can't improve on perfection. It's just a good way to spend a few hours," Ruth said, with a smile.

"Go ahead, you both could use some help," Yale laughed. Lisa started punching him playfully.

"Get him good," Ruth said.

"Thanks, Ma. I knew I could count on you to add your two cents."

"Two cents! Lisa, give him a dollar's worth for me."

Yale grabbed Lisa's hands and pinned them behind her. "Now what are you going to do?" She raised a knee and he backed away with his body, laughing, "Oh, so we're going to play dirty, are we?"

She pushed her body up against his, "Okay, do what you will with me. I surrender. I know when to quit."

He still held her hands pinned behind her, "What, no more fight left?"

She looked at him, her expression turning serious, "No, honey, no more fight left."

He let go of her hands, touching her face gently, "I love you, Lisa."

"I know," she whispered, with pain clutching her heart, while she looked hard into his eyes.

"Well, I know when to leave," Ruth said, rising from the sofa.

"Aren't you going to show me what you bought first?" Yale asked.

"Nope. We'll surprise you. Right, Lisa?"

"Right. Let's call and see if Pierre can take us fairly early, so we can relax before the show."

"Tell you what, Ma," Yale said, "I'll have a limo pick you up and then come here for Lisa. I have to be there early. That way the two of you can come together, and you won't have to take your car. The two of you don't need to leave for the show until seven-thirty."

"Good idea. Is that okay with you, Lisa?"

"Sure."

"What time are you taking off for the east coast?" Ruth inquired.

"Early the following morning," Yale replied. "I'll have Victor pack everything tomorrow night."

"Okay. I'll go now. Lisa wore me out, schlepping me from store to store all day long."

"Right, Ruth," Lisa smiled. "Don't listen to her, Yale. I couldn't keep up with her. I'm the one who should be tired."

"Are you?" he asked.

"Depends. What do you have in mind?" Lisa asked, rubbing against him.

"Bye, Ma. Talk to you tomorrow." Yale was rushing Ruth to the front door, his hands on her back, as she laughed. He gave Victor the rest of the day off, then came back carrying a bottle of champagne and two glasses.

After closing all the window treatments, so the room was dim, Yale sat next to Lisa. She put her head on his shoulder. The stereo played soft music as they held each other. "Dance with me, Lisa?" Yale asked.

He pulled her into his arms, swaying with her as their eyes held. He guided her closer to him, dancing her slowly around the room. He smelled the freshness of her hair, feeling the softness of her against his body. Kissing her gently, he brought her even nearer. He put his arms around her waist. She wrapped both her arms around his neck, and like one branch growing within another, they stood with their bodies entwined, as their hearts were interwoven.

Her hands moved from his neck, sliding up beneath his hair. His hands slid slowly across her back. He pulled her to the floor with him, and buried his face in her neck. Currents sliced through them. She pulled him to her, straining to feel his body braced against hers. Passionately drawn together, his body fused to hers, as she parted her lips even more to his probing tongue. They held each other, smoldering with passion, while his hardness pressed against her.

He moved off her and she looked deep into his eyes again. The reflection of her love was mirrored in the blue sparks. He stared at her face for a long time. He opened her blouse, running his fingers inside her brassiere. "I love you, Lisa."

He was over her, on his knees, her legs inside his. He reached under her, unhooking her bra, exposing her ripe breasts. His fingers were gliding over her like feathers. He circled her nipples gently. She couldn't take her eyes from his gaze.

He bent, kissing her face, her neck, moving to run his tongue across her breasts. She stroked the side of his face, holding herself arched to his mouth on her nipples.

He sat up, peeling off the rest of her clothing, as he touched every part of her body with loving tenderness. She gave herself to the sensations floating through her. He removed his clothes swiftly, unable to harness his need.

He moved over her, blanketing her body with his, as she guided him in. She closed her legs, wrapping around him tightly. She pushed to meet his every thrust. He was imprisoned while she rammed against his stiffness. The craving was paralyzing his mind, as his need was shattering his ability to withstand the impact of her movements.

Her body shivered, feeling his shaft rub against her, bringing her to heights she had never experienced before. He grabbed her, screaming, "Lisa" as she felt her climax merge with his. He felt her shudder beneath him. She held to him, tightly, long after. Neither wanted to break the connection.

He looked at her lovingly. Her eyes filled. She touched his face, tracing each feature with her fingers. "Are you memorizing my face, Lisa?" he whispered.

"I never want to forget this moment. A fairy tale came true, just like in a storybook. I feel like a princess."

"You will always be my princess, Lisa, just like in the books, even if we're not side by side in the same ivory tower." He kissed her again, tasting the salt of her tears.

"Do you know what you mean to me, Yale?" she asked, holding him tightly.

"Yes," he answered, braced against her. He looked tenderly into her eyes, "I know."

Chapter
40

Yale took the champagne and glasses into the bedroom, turning down the bed, while Lisa filled the tub with warm water. She climbed in and he followed, sitting in front of her. He rested his head against her breasts, while she sponged his chest. "Are you okay about going back on tour, Yale?"

"I think so. I know what I have to do. I'm going to do it, or at least, give it my best shot."

"That's all anyone can do, Yale. Give their best and take it from there." He knew she wasn't merely referring to his concert tour.

"What if you're not happy after you've tried your hardest, Lisa?"

"You make a change, Yale. But only when you're positive that making a change is the right thing to do."

"There are no guarantees, are there?"

"No. Just hope, and putting one foot in front of the other."

"I've decided to try and find my father after this tour. I have no expectations. But I need answers to some questions, before I lose the opportunity to ask them."

"Are you prepared to accept what might result in more pain?"

"Pain eventually eases, but questions left unanswered never go away."

"I know." Both felt the blow from that statement. "Nothing is ever easy, Yale."

They stayed emerged in the water, like infants in a womb, fearful of the voyage that would force them to emerge into the unknown.

After they dried each other off, they climbed into bed. Neither was hungry for anything but the other. She couldn't think straight, consumed with overwhelming emotions. She didn't want him away from her. He wrapped her in his arms, as a chill ran through her body. A sob she couldn't suppress escaped, "I love you so, Yale."

"Lisa. I want you in my life. Lisa." She stopped him with her mouth. She pulled his lips to hers, holding him as her body trembled uncontrollably. She moaned, when his hands ran over her body. Her mouth was locked with his. She pulled at him as he pushed against her, unable to stop. "Oh God. Oh God, Yale," she sobbed, tearing at his body. He kept repeating her name, hoarsely, as he pushed himself inside her. They moved violently, with urgency consuming them, unable to feel close enough. He pushed, intent in absorbing her completely.

"I love you, Lisa. I love you." She held him sobbing, feeling his tears merge with hers. She arched her body, screaming his name as they convulsed. Their bodies fused. They remained, clinging to one another.

The storm was still raging through their bodies, although their energy was expended. She was unable to stop her body from shaking. He cemented himself to her. They remained united and finally slept.

They tended to inconsequential matters the next morning, moving from room to room, avoiding any confrontation, holding tightly to their emotions, pretending calm. Needing a diversion, they both felt relief when Ruth arrived. Their facade was unsuccessful, and Ruth's attempt at joviality a failure. She regarded them closely, watching their frailty render them helpless.

"Ready, Lisa? Let's go get gorgeous," Ruth finally said.

Lisa followed Ruth to the front door, her decaying composure speeding her feet.

"See you later, Yale," Ruth said, unable to think of anything to say to assuage the fear she saw in his eyes. They got in the car with Ruth rambling on, trying to distract Lisa from her apparent nervousness. "Don't worry, honey. After everything you've gone through together, tonight will be a piece of cake." She hoped it was Yale's apprehension about touring that was responsible for their dispositions.

Lisa looked at the woman she had come to love, tears surfacing, "Not a piece of cake, I'm afraid. But we'll survive."

Ruth tried to ignore her own apprehensions, driving over the speed limit to the salon.

Primped, but not calmed, they arrived back at Yale's house after three. "I'll see you about seven, Lisa," Ruth said, staying in the car.

"Aren't you coming in?"

"No, honey. Maybe Yale needs some time alone with you before leaving for the theater."

"I'll see you in a little while then." She leaned over, kissing Ruth on the cheek. "Thank you, Ruth."

"What are you thanking me for, silly girl?" she admonished.

"For being who you are, Ruth. Bye." She rushed from the car, unable to suppress her emotions.

Victor was in Yale's bedroom, packing the suitcases, when Lisa asked if he expected Yale back soon.

"No, Miss. I think he's going for a rehearsal. He said he'd see you at the theater. I have dinner prepared, anytime you'd like to eat. Yale usually doesn't eat before a performance. He left a note in the other bedroom for you."

"Thank you, Victor." She walked to her bedroom, finding a sealed envelope and box on the bed. She sat down, opening the envelope.

Dear Princess,

You once said we both wear our hearts on our sleeves, making us more vulnerable than many. You were right. I can't pretend. I never could. There are no words for what I'd like to convey to you, Lisa, and you already know what is in my heart. I hope you will wear the gift in the box tonight, knowing that you have brought more to my life than love. You have taught me the true meaning of courage. You have shown me what caring is all about. I am more because of you. I feel more because of you. I will always love you. See you later.

Forever, Yale

She opened the small box. Inside was a gold koala bear. Its ears were made of sparkling diamonds, the eyes of blue sapphires, as blue as Yale's eyes, and around its neck, a tiny bow of red rubies. She turned the bear over to open the clasp, and engraved on the back was a heart with 'I luv you' etched inside. She squeezed the pin in her hand, rocking back and forth as she sobbed.

When Ruth went through the gates to pick up Lisa, there was a black limo in front of Yale's front door. The driver was loading Lisa's suitcases, the same ones Ruth remembered Lisa arriving with weeks ago. Ruth approached Lisa, looking at the beautiful woman standing in front of her. Lisa was dressed in the black flowing silk dress, adorned with only one piece of jewelry, a gold and diamond koala bear pinned over her heart.

"Ruth," Lisa attempted, unable to go on. Ruth took her

hands, squeezing them with understanding.

"Sometimes the timing is just not right. Lisa, you take more than one heart with you. If I had one more wish, it would be for a daughter, and for my daughter to be you. Gosh, I'm going to ruin my makeup," she sniffed. "You know what I mean." She hugged Lisa, hurrying to the gates. "I'll meet you there."

"Yes, Ruth." Both felt the impact of the other's laden heart. They left in separate cars for the theater.

Lisa walked in beside Ruth. David approached to escort them to their seats. Lisa saw Myra Sullivan, and paused to embrace her. She walked past Sergeant Joe Daly, who stopped her to tell her how lovely she looked. He introduced her to Jeff and Peggy Rose, and quickly explained that they were responsible for the videotape. He added that Jeff had just been offered a partnership with the law firm of Hall and Davis. Yale had given them special seats for tonight's show. She hugged them all, then followed David as the lights began to dim.

She sat directly in front of the stage as Yale emerged to a standing ovation.

He began the performance by singing an old Everly Brothers song, "Let It Be Me," bending to hand her a white long-stemmed rose. He looked splendid in his black tuxedo, and he sang magnificently. He stopped at one point, joking, "I may not be Elton John, but I think I'm okay."

While the crowd cheered, he winked at Lisa.

Their eyes met several times throughout the show. Lisa knew this concert was really meant for her.

As the show was concluding, he stopped, center stage. He held up his right hand until the audience quieted. A tray was wheeled out onto the stage, holding the bottle of champagne she and Yale had never opened the night before. He poured the liquid in both glasses, handing one to Lisa. He extended his hand, with the other glass of wine, to the heavens. "L'Chayim. To life." He sipped from the goblet. Lisa did the same.

She met him after the show. Their eyes were glistening. He held her hand while walking with her to the door. He stepped outside the door with her, thinking again how beautiful she was. She stood facing him and he touched the koala bear, smiling. They looked at each other without speaking, eyes brimming with tears. He didn't say a word, just put his arms around her, holding her tightly. They stood clinging to each other, until she finally whispered, "Yale, I need you to let go."

He stroked her hair, finally whispering back, "I know." He touched her face softly, one last time. "I'll always love you, Lisa."

She got in the limo without turning around to look at him. She couldn't.

The driver said, "We'll be at L.A. International in plenty of time for you to catch the red-eye flight to Canton."

"Thanks," she said, fixing her eyes on the dark floor of the car, clutching the koala bear pinned over her heart.

When he dropped Lisa in front of her terminal, the limo driver said, "You know, I'm originally from the Midwest, myself. I've heard people say they prefer the Midwest. That life out here is like a fantasy. Do you like things better here or in the Midwest, miss?"

She looked at him, before following the porter inside, "That's what I'm going to find out."

About the Author:

Libbie Richman resides in Michigan and is currently working on a new adult novel. A sequel to *Let It Be Me* has also been completed. She has also penned five volumes of poetry and lyrics and several stories for children. When Libbie isn't writing, she enjoys painting with oils, and lending her support to assure that the memory of the Holocaust and its victims is never forgotten.

Printed in the United States
1341700005B/118-120